About the Author

Gavin de Bier lives with his wife and family near Edinburgh.

Consider It Done is his second novel, following the critically acclaimed *Bobbing Heads*.

Praise for Bobbing Heads

A fast-paced contemporary crime thriller, finishing with a jaw-dropping denouement. **Sunday Mail**

Hard to put down. A real page turner. Cancel all engagements before you start reading Bobbing Heads! **Katharine Merry, Broadcaster**

A breathtaking debut novel. Bobbing Heads stands out in a crowded market. **Geoff Wightman, Author of Sport Armageddon, London Calling and Diary of an Also Ran**

Bobbing Heads has more twists than a Highland road. The author does an excellent job of keeping all the plates spinning. **Mike Kernan, Author of The Fenian**

This novel twists and turns at break-neck speed keeping the reader entertained throughout. There are dodgy characters and about-turns aplenty, with lots of black humour thrown in. I highly recommend it. **Catherine Simpson, Author of Truestory, When I Had A Little Sister and One Body**

Sets out and continues at pace. A very cleverly constructed thriller. **Allan Jardine, Author of Never Mind the Bagpipes**

A gripping read. **DRD Rollo, author of The Blitzkrieg Casino Scam, The Big Bust: The Blitzkrieg Casino Scam 2 and The Doublet Detective**

East Lothian Life Five Stars

TC Magazine Four stars

Consider It Done

Gavin de Bier

Stand your ground; no need to run.

If something needs doing, then consider it done.

PART ONE

Chapter One

October 2018

I stared out of the bus window watching the rain fall and could hear the minister's deep voice go round in my head:

I know that my Redeemer lives, and that at the last he will stand upon the earth; and after my skin has been destroyed, then in my flesh I shall see God, whom I shall see for myself, and my eyes shall behold, and not another.

I had just attended the funeral of my Aunt Isa and was now on the National Express service travelling from Solihull to London on a wet Wednesday. She died two years after a horrific experience which involved being kidnapped and held at knifepoint by a psychopathic thug. Isa had bravely hung on, but her spirit was broken. For the last two years of her life, she lived in the front room of my parents' house, having increasingly retreated into herself.

Aunt Isa's nightmare began after I found a small wallet containing a driving licence along with some numbers written on a Post-it note. On returning the wallet, I discovered the owner of the driving licence dead, with the perpetrators still in his house believing that I had a code which they desperately needed. As a result, my eighty-three-year-old aunt was kidnapped to force me to find this code. It was a race against time and somehow I succeeded. Vicky, an old friend from university, appeared to help me, but she was actually part of the gang and had strung me along to the point of waiting for her partner to kill me before, mercifully, the police intervened.

Vicky and the kidnapper were jailed, and her partner was killed while on remand, but I have found that of little comfort. My family blamed me for Isa's plight and no doubt ultimately for her death, and ever since, I have bitterly regretted the choice I made that afternoon which pitched me into the brutal realities of organised crime.

My thoughts returned to Isa's funeral. I closed my eyes and could see her coffin in the church as the minister addressed it:

We receive the body of our sister Isa with confidence in God, the giver of life, who raised the Lord Jesus from the dead. "I am the resurrection and the life," says the Lord. "Those who believe in me, even though they die, will live, and everyone who lives and believes in me will never die."

If only I could believe these words, I thought. Thinking back to Aunt Isa's funeral had induced an almost catatonic state, and luckily there was no one sitting next to me on the bus as I slouched and ruminated. Over the past two years the relationship with my parents and sister had just about been bearable, but there was definitely an underlying resentment towards me over what they believed I had caused. I didn't believe most of the minister's words, but I did feel that at least Isa's suffering was now over. However, I felt huge guilt at unwittingly causing that suffering.

My thoughts then turned to Vicky Monteith, now into the second year of an eight-year stretch inside. I had genuinely believed I was about to embark on the defining relationship in my life, but all along she had used me and was prepared to watch me be killed for her own selfish, twisted means. Vicky was intelligent, witty and absolutely gorgeous, with a shock of thick auburn hair. We had met at university and kept in touch over the years. During the traumatic weekend of Isa's kidnapping, as she helped me deal with the demands of the gang, we had finally slept together. At that time, I felt we had formed an unbreakable bond, one which gave me the strength to carry on and try to get Isa free. Her ultimate betrayal and the dangerous cold look in her eyes as I was held at knifepoint still sent shivers down my spine any time I thought about it, which was often, and was what my doctor believed was the trigger for my post-traumatic stress disorder.

My ongoing treatment for PTSD was getting it under control and I had been told that I was moving from the initial phase of the condition to stage two. However, my confidence and trust in others had been damaged almost beyond repair. I often felt depressed and anxious, and going against medical advice, I found myself resorting to regular drinking, which included the occasional binge. As well as losing my job as a college lecturer, my condition had contributed to the breakdown of existing relationships and problems forming meaningful new ones. I now worked for a charity called West London Action Group (WLAG), which provided help to immigrants on finding employment, advice on benefits, registering with relevant agencies and providing English language classes.

Seeing how Isa ended up and reflecting on my parents' circumstances caused me to consider my own life, which had been a content one up to that afternoon of *what ifs* which had caused my happy-go-lucky world to come crashing down. Before Isa's kidnapping, I had an active social life, much of which revolved around my job at West Thames College. I played five-a-side once a week with colleagues and students and enthusiastically took part in other extracurricular activities when they came along. However, since leaving the college, I'd had no contact with any of my former colleagues.

On the day I received the call telling me that Isa was dead, I had been drifting along at work. My father didn't offer any pleasant or even neutral preamble but simply stated, "She's dead." When I didn't answer as I took in this news, he repeated it: "She's dead."

"Oh my God," was all that I could come up with.

"She won't suffer any more. Here's your mother."

"Hi, Mum."

"Greg, it's so sad," she said, and burst into tears.

"When's the funeral?" I asked, as I pressed the phone to my ear with a shaking hand.

"We'll let you know. Bye, son." And before I could ask any more, she was gone. Two days later I had another awkward call from my father in which I was told the date and time of the funeral. Following that call, I booked a day's return bus ticket to avoid having to stay at my parents' house.

As I continued to stare out of the bus window, I noted that we were now on the outskirts of London. It took another thirty minutes or so to get to the bus station and then I made my way to the underground at Victoria and boarded a District Line train to Ealing Broadway before a short walk of around ten minutes back to my flat in West Ealing.

For the past eighteen months I have stayed in supported accommodation for vulnerable adults and young people who need help to live independently. I hadn't felt able to stay on my own anymore and jumped at the chance to stay at Ragmore House. My flat consisted of a single bedroom, a living room with a kitchen off it, a small bathroom along with access to a communal lounge, laundry room, shared garden and courtyard.

It was late afternoon when I got back to the accommodation block. Access to all apartments was through a main entrance which opened on to a foyer. I made my way through it, went up one flight of stairs and along the corridor to my flat. There were a few flowerpots and prints on the wall in an attempt to make the building homely. The foyer was carpeted with a tan industrial coir weave and the corridor and stairwell were floored with highly buffed grey linoleum tiles. The combination of coir entrance matting and heavily polished lino gave off an indeterminate frowsty smell which I found strangely comforting each time I walked to and from my flat.

I let myself in, put the keys in the back of the door and picked up the post on my way into the living room. It felt strange being home at this time on a working day. I hung up my coat, went into the kitchen, flicked the switch on the kettle, and returned to the living room to put the television on and open my mail, but there were no letters as such, just junk mail and circulars. The kettle had boiled, and I returned to the kitchen to make myself a cup of tea. As I was doing this, the doorbell rang, which gave me a slight surprise. Virtually no one came to visit me, and I wondered why someone would be at my door on a Wednesday afternoon. The only people who knew about the funeral were the warden of the building and my manager and receptionist at work. It crossed my mind, however, as I went to answer the door, that sometimes one of my neighbours took in a delivery on my behalf when I was out and so it could be a courier with a package to be signed for.

I walked along the short hallway and bent to look through the peephole in the front door, a habit that had developed over the past couple of years. After looking through the peephole, I stood back and swallowed hard as my heart began pumping very quickly.

The person waiting on the other side of the door was Vicky.

Chapter Two

Two years previously – my day in court

I had been dreading Vicky's trial, and acting on advice from the police and my lawyer, I regularly practised my presentation skills in front of the bathroom mirror while recounting my part in the tragic chain of events that I became embroiled in.

However, a few weeks before the set date, I received an email from my lawyer telling me that Victoria Monteith and her accomplice Darren Jackson had pleaded guilty to accessory to murder and kidnap. There would be no trial now, just a date set for sentencing.

To exorcise my demons, I went along to the Central Criminal Court, better known as the Old Bailey, for the sentencing. Vicky's case was being heard in Court 11. It felt odd walking up the stairs and entering a building which from the outside at least was so familiar. I navigated past excited tourists and bored teenagers accompanied by their parents as they proceeded to the high-profile trials. I found Court 11 after asking an usher and made my way to the public gallery, which contained fifteen to twenty people and was about half-full.

I wasn't surprised that none of my family were attending, but I was disappointed that neither my parents nor my sister had even bothered to phone or send a message of support. As I studied the faces of those around me, I saw a thickset black man staring ahead, and our eyes met as I looked at him whilst his bored into me. I assumed he may be a relative of Eustace Barrington, the poor sod who was stabbed to death in his own home by Vicky's partner Kevin Osborne.

After the formalities of the court were over, the judge began by giving a summary of the chain of events that had occurred the previous October and, as he recounted them, I thought how ridiculous this must sound to someone not familiar with the details of the case.

Kevin Osborne and Vicky were cocaine dealers with a number of high-spending clients. This included a Russian businessman with a serious habit who offered them polonium in return for coke. It was a seven-figure deal. However, the Russian double-crossed them before they got the polonium. Unfortunately for Osborne and Vicky, they had already arranged the sell on of the polonium to someone several notches up the London crime ladder.

Eustace Barrington was a mechanic who, to store the polonium, had adapted an Audi A7 to create a secret compartment under the floor of the front passenger seat which was accessed by a code. The hunt for the code was Osborne's desperate search for the polonium before the major player got seriously pissed off. Eustace was tortured and killed in a bid to get the code, and I had stumbled upon the aftermath when I went to his house to return a small wallet containing his driving licence and a piece of paper with some numbers on it that I had found in a second-hand waistcoat. Osborne immediately thought these numbers were part of the code and that I must know where the rest of it was kept. He therefore kidnapped my aunt to force me to help, and I did eventually stumble upon the rest of the code and the polonium was found. Luckily, however the police got involved, and Osborne, Jackson and Vicky were arrested.

Kevin Osborne, who as well as killing Eustace, had also arranged for Jackson to kidnap Isa, had been killed while on remand in prison. At the time I was glad of that, but now I wished that he was standing in the dock alongside Vicky and Jackson.

First up was Darren Jackson, the bastard who kidnapped my Aunt Isa and held her at knifepoint. The judge gave a summing up of Jackson's crimes and he was sentenced to fifteen years with a minimum recommended term of ten years. It was the first time I had seen him in the flesh, and my hatred for him went off the scale. He looked comfortable in his suit, totally unconcerned and ready to serve his time.

Then it was Vicky's turn. She appeared very nervous, avoided looking around the court and kept her attention fixed on the floor. I didn't think she was aware of my presence. I had met her parents and sister once and scanned the public gallery to see if they were sitting there. I didn't see her parents but saw someone who I thought might be her sister, although I couldn't be sure as it was some years since I had last met her.

Vicky was wearing a lilac two-piece suit which set off her thick auburn hair perfectly. Her skin had the sheen of alabaster, and she had the appearance of a porcelain doll. This was no doubt done under the instruction of her lawyer to make her look more vulnerable and get some sympathy from the judge. After the formalities from the clerk of the court and the judge, Vicky spoke in a very quiet voice to confirm her name, that she understood the charges and that she pleaded guilty to both charges.

The judge then began his summing up of her role in the death of Eustace Barrington and the kidnapping of my aunt, Isa Braithwaite.

"Victoria Elizabeth Monteith, you are charged with accessory after the fact to murder and accessory after the fact to kidnapping.

"You have accepted responsibility for your involvement in this matter, which led to the unfortunate and senseless murder of Eustace Barrington and the kidnapping of Isa Braithwaite. Isa Braithwaite, who is not well

11

enough to attend today, has made it very clear in her witness statement that she has not recovered from her kidnapping and fears she never will, and you accept that you played a major part in that."

The judge then got to the sentencing,

"You are thirty-eight years old, have no previous criminal convictions or cautions recorded against you and numerous people have attested to your positive good character, but you have shown no remorse for your crimes at all. Your reputation and career are forever sullied, and you have no one to blame for that but yourself.

"Given that you pleaded guilty and so avoided the need for a trial, I sentence you to eight years for accessory to kidnap and eight years for accessory to murder. Both sentences to run concurrently. This will give you ample time to reflect on your crimes.

"Take her away. This court is now adjourned."

Vicky looked stunned as the clerk of the court announced, "All rise." The judge then got up and left.

There was a mumbling from the public benches and some coughing as the court officials and police conferred. Vicky stared straight ahead as she was handcuffed and led from the stand towards the stairs at the side of the court. I looked for the person who may have been Vicky's sister, but she had already left the court.

It was hard to explain how I felt. Hearing the crimes recounted created a rage within me as I thought about my poor aunt and also what I had been put through. I had an incomprehension at what Vicky had become, and no sympathy for her on being jailed.

As I left the court I bumped into the man who had stared at me at the beginning of the session. "If I ever see her again I will kill her," he told me intently in a strong West Indian accent. He seemed to hold me partly to blame. I'm not sure if he had made a connection between me and Vicky or if he spoke to me simply because our eyes had met earlier. I gave him eye contact, nodded earnestly and sympathetically, but kept walking. I desperately wanted to talk to someone and let off steam, but not with him.

As I walked along the echoing corridor of the court building, I heard my name called out from behind. I turned and saw DI John Stevenson waving for me to stop. I waited as the detective who had worked the case, interviewed me several times and even locked me up while he carried out his investigation, caught up with me. He looked relieved and happy.

"Greg Stewart as I live and breathe. Well, Greg, we got a result," he said enthusiastically as he patted my shoulder. "They both got good sentences. What they deserved." I nodded less than enthusiastically.

"Cheer up, you have closure – it's all over. Let me get you a beer."

I nodded again and followed him out of the building. Stevenson wasn't my first choice of drinking partner, but any port in a storm I thought as we made our way along Newgate Street towards a nearby watering hole.

I intended to sink a few as I contemplated *closure* and my new life.

Chapter Three

I wasn't sure if Vicky could see me, or my shadow at least, through the fisheye peephole. I recoiled and ran into the kitchen in shock.

I couldn't understand how she was out and how she could have found me. My instinct was to run, and I trusted that instinct. However, I was on the first floor and the windows in my block were double-glazed, about a metre square and had catches to prevent vulnerable people fully opening them and either falling or jumping out. I dashed into the living room, and using my adrenaline-charged strength, yanked at the handle of the window. After several attempts and loud cracks, it finally gave and the window opened inwards, allowing me to duck my head under and look out. There was no one sitting on any of the three concrete benches in the centre of the drab paved courtyard below.

I had climbed out of my previous flat when my Aunt Isa was kidnapped, so this wasn't altogether new territory and the descent wasn't as high as in my last escape. However, the drainpipe was plastic, unlike the wrought iron one at my old place. I reckoned that speed was of the essence and stretched out of the window, grasped the drainpipe with both hands and immediately started to shimmy downwards using my feet, and to a lesser extent my elbows, to help slow me down.

Safely down and nursing a couple of sore elbows, I didn't take time to consider my options apart from getting away. Vicky's face was imprinted on my mind. She looked the same gorgeous but dangerous combination. I walked quickly across the courtyard towards the door leading into the corridor containing the laundry room. There were a couple of residents in the room reading magazines, and I hurried towards the foyer before they saw me.

As I was making my escape, I considered my options, which were limited. I didn't think I should go to my work, and I had no close friends, which just left Brygida, who was a Polish acquaintance of mine. Brygida was the wife of Piotr, who was a student from when I had been a teacher of English as a Foreign Language. He had helped me in getting Aunt Isa free, but he had then turned out to be a serial car and motorbike thief hiding behind the veneer of a cleaner in a leisure centre. Piotr took the top-of-the-range Audi which had contained the polonium and then promptly disappeared with Cassie, the fourth and final member of the gang, who was Kevin Osborne's accomplice in the murder of Eustace Barrington. Neither Piotr nor Cassie had been seen since.

As Brygida spoke little English at the time, I had helped her fill in forms and accompanied her to attend social work and housing benefit interviews. We had slept together before the court case, something which at the time I had immediately regretted, but as time wore on, my feelings of guilt lessened as occasionally when we met up we would have some physical contact which we now recognised in our current circumstances was mutually beneficial.

Brygida's flat is a fifteen-minute jog from my place. I considered hailing a taxi but decided I could go more directly by running. I felt self-conscious as I was still wearing my funeral attire of dark suit and black shoes. My shoes were only worn for formal occasions, because they were stiff, uncomfortable and the leather soles were hopeless in wet or icy conditions. Rather than running full pelt, I strode and then ran two or three paces before returning to striding, in the way that people do when not dressed for exercise but needing to move more quickly than walking pace. I made my way along the busy pavement before turning left and entering the park from where I would cut directly across to get to Brygida's. My strange gait meant that I attracted a few curious glances as I didn't blend in with the joggers. I occasionally looked back and thankfully couldn't see a red-headed pursuer. I made it through the park and crossed a couple of residential streets before approaching the main road and the maisonette block which contained Brygida's flat.

I charged up the common stairway to the second floor and I could hear Ania, Brygida's toddler, crying as I banged on the door. There was no response, so I banged again. Despite seeing Brygida once or twice a month, I had never asked for or been offered a key, which suited us both. I was about to shout through the letterbox when the door was opened tentatively and kept on the chain.

"It's me," I gasped.

The door then opened wide. Brygida is elfin-like and always has a slightly worried look, which today was magnified by my sudden appearance. "What is wrong?" she asked in her strong Polish accent.

"It's her – Vicky - she was at my door."

"She is in…" She hesitated, trying to remember the right word.

"Prison," I finished for her. "But she's not. She was at my front door."

Brygida frowned at me and looked at Ania. "Sorry," I said, "but what do I do?"

Brygida was confused, because usually it was me offering advice and support, but now the shoe was on the other foot. "Come in," she said, and stood to one side. I went into the living room but didn't sit down as my agitation wouldn't allow it. Instinctively I reached for my phone, and not finding it in the usual place of my breast pocket, I started patting myself down before realising that I had left it in my flat.

"How could she find my flat?" I asked. Brygida said nothing, and Ania looked at me with a worried expression. "It must be from my work," I continued. "But how could she find it? Why isn't she still inside? Do you have my work number?" I asked Brygida. She went and got her phone and scrolled to it, then passed the phone to me. I quickly pressed dial. "West London Action Group, how may I help you?" I recognised the voice.

"Hi, is that Di? It's Greg. Can I speak to Maggie? It's very important."

"Hi Greg, how are you? How was the funeral, if that's not a silly question?" Di was well suited to the receptionist role in many ways as she had a genuine interest in people, but unfortunately she could talk for England as well, which often got in the way of her work. She was quite new to the organisation but had a confidence and easy-going manner which belied her inexperience in the role.

"Fine. Is Maggie in?"

"She has just left to go to a meeting. She'll be back in a couple of hours."

"Look, maybe you can help me. Someone who was uninvited and unwelcome has turned up at my flat. I think she must have got my address from work. Do you know anything about it? Did anyone phone or turn up asking for my address?"

"Funny you should say that. Yeah, someone did. I said that we don't give out addresses of staff, but she said she was your sister just back from Australia and that she had lost her phone with all her contacts in it. She sounded very upset so I said I would put her through to Maggie."

Maggie Gray is a lovely person, but overwhelmingly middle class, lefty, right on and every other similar cliché. She only sees the best in people, and for our job that is a positive trait, but she is so gullible. She has an upper first in philosophy from Cambridge and numerous other qualifications. I don't like using a cliché to sum someone up, but in this case *more brains than sense* would do her justice. She would have felt sorry for my "sister" and given out my address in a heartbeat.

"Di, I don't have a sister in Australia. Tell Maggie I called, and if my so-called sister calls again, try and get her number, but don't give her any details about me. Do you understand?"

"Yeah, of course, Greg – very sorry. Is there anything else I can do?"

"Just tell Maggie that I'll call later, and I may be off work for a few days."

"OK, Greg, will do."

With that, I hung up. At least I had established how Vicky had got my address, but not how she was out of prison or how she had found out where I worked.

Brygida had been in the kitchen when I was on the phone and returned with a cup of tea. I gulped the tea down while Brygida knelt on the floor and busied herself with Ania, who was pulling a variety of toys out of a shoebox and throwing them about the room. I tried to put my random collection of thoughts into some coherent order but failed miserably. I simply could not think of what to do next. Just then, Brygida's phone rang. She answered it and handed it to me.

"Is that you, Di?" I asked with a dry throat.

"No, it's Vicky," came the reply.

Chapter Four

"What?" I screamed at the phone. Brygida stared at me in terror.

"Where's Di – what have you done with her?" I shouted.

"I'm holding her," she replied.

My PTSD has a number of unfortunate manifestations, including flashbacks and, at times, an uncontrollable fear of everything, which can make me unable to do almost anything. However, on the flip side to that, I can also get a flight adrenaline surge, which is what I suddenly experienced as I stood in Brygida's flat. I threw the phone onto the floor and ran to the front door. Ania screamed and then Brygida charged after me as I yanked open the door and, using a strength I didn't think she was capable of, pulled me back and spun me around. The speed and ferocity sent me spinning on to the floor of the hall. "Don't!" she screamed. "Don't!" she screamed again even louder.

Ania kept up her wailing as well. A neighbour burst out of his flat and started grappling with me. He must have thought I was attacking Brygida. Brygida screamed again and pulled him by the hair and scratched at him, shouting, "Get off, get off!" I pushed him away and got up. "He is OK – it is not him. Leave him alone," she shouted at her neighbour.

"Fucking idiots," he shouted breathlessly. "I'm calling the cops. Coming over here and fighting with each other…" he added as he stormed off.

I was too distressed with the Vicky situation to care about him and just said to his back, "We've got an emergency. Go away."

"Fuck you," he shouted back. Some other neighbours had now collected around the stairwell.

I closed the door. "Brygida, Brygida, help me, please, what do I do?" I implored.

She put her fingers to her lips and made a shushing gesture and pointed at the phone. "You must speak," she said, and then she picked it up and handed it to me. My heart was racing and my hands shaking as I took the phone. I pressed the screen and saw that the call from Vicky was still live.

"What do you want?" I shouted. "Haven't you caused me enough misery to last a lifetime?"

"Greg, calm down. What's been going on? It sounded like a riot down the phone line," she cooed.

"What do you expect? You've just thrown my life into turmoil again after ruining it in the first place. What do you want?"

"Greg, what I want is for you to calm down and make your way back to your flat. Tell Brygida to stay in her flat and not to tell a soul. Also, come on your own and don't tell anybody. If the police arrive at Brygida's following your meltdown tell her to tell them it was a domestic incident that has been resolved. If you do that, I will let Di go. It is getting quite tiring holding a knife against her throat. You have got an hour, starting from now." She hung up. I stared at the phone and then Brygida.

"She's got a colleague from work at my flat and is holding a knife against her throat," I croaked. "I've got to go there in an hour or she'll kill her..." I trailed off.

"You must go," Brygida told me.

"Why? Let's call the police," was my response.

"No, no," Brygida insisted. It may be because of her husband Piotr's criminal activities that Brygida had a strong mistrust of them.

"Also, how are they at my flat when I was speaking to Di on the West London Action Group phone number?" I added.

"I don't know, but you must deal with it. Go, go do what you did the last time."

I assumed Brygida was referring to when my Aunt Isa was kidnapped and I managed to solve a riddle and not get killed by Vicky's gang. I really liked Di and had a huge feeling of guilt that someone who only saw good in people and wouldn't harm a fly was being held by my deranged ex friend. I decided I had to go. I made up my mind that if this was a hostage situation then if necessary I would put myself forward as the hostage instead of Di.

"OK, I'll go," I said to Brygida. "I don't even have my phone – it's in my flat. Write down your number and I'll call in an hour from some device if I can't get mine," I instructed hurriedly. She nodded.

"Don't call the police," I added rather unnecessarily, and then gave Ania and Brygida a cuddle. "I love you," I blurted out. This confused Brygida, because despite our occasional functional lovemaking I had never expressed my feelings for her. Come to think of it, my exclamation came as a surprise to me as well. I saw Brygida mainly as someone requiring my help, but also at times as something of a kindred spirit, but never as a partner. I gave a sort of wave and left the flat. There was no one on the stairwell fortunately, although as I made my way from the building I sensed curtains flickering and blinds being shifted to allow the neighbours to catch a glimpse of the person who had caused the commotion.

I retraced my journey through the park and back to my complex. I walked briskly but didn't run as I needed time to gather my thoughts and prepare to meet Vicky. I was unsure how she would have made her way with Di to my flat and had no idea what state of mind she was in and how she intended to treat me. She sounded calm on the phone, but I remembered with a shudder how calm she had been when Kevin Osborne had held a knife to my throat. In many ways, since that episode with Vicky's gang, I had come to think of life as cheap. I now accepted there wasn't always a happy ending and had felt at many times, *what is the point*? The value I now placed on my own life had definitely diminished. However, Di had been dragged into this. It wasn't my fault, but as ever it seemed I was the cause of it. I had to try and be calm, find out what Vicky wanted and where I fitted into her plans.

As I approached Ragmore House I slowed down to a stroll, took deep breaths and entered the building. I didn't have a key as I had dived out the living room window, and was wondering how Vicky had got in. I was dreading meeting Vicky again and part of me was hoping that she wouldn't be at the flat. However, if that was the case, I reasoned, then how could I help Di? I didn't pass any neighbours as I went up to the front door. Everything seemed normal. I tried the door – it was locked. I rang the bell. There was a pause, then the door was opened slightly.

"Hi Greg, are you alone?" she said calmly.

"Yes, of course. I have done what you asked."

"Don't try anything silly, Greg. I will open the door and I want you to look straight ahead and walk slowly to the living room."

"OK," I grunted, then asked, "how did you get Di here so quickly from WLAG?"

"Easy. We have been here for a while. I used call divert. When you called the WLAG number it diverted to my phone and she was here when she spoke with you," she explained, as if she was talking to a child.

The door slowly opened inwards, and I walked into my hall. I did as I was told and looked straight ahead. I could feel Vicky behind me, and my racing mind was in turmoil as I turned into the living room, having visions of Di shackled up and gagged, or even worse, with her throat slit.

"Sit down," Vicky ordered as I entered the living room. I did so and sat on my favourite chair. There was no sign or sound of Di, which heightened the tension as I imagined what fate had befallen her. Wrong place, wrong time, I thought, and inwardly cursed Maggie for being so easily tricked into giving out my details to Vicky. Because of that, one of her staff, her completely innocent staff, had probably had her young life taken from her.

I needn't have worried, because as I was thinking this, Di called through from the kitchen, "Like a cup of tea, Greg?"

Chapter Five

"How are you doing?" Di asked breezily.

"What?" I spluttered. "What the hell is going on?"

"You two obviously know each other. Have a cup of tea, Greg, we have a lot of catching up to do," Vicky said. She seemed relaxed and in control. Not the porcelain doll that I last saw two years ago in court. I accepted a cup of tea mechanically and sat open-mouthed.

"Cat got your tongue?" Vicky asked.

"What do you want from me? I have nothing. Look where I live. You caused this and now you're back for more. What did I do that has made you treat me like this?" I trailed off.

"Greg, believe me that I didn't want you wrapped up in the incidents, but it was chance, and I suffered too. I was put in jail."

"Incidents? Incidents? You chose to do what you did. My aunt was kidnapped, for Christ's sake," I roared.

"Yes, yes, it was very unfortunate, and I am deeply sorry. I truly want to make things up with you."

I found this hard to comprehend. She had been sentenced to eight years and yet was sitting in my living room after just two of them. "You can never make it up to me," I asserted.

"I'll try, but first I need some help from you."

"I have nothing to give," I said.

"Oh, but you do. Remember your friend Piotr and my accomplice Cassie?"

"Of course I do," I said.

"Well, you may remember that they made off with the Audi. They didn't know it, but it contained a large wedge of cash along with a second consignment of polonium. You found one hidden compartment, which contained four phials of the stuff, but there was another one, containing another four. That was why Kev was killed on remand, because the gang that Kev was dealing with thought he had double-crossed him. His police informant had told him that four phials were recovered so he assumed Kev was holding the other four back from him, but Kev wasn't. Neither of us knew that there were two hiding places in the car, we just assumed it would be one and so Piotr and Cassie have got a lethal consignment worth around one million and a stash of money and I want it back."

The large sum of money and the additional four phials of polonium was news to me. "How did you find this out?" was all I could say.

"I have been held at Bronzefield Prison for the past two years. It's for category-A prisoners, so some of them have done serious shit."

I noticed that Vicky's accent and vocabulary had hardened somewhat.

"There are about a hundred and forty screws, with a fifty-fifty split between men and women. I've never been inside before so I didn't know what to expect, but I was surprised at its lax regime and high staff turnover. I got friendly with one of the screws. A sad old git in his fifties who I used to flirt with and treated him like my favourite uncle. He responded as I knew he would, and I had him twisted round my little finger. He probably went home at night and bonked his wife thinking of me.

"Well, this old screw had previously been based at Bedford, which is where Kev was kept on remand, and he told me there was a grass in Bedford who confirmed to him that Kev's killing was a hit done by a prisoner with little more to lose, but whose family outside would benefit."

"OK, but what has this got to do with me? I know nothing about where they are. I haven't heard from either of them since the day they left me holding the four phials of polonium that you know about. I never knew Cassie. I thought I knew Piotr, but obviously I didn't."

"Come on. You are, shall we say, *pals* with Brygida. That's how I found you so easily through her social media. You must be teaching her English well. She gushes about you."

"You aren't allowed mobiles in prison I thought?"

"You're not, but it's easy. Especially if you are the screw's favourite. Brygida must have heard from Piotr from time to time?" Vicky asserted.

"Never. Not once."

"But he has a child."

"Yes, I know, but he hasn't been back or in touch at all. I'm sure the police would let me know if they caught him. DI Stevenson gets in touch with me once in a while."

"We need to find Piotr, Greg. I will make it worth your while."

I tried to shift the conversation. "How did you get out?" I asked.

"Easy. I was on a work placement that my favourite screw helped get me on. A fellow inmate that was released last year whose dad is a crime boss did the planning. I was spirited away in a laundry van from gardening duties at a residential care home in Kent while the guards were drinking tea and flirting with the staff. I bet it would have been an hour before they even noticed I was missing.

"Di's sister, who is still inside, had made the link to you. I was following Brygida on Facebook and sharing this with Sharon, who is Di's sister. I told her where you worked, which I got from Brygida's Facebook, and so we got Di to get a job where you worked. Simple."

Di smiled as her role was explained. So, it wasn't Maggie inadvertently giving away my details. It was Di, and all planned by Vicky. I remember when Di arrived on her first day looking nervous and shy and that I took her under my wing and introduced her to everyone. I watched as each day she got more confident, to the point where I would want her to shut up. She was just like Vicky, another actress.

"I can't and won't help you," I stressed, looking at Di but speaking to Vicky.

"That's a shame," she said. Vicky then took out her phone, keyed in her password and selected a photo. She turned the phone sideways to give me a landscape view. My worst nightmares came flooding back as she handed me the phone. There was a woman with her mouth taped over and terror in her eyes as a large kitchen knife was being held against her throat.

It was my boss, Maggie.

Chapter Six

The image of Maggie was still in my mind after Vicky had taken the phone back from me and was now keying something in. A few seconds later I could hear someone speaking. Vicky had put the phone onto FaceTime, and I could hear Maggie's heavy breathing.

"Hi Suzi, how's it going?" Vicky asked.

"Not bad. This fat cow hasn't put up much resistance. Just hard to move her cos she's so big." Her accent was Scottish, possibly Glaswegian.

"Yeh, well, I've got Greg here. Wave to Maggie, Greg," Vicky told me.

I refused and just looked at the screen for a few seconds before looking away. Not only was the scene nauseating and terrifying, it brought back vivid memories of my Aunt Isa being held in similar circumstances two years ago.

"Got to go, Suzi. Keep in touch. Bye Maggie." Vicky waved the phone in front of me and I could see the whites of Maggie's eyes. I couldn't imagine her terror. Someone as trusting as her being treated like this, and yet again all because of me. I noted that Vicky had used Suzi's name and was obviously not bothered about Maggie knowing it. That frightened me.

"Di has put an out-of-office message on the West London Action Group website and emails and the office will be closed until next week. That will give you enough time to track down Piotr and Cassie. You don't need to bring them back; you just need to find them. When you have done that and given me the details, then Maggie will be let go," she said.

"You're right. I do see Brygida quite regularly and we have become friends," I said flatly, and Vicky winked. "But...how can I get you to understand? I have no idea where they are. None at all. They left with the Audi and a BMW motorbike over two years ago and I have seen or heard nothing since. As far as I know, Brygida has heard nothing. Believe me, if she had heard something then I would have found out."

"How is she supporting herself and her child and living so comfortably?"

"She gets some benefits."

"Such as?"

"Housing benefit and universal credit," I mumbled.

"How much is that a week?" she asked.

I shrugged and said nothing. After Piotr fled, I had found a stash of his ill-gotten gains hidden under the floorboards in their flat, which came to just over four thousand pounds. However, Brygida would have spent all of that by now.

"She is getting money from somewhere Greg, and I bet it's from Piotr. Use that brain of yours that helped get me convicted and find out where he is." She nearly spat out the words.

Again, trying to buy time, I asked, "Are you on the run? Won't the cops be looking for you and come here? They know the connection between you and me."

"Yes, they will be looking for me, but Suzi's dad is making arrangements for me to disappear, and will only do that when Piotr, and more importantly his car, is found. He has given me five days."

I scoffed, then said, "You're having a laugh. You've got five days on a wild goose chase with the cops on your tail?"

"That's why you are going to do the legwork. I am going underground, so to speak, and you are going to find Piotr," Vicky replied.

"What if I refuse?"

"Well Maggie will be killed, of course, swiftly followed by Brygida and Ania." Vicky straightened up and walked around the room before leaning against the sideboard. "Suzi Moore is a hard cold bastard. Her dad is Clinkie Moore, who runs an outfit in Glasgow's East End. She's just finished a ten-year sentence, most of it in high security, and got out after seven. As I said, and to repeat what I have already told you, my favourite screw, the one I told you about, is bent." I noted the old lag speak.

"He passed a message to me from a third party regarding the Audi. The person who was supposed to be getting the polonium from the white Audi was looking for eight phials. There were only four found so there must be another four in that car. He is very serious about getting them back and thinks that I know where they are. I am on a deadline. That's why I got in tow with Suzi. I had already got to know her and cultivated a relationship, if not a friendship, because I could see that she had influence inside and would be of help to a posh girl like me. When that message came in, she was the obvious first port of call. It couldn't have worked out better.

"Clinkie likes the idea of having some polonium. It would shift him up the UK crime ladder by several notches. Suzi doesn't want to let her dad down, as she got him involved. So, you finding Piotr would make three people very happy and prevent a few ending their days prematurely. Brygida knows something and you are going to get it.

"The only problem is that Clinkie got me out of jail and now I'm in his debt. I want nothing to do with either the polonium or Clinkie." She looked over at Di as she said this. Di winked.

"When you find Piotr and the polonium or point Clinkie in the right direction, then hopefully our Mr Big will be on Clinkie's tail, take Clinkie out and head off into the horizon. And I will be doing similar. Job done."

"Vicky, as ever, you have got it all worked out. Where do you fit in, Di?" I asked. I wasn't trying to buy time. I was genuinely interested. "What do you do, where do you go when this is all over?"

"Hopefully Maggie will still be alive, and she will keep me on at WLAG," she replied, and then winked at me.

Chapter Seven

As a result of my PTSD there are times when I feel unable to move and experience intense anxiety in just going about everyday life. I usually don't have more than a couple of hours' unbroken sleep at a time and experience regular night sweats.

My muscles and joints are often painful from being so tense, and I have chipped front teeth from grinding my jaw. I am very anxious and find it difficult to relax, and as a result, I am irritable, have angry outbursts and difficulty concentrating. My doctor has prescribed beta blockers, which work to an extent in managing my hyperarousal, which she explained is the medical term for this feeling of being on edge. However, I am taking more than the prescribed amount on a regular basis and use them at the first signs of any type of stressful situation.

I have adapted to live for the moment and can't and don't make any medium- or long-term plans. Now Vicky wanted me to track down Piotr and Cassie with no clues whatsoever as to their whereabouts in five days at the behest of a major crime boss or we would all be in deep shit. I spoke from the heart. "Vicky, I don't think you understand how affected and ill I have become as a result of Isa's kidnapping and the attempted murder of me. I maybe happened to get some things right at that time to help get the code, but they were unprecedented, and I haven't the will, strength or resolve to repeat them. I have been diagnosed with PTSD and am on medication and attend counselling.

"What you are asking of me is even harder than what I had to do two years ago. We have no idea where they are. No idea at all, and my brain isn't functioning like it used to. I have no confidence. I have no nerve; my concentration levels are not what they used to be, and I am constantly on edge. I am on medication and will be a liability and no use in dealing with a ruthless crime gang."

"Greg, think of Maggie. Now think again about what I am asking you to do."

"I expect they are abroad, which makes it even harder," I said forlornly.

"Why abroad? What makes you say that?"

"I don't know, just that they would have got money from selling Piotr's motorbike and it somehow seems natural when you are fleeing a crime to leave the country. I had a vision of them as some sort of Bonnie and Clyde. What will Clinkie do if you can't find them?" I asked.

"If we can't find them you mean," she replied with emphasis. "Don't worry about me. It is now nearly five o'clock on Wednesday. By Monday at five, Clinkie needs to know where they are."

"Yes – what are you going to do if we can't find them?" I repeated. "Also, the cops could be here any time now. Stevenson is bound to get the nod and come looking for you here."

"Yes, Greg, it is serious shit. But you are going to help sort it."

"But I'm not a miracle worker or a mind reader."

"Come on, Greg. You know Piotr, you know Cassie. You know Brygida and how she thinks."

As I considered the implications of what I was being told to do, my heart rate was all over the place, and my body, which had been slightly shivering from the moment Vicky had turned up at my door, was now noticeably trembling.

"I need my tablets please," I said. "Di, go to the bedside cabinet. The pills are next to the light. Bring me two and a glass of water." I think Vicky could see that my distress was genuine as she nodded to Di. Di did as I asked, and I gulped the pills down with the water. It would take at least thirty minutes before I felt any benefit.

"What are your initial plans?" Vicky asked. She could obviously tell that I was broken and therefore malleable.

"I'll go to Brygida's and try to get the details without her knowing why," I answered absently.

"Good, that's a start. How do you intend to do that?"

"Probably start off by getting her pissed."

"Sounds like a plan, Greg. The quicker you get this done, the quicker it's over for all of us. This time tomorrow it could all be done." What a thought. However, given how things had panned out in the past with Vicky, I somehow doubted that would be the case. She then said, "I know that Brygida messages him just about every night."

"What? How do you know that?"

"Suzi used her connections, so to speak, to hack Brygida's phone, which was pretty easy. You know the café near the station?

"Yes. I've met you there before."

"Of course, that's right. Well, that's where she meets a friend sometimes and it's where she uses the free Wi-Fi. It's easy to hack that. By the way – she likes you, but misses Piotr."

My mouth was hanging open, and I resented Vicky's flippancy at such a time but couldn't think of anything to say.

"Right, you get back to hers. Tell her I just wanted to see you to give my heartfelt apologies for what I had caused before disappearing forever. Tell her that everything is over and you can move on. She likes you, Greg. Be her big brother or shag her brains out – do whatever it takes. Just find out where Piotr and that car is or what he has done with it."

"If you've got into her messages, how come you can't you find out?" I asked.

She sighed. "Remember, it's Piotr who we are dealing with, and he's smart. They don't refer to each other by name and there are no locations ever mentioned in any message. Most names used are probably codes for something else."

"So how do you know it's him she's speaking to then?" I asked tartly.

"It's obvious from the language used that it's doublespeak."

"Maybe it's just because you're reading a translation?"

"No way. Suzi got into the phone thanks to one of her dad's cronies who know this inside out, and they're convinced it's Piotr she's speaking to."

"If you can get into her messages so easily why can't the cops?" I asked.

She sighed again. "Because they aren't interested. Two key players are dead, me and Daz are in jail. Piotr was never a suspect and Cassie, while involved, was so at the behest of Kev. They probably feel sorry for her while they are feeling their hard-ons. The cops don't have the resources to deal with one small part of a chain that has been broken. They may start looking again now I'm out, which makes it even more important that you get this done quickly, Greg. Get back to Brygida's and use your charm, guile, lateral thinking, whatever, to get a result."

As I watched and listened to Vicky, I found it hard to comprehend how I'd had a friendship for seventeen years with her before it all blew up. This was a different person. She had been lovely, quirky, witty and very sexy. What had happened – what switch had been flicked that caused this?

Back to reality. "Vicky, I have thirty pounds to last me until next Tuesday when I get paid. I'm on minimum wage."

She went to her bag and peeled off five fifty-pound notes and gave them to me. She returned my phone that I had left in my flat when I had fled and handed me a piece of paper.

"Here is a number to get in touch. Never use my name and only text. I will be changing phones regularly. Each time I change it, I'll text you from the new number with a message that starts with 'Ealing'. In an absolute emergency call Di. This is her number." She handed it to me. Di winked. "No one knows Di's role in this, and she will return to work for a short time next week assuming you have done the business and tracked down Piotr and Cassie. Maggie will return to work hopefully and Di can be the sympathetic secretary helping her boss for a while."

"And what about you?" I asked.

"Don't worry about me, Greg. If you do your stuff then I will be absolutely fine."

"What about your parents and sister?"

"What about them? They no longer exist."

"By the way, how did you get into my flat?" I asked, changing tack.

"Di explained to the warden that I was your sister over from Australia and that my flight had been delayed causing me to miss my aunt's funeral. I cried a lot and he was very sympathetic."

Di winked at me again, which was becoming tiresome and making me more agitated. In this day and age where I thought that nobody trusted anyone, here was an example of how easy it still was to con your way into and screw up people's lives.

"Don't come back here until you have completed your task," she said. "Text every two hours up to midnight and then start again in the same pattern tomorrow from seven. If there are any cock-ups or you try to be smart, then Maggie is a goner."

"Vicky, you're desperate. How do I know you'll keep her alive?"

"I'll send you a picture each day with her holding the morning paper if you want. But I'm warning you, Greg – I am desperate, and I have got nothing to lose. I am not going back inside, so if you screw up, she's a goner."

I felt as if there was some kind of weight in the pit of my stomach, almost like a bad dream where some invisible force was holding me down and I couldn't get up and move away from danger. My legs were trembling, and I was sweating profusely.

"Di, there's a bottle of vodka in the cabinet over there and fresh orange in the fridge. Please pour me a large glass."

"Oh, here we go again, Greg – this is just like the last time. Reaching for the bottle every time you have to do anything."

"What do you expect? I need it. You've caused all of this," I hissed. "And if you want any help then you better let her bring me it," I growled.

She nodded to Di. Di brought me the drink and handed it to me. I gulped it down, then I asked for another, which I used to wash down a couple more pills. I sat for five minutes, then went to the toilet and left. I

didn't say bye. It was time to get to work.

Chapter Eight

On my way to Brygida's I went into a café, ordered a coffee and sat down. I hadn't told Vicky, but it had dawned on me when she was talking about hacking Brygida's phone that I didn't need to do that because I almost certainly had her logins for Facebook. After Piotr left, I had accompanied Brygida to numerous meetings with social services, jobseekers and charities. I had helped her plan a budget, gave her English lessons and I had set her up with an email account.

I took out my phone, clicked on the Facebook icon and logged out of my account. Then I put in Brygida's email address and the password that she used for her email and I was in. I went to the messages, used the translate app and worked my way through them.

Brygida was indeed in regular correspondence. However, it was with someone called Jess. From the nature of the messages, it appeared that Jess was female, which I guessed was the intention. There were lots of messages along the lines of *today I went to...*, which was invariably a visit to the shops, the bank, café or museum. There were never any actual place names for either the location or the name of the facility that *Jess* had been to that day.

I concurred with Vicky's summation that this would very probably be Piotr she was conversing with and they were using a very basic code. It dawned on me that I could have checked this at any time because I had wondered quite regularly where he was. I decided though that I was glad that I was a respectful person and not the naturally prying type. I finished my coffee and left to go to Brygida's. When I arrived, it took a while for Brygida to let me in. She had been reading to Ania, who looked startled at my sudden reappearance. Poor child, I thought; first, her father vanishing, and now having to deal with me, who she will grow up thinking of as a complete idiot.

"Hi," I said.

"Hi," Brygida said back. "What does Vicky want?" Brygida sounded nervous as she asked.

"She thought I had a code from the time when Piotr ran away. Do you understand?" She nodded.

"I have convinced her that I don't have anything. She believes me, and she doesn't want any more from me," I lied. I'm not sure that Brygida was fully convinced.

"Where is she now?" she asked.

"I don't know where she's gone now, and she obviously hasn't told me as the police are after her. The main thing is that Vicky is away and won't bother us any more." Only a few minutes ago I was inwardly praising myself for not prying into Brygida's affairs and now I was finding it so easy to lie that it was a bit disconcerting. I couldn't tell if Brygida believed me. It was now nearly six o'clock.

"Has Ania had her tea?"

"Pardon?"

"Have you fed her?" I said, pointing at Ania.

"Yes," she said.

"Let's order some food for us. I feel we need to have a celebration because Vicky is gone for good," I said with my best false smile as Brygida looked at me a bit uncertainly.

"What do you want? Fancy an Indian?" I wanted Brygida to have something hot and spicy to make her thirsty, as I was going to get her drunk. Brygida had never been much of a drinker, but she was starting to adopt some British characteristics, and one of them was a liking for Prosecco.

"I'll phone the Bombay Palace and get your usual," I said breezily.

"Not very hungry," she said.

"It'll probably take an hour to arrive and you'll be hungry by then," I said encouragingly, and she nodded somewhat reluctantly. I had the number of the restaurant on speed dial and rang and placed the order. I had decided to use the Bombay Palace because they delivered alcohol as well. I ordered a bottle of Merlot for me and a Prosecco for her. Normally I would supply my own booze at this time of night, but I didn't want to have to let Brygida out of my sight. I tried to appear nonchalant, and we made small talk and played with Ania while a kid's programme was on the television in the background.

"How are you, Greg?" she asked.

This slightly threw me. "What do you mean?"

"You were, were…" She was struggling to find the correct word as she acted out what I assumed was someone who was stressed or agitated.

"Agitated?" I suggested. She nodded gently.

"Well yes, I was, but I'm better now that Vicky is away. I'll take a couple of pills when our food arrives." She nodded, as she was used to me taking my prescription drugs.

The food finally arrived, and in my enthusiasm I overtipped the delivery man using some of the wedge that Vicky had given me. He quickly took my money and hurried away gratefully before I changed my mind. I went straight to the kitchen and poured a large glass for Brygida and a tipple for me. "Cheers!" I said with hearty fake enthusiasm.

"Cheers," she replied in her timid voice with a sad-looking smile.

"I'll serve up the food," I said cheerily.

I plated our helpings, hers a nice hot jalfrezi curry and mine a more moderate korma, put the pitta bread, chicken samosas and pakora on separate plates and brought everything through and set them down on the small table across from the sofa. I made sure that the additional hot spicy full-on chilli chutney was next to Brygida's portion. She wanted a glass of water so I brought her a small cup of not particularly cold tap water. Her Prosecco bottle was chilling in the fridge and I topped up her glass. We both ate about two-thirds of our meal. "You sit with Ania," I said. "I'll clear up." I took a couple of my pills along with a large glass of water. I returned to the living room and sat beside Brygida on the couch and put my arm around her. She rested her head against me.

"Greg, I am frightened. Is Vicky gone away forever?" she asked.

For a few minutes during our meal, things had felt almost normal. Brygida's question jolted me back to reality and my heart started racing again. "Yes, she is, so stop worrying. Let's have another drink to celebrate," I said, gesturing a drinking motion as I took her glass and went to the kitchen and filled it up again. We sat pretty much in silence, observing Ania as she watched television. After about thirty minutes Brygida decided it was time for Ania to go to bed, and when she returned ten minutes later it was time for me to get to work. I topped up her drink again. "Be careful," she said, "this will make me sleepy."

I moved the conversation on to her and Piotr. "Do you miss Piotr?" I asked.

"Yes, of course."

"Will he ever come back?" I asked. She didn't answer. I had often seen Brygida upset, but I had never seen her annoyed. Her brow had furrowed when she said this, and it was the nearest I had seen her to being angry.

"Where do you think he is?" I said softly. "Is he in the UK?"

"Why do you ask me this Greg?" She looked sad when she said this.

"Because I love you, Brygida, and want to live with you." I felt that my voice carried the correct level of sincerity, calmness and affection. She looked startled and gave a small gasp.

"But, but I like you, Greg..."

I interrupted, "I want to live with you and adopt Ania," I said. "She can become Ania Stewart." I couldn't believe that I was saying these words. Brygida looked even more worried. I carried on in a similar vein for another fifteen minutes. Brygida's drinking rate had increased. I was pleased on the one hand because my plan appeared to be working, but guilt was beginning to creep in at the way that I was shamelessly lying to Brygida. However, I was desperate, so needs must.

As Brygida slurped through her final glass, she said, "Greg, I like you, but I can't stay with you."

"Why is that?" I asked.

"Because I am going to stay with Piotr."

Over the past two years I had become something of an expert on Jobseeker's Allowance and Housing Benefit because I had been finding out and filling out forms, arranging meetings and assessments on behalf of Brygida. I had always felt quite detached when I carried out any of those tasks, although I felt good that I was helping her. However, Brygida's revelation of her plans had now sunk in and I cast my mind back to earlier when I blurted out, *I love you* and realised that subconsciously over time I had indeed developed feelings for her. Suddenly Brygida's news felt like a huge kick in the balls, and I realised that I was hurt and jealous. She wasn't reciprocating. No doubt she liked me, but more importantly, I was useful to her. I had to put that to the back of my mind for the time being and get the information for Vicky to try and finally bring this relentless nightmare to an end.

"Oh, I see. Sorry, Brygida, I thought that with him vanishing and us becoming, you know, close, that Piotr was gone for good. I'm sorry. I don't make a habit of shagging people's wives…"

"Greg," she said with furrowed brows. My English lessons, given freely and often, must have been good, I thought bitterly, as she could now clearly understand slang.

"No – I just thought that Piotr was gone for good. You never gave any indication that you were in touch or that he was coming back. We see each other a lot, we sleep with each other. I honestly thought that we were an item."

"What is item?"

"I mean that I thought that we were becoming a couple…" I said weakly.

"I like you very much, Greg. You are so good to me and Ania. I love Piotr though. He is my husband."

"But you've slept with me lots of times," I said prissily.

"How you say? – needs must," she said as she turned away.

"What the hell does that mean?" I responded angrily. I didn't need any acting skills here. The role that I was now playing was genuine. "When were you going to tell me?" I almost whispered.

"Soon."

"Oh that's great. Where is he?"

She looked at me in a strange way. "Don't worry, I'm not going to the police or anyone else for that matter," I lied. "If you don't want to tell me, don't bother. Vicky's gone. I thought we could stay together, but if that's what you want, I'll be gone. I have really felt good about helping you and Ania and I hope that Piotr becomes the father and husband that he should. Please don't tell him about us..." I tailed off.

"Greg, I will always be your friend, but I can't be with you. I must be with Piotr."

"I understand," I said stoically. I'll head back to my place and not come round here any more. It doesn't seem right."

"I understand," she said. "Can't we be friends for a bit longer?"

"What on earth do you mean by that?"

"Can you help get me tickets?"

"What do you mean, Brygida?"

"I need to go to Spain to join Piotr– can you help me?"

Chapter Nine

"Piotr's in Spain?" I asked breathlessly.

"Yes."

"How long has he been there?"

"Most of the time."

"You mean over the last two years?"

"Yes."

"And how long have you known?" My heart was pounding.

"Most of the time," she said quietly as she looked away from me. "Can you help me please, Greg?"

Despite my feeling of being double-crossed in the relationship game yet again, I was being delivered the details I needed for Vicky on a plate. "Brygida, you have got to realise that I am very hurt. I thought we had something and now you want to escape from me."

"It isn't that," she said in her small voice. "It's not an escape, but I need to be with Piotr. She needs to be with him," she said, pointing at Ania.

"OK – what do you want me to do?"

"Get us to Spain and speak to the council about my flat. Get rid of it."

"What about your possessions?"

She looked blankly. "All this stuff." I swept my arms around, indicating the contents of her flat.

"Not care," she said.

The teacher came out in me. "You mean you don't care," I corrected, and sighed theatrically. "OK, give me the details. What airport do you want to go to and when? Do you want me to book a hotel?"

"No. Don't need."

"Why is that?"

"Because we stay with Piotr."

"Ah, of course," I said, and tried to smile. Time for a little gentle probing. "What is he doing over there?"

"Works on boats."

"Doing what?"

"Helping on boats."

Not much clearer. "Does he stay on a boat?"

"Not sure."

"I could arrange for a transfer from the airport to his apartment if you want." I was hoping that she was so gullible that she would give me Piotr's address. Unfortunately, she wasn't, so it was time for a different approach. "Brygida, I have had too much to drink tonight and I'm very tired. I'm going home now, and tomorrow, after a good night's sleep, I will come back here and make all the arrangements." My heart was racing, and I went into the kitchen for a glass of water and two more pills. I returned to the living room. "Don't tell anyone of your plans. OK?"

"Of course."

"At this stage, don't even tell Piotr. I'm not sure how you communicate with him," I lied, "but don't say a word just now. Do you understand?" She nodded rather reluctantly. "It may take a few days for me to get everything together and you must be patient. I'll come round tomorrow and we will get everything underway. OK?"

"OK," she replied. She still looked worried and not very reassured. Time to lay it on.

"Brygida, I did think we could become an item, but obviously you and Piotr are still together. You are married, for God's sake, and have a child. I completely respect that, but I thought he was gone forever, and I would never have slept with you otherwise. I'm not that type of person, and I hope you understand that."

"I do, Greg, and very sorry for how it ends." She held out her arms in a resigned fashion. I stood for several seconds, then walked slowly over to her. I put my arms around her, we gently cuddled and then kissed softly.

After a few seconds the kissing became more passionate and our cuddling became more active. I put my arms around her and squeezed her tightly. Her hands were underneath my shirt. I followed suit and we frantically tore at each other's clothes. We didn't make it to the bedroom and dropped on the floor in a welter of frenzied almost violent lovemaking far removed from our usual cautious, respectful approach.

Afterwards, we lay on the carpet in each other's arms for around ten minutes while we cooled down and our heart rates returned to normal.

"Thank you for everything, Greg," she said softly.

"Don't thank me, Brygida, you deserve it. I still think it is best if I go home. Do you understand?"

"Yes, I understand, of course."

"OK. I will be back tomorrow," I said sincerely.

I got up, dressed slowly then kissed her on the forehead. I went into Ania's room and kissed the sleeping child. "Bye," I said softly to her, with tears in my eyes.

"Bye," I said to Brygida, with more tears in my eyes.

I walked slowly to the front door and opened it as quietly as I could. I turned round and gave a gentle wave to Brygida, then left the flat and closed the door behind me. I made my way downstairs and out of the building. As soon as I was out of sight of Brygida's building, I took out my

phone. It was time to call Vicky.

Chapter Ten

It was just after eleven as I walked along the quiet street. I rummaged in my trouser pocket for the scrap of paper with Vicky's number on it. Then I stood under a streetlight so that I could see the number and dial it. It was answered on the first ring. "I told you to text every two hours. I get nothing and now you call," she hissed.

"I'm sorry," I mumbled, "but I have got lots to tell you. Piotr is in Spain and I will get his address tomorrow. Brygida is going to go and stay with him and she wants to take Ania."

"What about Cassie?" she asked angrily.

"Oh I don't know, I haven't got that far yet," I replied.

"For Christ's sake, Greg – we need the full picture," she demanded.

For some reason, while I had been talking to Vicky and making my way back to my flat, I was deliberately keeping my voice down to prevent any eavesdropper from hearing what we were discussing. That went out of the window. "Listen to me!" I shouted into my phone, and a passer-by looked at me and gave me a wide berth.

"On the first day and in a couple of hours I have got nearly everything you want, you ungrateful bitch, and this is how you thank me." Despite the bottle of wine and numerous pills, my anxiety level had suddenly shot through the roof and I could take no more.

"I can't do any more, Vicky. Too bad if Maggie gets killed – there is nothing I can do about that. I can't cope – I can't take any more of this, so just leave me alone. You deal with Clinkie." With that, I ended the call and realised that I had continued along the street as I ranted and was now leaning against railings on the side of the road in front of a taxi rank. There were three cabs in the parking bay and the drivers looked at me suspiciously and no doubt breathed a sigh of relief that I didn't approach any of their cabs when I started walking again.

My tirade to Vicky was no bluff. I couldn't do this again. Before she had re-emerged into my life I was just about coping, but it took very little to trigger anxiety, panic, depression and other negative emotions. Her latest requirements took this to a new level and one which no amount of alcohol or pills could keep suppressed. Paradoxically, although I was extremely agitated and anxious, I wasn't scared. I needed to blurt out to Vicky and was glad I had done so. I considered that as Vicky was on the run and needing to keep her head down, there was little she could do to me. I really liked Maggie and was absolutely appalled at what Vicky had done with her, but I couldn't help. This wasn't like the last time when I got lucky in my desperation to find a code and get my Aunt Isa free. That was a one-off, a random set of circumstances and it wouldn't happen again.

I decided I was going home, not answering my phone on my way there and then packing a bag and disappearing for a while after having first phoned DI Stevenson. Surprisingly, on my way back the phone didn't ring, and no texts were received. In some ways I was glad, but in others this worried me, as I wondered what Vicky was up to. I approached my block and suddenly realised I didn't have a key. When I had left several hours before, Vicky and Di were there, and in my agitated state I hadn't considered how and when I was going to get back into my flat. However, I kept a spare key underneath a plant pot that housed a tired rubber plant which sat beside the front door.

As it was after nine, the front doors were locked. I had to press on the bell three times before the night porter arrived. Luckily, he recognised me and opened the door straight away. He asked if I needed his master key to open my front door, but I explained that I had a spare key hidden in the corridor. I didn't want him anywhere near the flat if Vicky or Di were still there.

I made my way there to find it locked and with the lights off. I retrieved the spare key from its hiding place and opened my door. I put the lights on and went into each room. There was no obvious sign that I had had visitors.

My first stop after the quick tour of the flat was to go to the fridge and take out a beer. I opened the can and drank thirstily from it. I was halfway through when I heard what sounded like a groan. I was in such a state I thought for a second that it was actually me giving out a spontaneous involuntary grunt as I swallowed my beer. I took another large gulp and heard it again, along with a slight tapping noise. That definitely wasn't me, so with my heart racing again, nerves on overdrive and armed with a kitchen knife, I went in search of the noise, which I was sure was coming from the hall cupboard.

I grabbed the handle of the cupboard door and yanked it open with my left hand and brandishing the knife in my right hand. Di sat cowering in the cupboard. She was tied up; her mouth was taped, and she was holding a picture of my parents.

She wasn't winking now as she looked pleadingly at me, reminding me of a frightened rabbit. I ripped the tape from her mouth, and as I used the kitchen knife to cut through the bindings on her wrists and legs, she implored, "Don't call the police. You don't know what trouble that will cause..."

She blurted out in heaving sobs basically what Vicky had already indicated to me earlier, that she was forced to get involved by her big sister and Vicky. "She told me to get a job at West London Action Group and find out your address. Then to check out the place where you stayed and get to know your lifestyle."

Well that would explain why she had become so talkative and friendly with me so quickly after joining the team at West London Action Group. And I had believed it was because she thought I was a great guy and good colleague.

"She was planning to break out as she had to try and track down Piotr and Cassie. When your aunt died and the funeral was confirmed, then that was a lucky coincidence for her."

"What?" I shouted. "My aunt dying was good news for you?"

She sobbed, "I didn't mean it like that. Vicky was planning to break out and she used your aunt's funeral as a way to get in here. Because I had access to staff files and all of Maggie's stuff, I found out the day and location of the funeral easily enough and sent an email to a false address that I had set up to make it look like you were asking Vicky to come over for the funeral and that she could stay at your flat.

"When she got here yesterday, after you left, she did her act in front of the warden and showed him her fake travel documents, which I had produced for her, along with the fake email from you. We even gave him the number of a phone that we said was yours and had a male voice on the voicemail to take messages. Obviously it went straight to messages, and the warden left a message which I think made him feel better because he then took Vicky to your flat and let her in. She let me know when I could come round, so I did that after you had left to go to Brygida's."

It had been so easy to get into what should be a secure building, I thought, as I considered the levels to which she could stoop. The residents all have some issue or other and all require support. That's why we stay there. That's why someone is on duty every night. I recall once Vicky stating that all men think with their dicks, and the warden of Ragmore House had certainly proved that. If I got through this then I would be having words with him, and perhaps his boss if I had the strength.

I picked up the photograph of my parents. It was in a frame and normally sat on the chest of drawers in my bedroom. My relationship with them was cool at best, but they were my parents and I still had a bond with them. "Why did she put this photo with you?" I asked angrily as I pointed at the photograph. "Is she seriously threatening that she will have them harmed?"

"It's a warning, Greg. She's desperate. She needs your help so much. Like it or not, she is part of a network now and some of them would think nothing of carrying out orders, and if that meant…" She tailed off.

When I thought back to Aunt Isa being seized, my chest tightened. I couldn't allow anything similar to happen again. As I was thinking this, I was looking at Di, but I couldn't speak. Di looked back at me and then said firmly and reassuringly, "I don't think that Vicky has done anything to your parents. The photo is just a warning to remind you of what the consequences might be. Think about it, she doesn't want Clinkie or his daughter to know that she is struggling to get anything from you. If she put them onto your parents they would know that something was wrong and Vicky was screwing up."

I considered this, and she had a point. However, that didn't give me any steer on what to do next. Despite this latest shit, I think I still actually liked Di. I knew what Vicky was like and that Di had no doubt been left in a position that gave her zero wriggle room. I needed her on my side for now.

"So, what now with me, you and Maggie? Where is Maggie?" I asked. "Any ideas?"

"I think she's being held by Clinkie's daughter somewhere, but Vicky hasn't told me. It must be nearby because she would have got her near our workplace."

"How would they get her in broad daylight?" I asked.

"Clinkie's daughter is a hard criminal bitch," she said, and looked nervous even talking about her. "She probably used a couple of Clinkie's gang to trick her into going someplace and then grabbed her."

"Where will she be then?" I demanded. Di still didn't directly answer my question.

"We don't have time to try and find out where Maggie is or if your parents have been got at just now. You need to contact Vicky and tell her that you've found me. Say you are sorry for your outburst, which she must understand was due to the stress you are under, and that you will do what she wants. Ask her how you give the information over to her and ask how you know that Maggie is unharmed and how she will be released and where.

"You have to work quick, Greg. Vicky is desperate."

That sent a shiver down my spine, as I knew from bitter experience what Vicky was capable of when she was desperate. I went to the kitchen, got a beer from the fridge then picked up the phone and texted Vicky.

Chapter Eleven

I got straight to the point in my text to Vicky.

Sorry about outburst – stress getting to me. I'll go to Brygida's tomorrow – tell me what you want me to do when I have the info.

I expected an immediate response, but none was forthcoming. An hour later I finished my third beer and decided it was time for bed, although I didn't expect to sleep. All the while Di had been playing on her phone or staring at the television, which was on, but with the sound muted.

"I'm going to bed. I'll get you some covers and you can sleep on the sofa," I stated neutrally.

I still liked, or at least felt sorry for Di, but I was in no mood for chivalry, because, after all, she had helped get me into this situation. If I was going to be tossing and turning all night, it was going to be in my own bed and not on the sofa. I got some spare bedding, handed it to her and went off to my room without any further words.

After a restless, sleep-interrupted night, I was roused by the tone of my text alert as I lay in bed. It simply said – *Go to B's, do your stuff then text me.* I replied *OK.* During the night I had again considered why Di had been bound up and left at my flat. I presumed there may have been a falling out and Vicky was showing Di who was boss, and she was also warning me as well.

My stomach was churning when I got up from my bed and went to the bathroom for a pee and a shower. I returned to my bedroom, got dressed and went into the kitchen past a sleeping Di who was breathing very gently. She looked almost childlike, and I found it hard to contemplate her role in this nightmare. I made her a cup of tea: milk, two sugars. I remembered that from work and went into the living room.

"Di," I said, but there was no response. "Di," a little louder and she still didn't respond. I then gently gripped her left shoulder which was outside the cover and rocked her. She had taken off her shirt and just had her bra on top and I felt a bit uncomfortable touching her exposed flesh. After about thirty seconds she awoke with a start and then screamed. I recoiled. "Shoosh!" I said, "It's all right, it's all right, it's me, it's Greg." I held her by both shoulders and turned her to face me, and after a few seconds her panic subsided. "It's OK, it's OK," I kept repeating.

Her breathing slowed down and she said, "Sorry, I was in a crazy dream when you woke me, and I flipped. I'm not used to this," she said nervously.

"Well I am, and it doesn't get any better," I replied bitterly. "Have a cup of tea." I told her I was off to Brygida's. "I want no sign of you here when I return, do you understand?" I asked. Vicky hadn't acknowledged Di at all in her text, but I wanted her gone by the time I got back. "Yes, that's fine," she said, but she didn't look fine to me.

I looked at my watch; it was nearly nine o'clock. I picked up my jacket, put it on and walked to the front door. "Right, that's me off to Brygida's. I don't know where you're going or what you're going to do, but if Vicky contacts you, tell her I'll get the information she needs and give it to her. I don't expect to see you again, and I hope Maggie is going to be all right." I looked at her pleadingly and accusingly at the same time. There was no point me issuing threats about what I would do if Maggie wasn't all right because she knew they would be pointless. With that I left. I could see the top of the warden's bald head as he bent to pick up a box underneath the reception desk. I was angry at his incompetence in allowing Vicky access to my flat, but accepted that she would have found a way in, with or without his unwitting co-operation.

As I was walking towards Brygida's I asked myself why I had left Di in my flat and not thrown her out at the same time I had left. I couldn't answer that question, which was worrying as I was about to embark on my latest and most important task. Before I knew it, I was at Brygida's. I rang the bell and waited patiently for the door to be opened. Eventually Brygida appeared and let me in. She was still in her nightwear and dressing gown and looked very dishevelled. "I am sorry, Greg," she said.

"Why are you apologising?" I asked.

"I feel…" She pointed at her head and stomach as her words tailed off.

"Hungover?" I suggested, and she nodded. I thought back guiltily to how much Prosecco I had plied her with the previous night. I reassured her, "Have a glass of water, get a shower and I'll make you a cup of tea. Has Ania had her breakfast yet?" I asked. She shook her head. "No worries. I'll get her something. What does she normally have?"

"Cereal," she replied.

"OK," I answered, and went looking for the Weetabix. I was surprised at how well I was acting in my role of Brygida's friend and helper, a role that up to yesterday was genuine and not a sham. I brooded as I began to think of life without her and Ania.

Brygida appeared dressed and looking a bit better. I handed her a cup of tea, which she took gratefully and sat at the table beside Ania, having given her a kiss on the head as she sat down. Ania had been remarkably friendly towards me despite witnessing the turmoil I had caused yesterday. "Get this tea down you. Do you want anything to eat – maybe some toast?" I asked breezily. Brygida shook her head.

"See to Ania and then we'll get on with this," I said encouragingly. My thoughts about both of them leaving had unsettled me and the butterflies were fluttering big style in my stomach. Brygida dealt with Ania by wiping her daughter's hands and mouth, speaking softly in Polish and then taking out some toys in the corner of the room for her to play with. She put on a kid's television channel for added entertainment and plonked Ania on the floor, who then immediately started playing with her toys.

"OK, let's get started," I said. As I wanted to appear businesslike and supportive, I suggested to Brygida that we begin with starting a to-do list covering all the key domestic tasks such as informing the council about her departure and listing all of the agencies she would need to contact. Brygida agreed and went to the magazine rack, from where she got a writing pad. She spent several minutes locating a pen that worked, and we were now ready to begin. Brygida said the name of each institution that she thought needed to be contacted and I would nod before she wrote it down. We quickly had a list of eight bodies, although she hadn't mentioned her bank.

"What about your bank account?" I asked.

"Leave it, Piotr will do it," she replied. My heart and stomach fluttered at the sound of his name. My future, along with Vicky's and Maggie's, depended massively on what Brygida was going to divulge, hopefully very shortly.

"OK. We'll start contacting them today," I said authoritatively, and pointed to her list.

"Have you decided when you are going to leave?" I asked almost too casually.

"We leave eight days from now," she said. My flutters intensified. The way she said this confirmed that after I had left her flat last night she must have spoken with Piotr and they had agreed and finalised their plans.

"Well, we don't have much time then. Let's get on with this," I said. We spent the next forty minutes going through old papers, searching online and locating what appeared to be the best contact details for each institution. I then typed up a template to use to inform various agencies, such as the council, housing association, health centre and drop-in centre of Brygida's imminent departure. I put my postal address as the contact details and told Brygida that if she gave me her new address I could then send on relevant communications or documents. She looked at me quizzically for a moment then got up and went to her bedroom. She returned to the living room with a scrap of paper and copied the information on it onto the writing pad, then ripped off that page and handed it to me. My heart sank. It was the Spanish equivalent of a PO number. Still, I had at least narrowed down Piotr's location.

I carried on with my charade. "Thanks for that. Hopefully there won't be much that needs to be sent to you," I said. She nodded in agreement. I spent another few hours with Brygida as we typed up and sent off her various notifications.

"Let's get on with booking your flights," I said after we had finished our first task. Brygida sighed.

"Don't you want to go?" I said.

"Yes, of course," she replied, "but all this, this..." She tailed off.

"Change?" I added.

"Yes, change. It makes me..." She mimed trembling.

"Nervous?"

"Yes, nervous."

"Well you'll be back together as a family, so that will be good," I said, and tried to appear happy for her and not show my genuine regret at her imminent departure as I needed to stay focussed. "Remind me of the date." She did. "And where in Spain are you flying to?" I asked.

"Tenerife," she answered.

The butterflies started fluttering in my stomach again as I took another step towards locating Piotr. After significant online searching, I made a flight booking with a budget airline from Gatwick to Tenerife in eight days' time and booked her and Ania on return tickets as it was cheaper than one way.

"Best that you let Piotr know what flight you are on. You better let him know as soon as possible," I added rather unnecessarily. However, I was getting carried away and hoped she may phone or text him while I was there and somehow I could look at her phone and get his contact details when she was distracted.

"Make sure you give him the flight number and time of arrival," I said. "Do you want me to send them to him?"

"No, I will do it," she told me as she picked up her phone. I picked up mine and pretended to be casually checking my social media on it as I surreptitiously watched what Brygida was doing. I could see that she was on Facebook and was messaging someone, who I assumed was Piotr. When she was finished, I asked for a cup of tea. She got up, checked on Ania first and then went into the kitchen.

I picked up my phone again, logged into Facebook as Brygida, used an app to translate, and checked her messages. Piotr had already replied. I read the bland exchange of messages between them again and did a couple of quick Google searches while Brygida made my cuppa. By the time the kettle had boiled, I had cracked their code.

I had narrowed down Piotr's whereabouts. He was indeed in Tenerife, living on a boat berthed in the harbour at Puerto Colón, in the south of the island, to be precise.

Chapter Twelve

"I think that's enough for now. Do you want some lunch?" I asked Brygida.

"No. I want to take Ania to park," she replied. I was glad I could get some time away from them as I needed to contact Vicky and pass over the details I had successfully got. However, there was a bit of me pissed off, or at least slightly sad, that after helping Brygida all morning it seemed that she couldn't wait to get away from me.

"OK. I'll head off for now. Should I pop by later?" I asked.

"Maybe tomorrow," she replied, looking sad. I picked up Ania, said *bye* and gave her a kiss. She smiled at me. Typical, I thought, just as I'm bonding with her she's leaving. I looked at my watch as I made my way down the communal stairs. It was past twelve. I'm not normally a lunchtime drinker but felt that in my current circumstances I deserved one. I headed into a pub at the edge of the park and ordered a pint and took a seat. I didn't want to engage with anyone so took out my phone and started playing with it. Before I contacted Vicky I went back into Brygida's Facebook page to see if there were any other messages between Brygida and Piotr; there were.

Her – *The cleaner has left.*

Him – *Good. Has cleaner got anything?*

Her – *No.*

Obviously I was relying on a translation and wouldn't pick up if they were using puns or other nuances in their native language, but it appeared that they were using the same code as ever: replacing one key word with another that may have some vague connection. In this case no doubt *cleaner* was chosen as it was neutral but suggested clearing up Brygida's affairs. The question from Piotr asking if the cleaner got anything I guessed was him asking if I had got his address or any hints of where it was. I was glad to see that she had told him I hadn't.

I scrolled back to their exchange from earlier in the day that had led me to Piotr's whereabouts,

Her – *My sister and niece are coming to visit.*

Him – *That's nice. I would like to meet them.*

Her – *OK. Where?*

Him – *Tell them that the harbour is nice.*

Her – *Which one?*

Him – *The one that makes you think of your stomach!*

Her – *Are there lots of nice boats?*

Him – *Yes, the Shark is nice.*

Her – *OK. I will let them know!*

I hadn't understood this reference so had then searched under *harbours in Tenerife* and found a list of harbours and marinas. Puerto Colón was fourth on the list. Piotr's English must have improved, I thought, as he had linked *colon* to *stomach* and Brygida obviously understood. I had guessed that the boat he was working on and possibly living on would be called the Shark, or perhaps the Spanish equivalent - *El Tiberon*. Bearing in mind they were writing in a foreign language that they had only learned over the past couple of years, I reckoned their coded communication was quite good. I was no Alan Turing and had only narrowed down Piotr's location because I knew he was in Tenerife.

Having gone back over many of Brygida's messages, which were all similar in style, I felt less treacherous at the thought of what I was soon going to do. She had obviously been in contact with Piotr from soon after he disappeared two years ago and yet she had never let on to me and had continued to play the victim and let me run after her. I was beginning to become quite angry and had to snap out of it. I went to the bar and ordered a second beer. It was time to contact Vicky. I sat down, had a large slug of lager and checked my phone for text messages from her. She hadn't sent any further ones since last night and so I replied to the existing number I had for her.

Got P's location. B flies out in 8 days.

Unlike last time, the reply was instant.

C u at B's pub in 15.

That was it. Not a "good" or "well done", just an instruction on where I was going to give her the information. I was quite proud of how I had worked out Brygida and Piotr's code so quickly and how easily I had squeezed information from Brygida. Of course, Vicky didn't give a shit about that – she just wanted the information as quickly as possible and screw the rest of us.

I assumed that "B's" as referred to in Vicky's text was Bonaly's, which was a slightly tatty pub near to Ealing Broadway station. In previous, happier times, I had had a drink there with Vicky once or twice, and I think she chose it because it had a front door and also a side one accessed from a lane which, given her current fugitive status, would make it easier for her to slip in and out unnoticed. At lunchtime there were always a few drinkers around attracted by very generous Monday to Thursday happy hours that lasted from one until four.

I finished my pint and headed for Bonaly's, which was around fifteen minutes' walk away, I wasn't going to take a taxi. Vicky hadn't asked my location and had just expected that I would be nearby and jump at her command. I decided that she could wait for me, and the walk gave me time to reflect and speculate. I felt that surely Vicky must appreciate what I had done for her as I was going to give her Piotr's location, which she would pass on to Clinkie Moore. This would allow Maggie to be freed and for both of us to somehow get on with our lives. I still couldn't fathom out what the knock-on effect for Di would be.

I had tried not to think about my parents too much, but hoped they hadn't been affected in any way by this latest twist and that Vicky leaving the framed photo of them with Di was simply a warning. I felt secure in the knowledge that if Vicky was indeed going to get a new identity and disappear somewhere, which was hopefully abroad, that would mean I would never see her again after today. The butterflies kicked in again at this thought, but this time it was in a feeling of anticipation rather than of anxiety.

My dawdling walk meant I made it to Bonaly's around twenty-five minutes after receiving Vicky's text. I ordered a pint and looked around the pub. There were a few Transport for London workers who had finished their shifts at the station and were having some good-natured banter amongst themselves, along with a sprinkling of office workers and student types. I couldn't see Vicky and made my way to a table at the back of the pub to wait for her. As I made my way there, I knocked against a table that was occupied by a studenty type reading a book and nearly spilled her soda water and lime.

"I'm sorry," I said, and gave a weak smile. She looked up from her book and said quietly, "You're late." I did a double take. It was Vicky. If she hadn't spoken then I would never have recognised her. Her usual striking auburn hair was now jet black and scraped back and held in place by a thick black plastic band. She was wearing small round glasses with thick black frames and had a nose stud. Black was the theme, as her T-shirt and trousers were black as well and she was wearing black fingerless gloves. She put her book down, which I noticed was *The French Lieutenant's Woman*, and beckoned me to sit beside her.

"Want a drink?" I asked.

"No thanks – let's get on with it," she said quietly but firmly.

Part of me wanted to milk this given the grief that Vicky had given me and how much she wanted this information. I handed her a piece of paper on which I had written Brygida's flight details, Piotr's PO box number in Spain and the name of the harbour in Tenerife along with name of the boat in both Spanish and English.

"Is there anything else you need?" I asked as she looked at the piece of paper. She continued looking at the paper for some time before folding it up and putting it in her rather large purse. "Greg – you're a star," she said, and leaned over and gave me a peck on the cheek. "I'll take a drink now – vodka and tonic."

Well her cheek hadn't left her. I had done all the hard work and now my reward was to buy her a drink. I took a large slug of my beer and went to the bar to order her drink and another one for me. When I returned to the table, she smiled and said, "We're nearly there."

"What do you mean – nearly there?" I asked. "We are there. You just need to let Maggie go, confirm that my parents are fine and that's it. I like Di, but she's no concern of mine and I don't know if she's innocent or a key part of your gang."

Vicky gave a half-smile and said, "Just one more thing... Clinkie." I had never met the man, but the mention of his name was enough to send shivers down my spine and put butterflies in my stomach.

"I've given you all the information you need for Clinkie. He should be delighted – it has taken less than two days from when you reappeared."

"Quieten down, tiger," she said in an affected soothing voice as she theatrically looked around the bar. This just served to get me more agitated. She put her hands on top of mine, looked me in the eyes as if we were a couple dealing with an argument and said quietly but firmly, "Greg, we are in a public place. Don't draw attention to us. We are nearly done, but be clear that Clinkie Moore makes Kev Osborne and his sidekick Daz Jackson seem like choirboys. There is every chance he has got men out looking for me – and you…" – she let that one hang for a few seconds – "and believe me they won't piss about, Greg."

I nodded and sat back and had a large gulp of lager while surreptitiously looking round to see if anyone appeared to be watching us. I was just so glad I didn't have to deal with Clinkie Moore, and all I wanted Vicky to do was give him the information she had on Piotr as soon as possible and be away from me forever. These thoughts were shattered by her next statement. "So, the final thing we need to do, Greg, is for you to go to Clinkie's house and steal my papers."

Chapter Thirteen

"What – are you having a laugh? You've got to be kidding," I said in a low voice that sounded like a wail.

"I'm not," she answered in an affected calm voice.

"Look, Vicky, I've done what you asked. I'm finished. Get off my back and let Maggie go."

"I'm sorry, Greg. I can't. I want my new identity papers and passport now."

"Why?" I asked. "Surely once you've given Clinkie the information he needs then you'll get your papers and that's you done with him?

"Christ, Greg, you are so naive. It doesn't work like that," she replied. "Once you are in the clutches of a guy like Clinkie Moore, then that's it. As far as he's concerned, you're his, to be used as and when he wants. I'm in debt to him and Suzi and this won't pay that off..." she said, pointing at her purse, which contained the information on Piotr that I had given her.

"So, what are you going to do?" I asked naively.

"When you have got my passport and the other papers, I am off, never to be seen again," she said quietly with a strange look in her eyes.

"And how am I going to get them?"

"Easy."

"Easy?"

"Yes, easy. It's Clinkie's youngest daughter Hannah's wedding tomorrow. The reception is being held in a marquee in the garden of his house. He has a large ranch-style house near a town called Carluke in Lanarkshire. It's about thirty minutes' drive from Glasgow. You need to get a job as a casual waiter at the reception, which will get you access to Clinkie's house. I have taken the liberty of registering you with an agency and they have hired you. You will get slightly more than the minimum wage."

Her flippancy was really getting to me, and yet again she had something all planned out in how she was going to exploit me for her own ends. She took out a letter from her large purse.

"So, here is your contract of engagement with Catering Solutions, which provide services to weddings and other functions. A minibus is picking everyone up from Buchanan Bus Station, Glasgow at nine tomorrow morning. Make sure you don't miss the bus."

"But, but..." I tailed off.

"Greg, it will be easy," she interjected.

"You keep saying that, but how? If it was so easy then why don't you get them?"

"Greg, don't be so silly. If Clinkie saw me anywhere near his house or family he would know that something serious was up," she asserted.

"And how is it going to be easy for me?"

"Last week I asked Suzi to prove that her dad had got my papers while I was facetiming her. She was back home and she showed herself walking up the stairs of her parents' house, going into an office to the right-hand side of the stairs and taking the papers out of the top left-hand drawer of a large desk. All you need to do is to find a way to get into the house, get up to the office, take the papers, hide them on you and then finish your shift and leave. Piece of cake." She picked up her drink and had a sip.

I couldn't look at her and was staring at someone playing the fruit machine as I said with controlled fury out of the side of my mouth, "Do you honestly think I am going to steal something from the house of Clinkie Moore? You must be off your head."

"Well, Greg – I wouldn't want Maggie to hear you talking like that. I will be looking after her while you and Suzi are at the wedding."

I looked at her and couldn't say anything to that. After about a minute's silence between us, which I felt that Vicky was using to exploit my weaknesses, I said, "What will you do with the details about Piotr that I got for you?"

"You ask too many questions, Greg, but they will help me to disappear."

"What do you mean?"

She ignored my question and took an envelope out of her purse. "Here's a ticket from Victoria bus station to Glasgow. Now hurry, it leaves in a couple of hours."

I took the envelope and put it in my pocket without saying anything. My second pint dutifully dispatched, I got up, went to the bar and ordered a third. I didn't ask Vicky if she wanted a drink, and when I returned to our table she was gone. When I sat down, I looked at the ticket and saw that the bus didn't actually leave until seven o'clock. I sighed, took a leisurely sip of my beer, checked the bar meals menu and decided what I would have to eat as I now had time to kill. I was actually quite hungry, but when the food arrived, I found I couldn't eat it. I pushed the plate to the side, got up and went to the toilets. I just made it into a cubicle before violently throwing up.

I hadn't yet met him, but Clinkie Moore already had his hot breath on my neck.

Chapter Fourteen

After an uncomfortable overnight bus journey involving numerous pickup points en route and a fifty-minute stop at a motorway service station at some ungodly hour, I arrived in Glasgow just a bit after seven. The journey terminated at Buchanan Bus Station, so that at least meant that I didn't have to find my way around the city in order to make my pickup with Catering Solutions.

I had spent much of the night unable to sleep on the bus. I was sitting two rows from the back in an aisle seat next to an extremely large middle-aged man. For pretty much all of the twelve-hour journey north I was jostled by passengers as they made their way to the toilet, which was situated at the back. Anytime I was drifting off to sleep, it seemed that someone would brush against me with never a word of apology. Whenever the toilet door was opened, the whiff of the chemical smell was overpowering.

The bus journey gave me plenty of time to think. However, to be honest, my thinking time was not very productive. I pondered what Vicky was going to do with the details of Piotr's whereabouts. All I could think of was that she would give them to one of Clinkie's rivals, Clinkie would get wind of this and realise she was using Piotr as bait to cause a bloodbath between two gang lords to give her the space to exit stage left.

All of these thoughts simply compounded my nervousness at the situation I had found myself in. I didn't know if I would contact Brygida or not. She would be wondering what had caused my non-appearance at her flat last night after our productive day together and I hoped she thought that it was because I was emotionally disturbed at not becoming an item with her.

I was naturally extremely nervous about going to Clinkie's and getting Vicky's papers, but perhaps even more scared about, even if I did somehow manage to get them, how I would do so undetected and then make my escape. These thoughts came back to me as I sat in the draughty bus station café drinking coffee and trying to eat a bacon roll. The thick pink meat was hanging out of the roll as I bit into it. Unfortunately, I had bitten into a large piece of yellowish fat which was sticking in my throat. I gagged and put my head down, retrieved the offending lump from my mouth and put it in my napkin. There were only two other diners in the café and neither seemed to notice. I put my food aside as I couldn't face any more of it. The roll certainly wasn't pleasant, but my loss of appetite was caused as much by my nerves and lack of sleep. I still had over an hour to go before being picked up, and I absently played with my phone. Vicky had supplied a new number to text her on and I was tempted to do so. However, I was on strict instructions to only contact her in an emergency, and texting her to complain about my bacon roll didn't quite fit the bill. It was a crap roll though.

After a while I went for several slow walks round the block and returned to the café for a third and final coffee. I visited the toilets to examine myself. The sink was relatively clean, so I reckoned it was safe to give my face a splash to wake up and psychologically give myself a boost. Before boarding the coach in London, I had bought a small bottle of aftershave at a chemist near Victoria bus station and now put some of it on.

The instruction from Catering Solutions that Vicky had printed off and put in the envelope along with my bus ticket, was to stand on the pavement outside the bus station opposite stance three, which was next to the newsagents. It turned out this was also right next to the café. I left the café, looked for and found the designated spot for the casual staff pickup and dutifully stood in line on the pavement.

The pickup time was given as nine am. The dress code for men was black trousers and a white shirt with collar and sleeves. It was eight forty-five and I was the first person there, which immediately induced mild panic as I thought I had the wrong place. Also, I hadn't noticed the bit in the instructions about clothing up until now. A few minutes later a couple of attractive young females approached and one of them asked me in broken English if this was where they got picked up for the wedding. I nodded enthusiastically and told them it was, glad I was no longer on my own. Within minutes another eight people had arrived and asked each other if they were in the right queue. I noticed that all but one of them appeared to be meeting the dress code.

At ten past nine, a mini coach turned up and a middle-aged woman got off. She was heavily made-up and looked like a drinker. Her make-up hadn't hidden the broken veins and lines on her face. "Good morning," she said. "I am from Catering Solutions." Her gravelly voice was that of a heavy smoker. "I will read out your name and then you get on the bus." She had a list on a clipboard and read out each name in turn and the person came forward, was marked on the sheet and got on the bus. I was second last to be called and my pseudonym of "Grant Douglas" was one of the few British-sounding names. Most of the surnames appeared to be Eastern European, and the murmur of conversations that I could pick up on the bus suggested that.

The woman, who had not given her name, told the driver to start up, he did so, and we were on our way. I had never visited Glasgow before, and so, despite my nerves at going to Clinkie's, I was vaguely interested in where we were going and noticed Celtic Park as we made our way out of the city, and not long after that we were on the motorway and picking up speed.

After that there was nothing much to watch, and I stared vacantly out of the window and tried to think about what I was about to do. Vicky had persuaded me to go to the house of one of Glasgow's most notorious villains and steal from it. I shuddered and surreptitiously slipped two of my beta blockers into my mouth. I looked at the strip of remaining pills in the silver foil sachet and was disappointed to see that there were only six left. Because I hadn't gone to my flat after seeing Vicky in the pub, I hadn't packed and therefore not picked up any extra supplies. I was on a repeat prescription but was using them so quickly that no pharmacy would give me another batch for at least a fortnight. Another entry into my anxiety top ten and, if I hadn't been so desperate, I might have found the irony of my anxiety levels being increased by thinking about tablets designed to reduce anxiety wryly amusing.

After about fifty minutes we were skirting a town which I think was the one that Vicky had called Carluke, before turning onto a country road. We drove for around another ten minutes and then took a turn up a lane. It was gated and had an intercom. The driver wound down the window, pressed a button on the intercom and after a pause spoke into it. The gate opened. We proceeded along the driveway towards a large ranch-style house which appropriately had a horse in a field adjoining the garden. We were directed by a security guard round to the side of the house. The bus stopped and the unnamed woman said loudly, "Please wait on the bus. I will check us in and then you will be given your duties." Perhaps because of the foreign element amongst the casual staff, she used lots of exaggerated arm movements when delivering this information. She left the bus and returned a few minutes later accompanied by a small middle-aged man, who although dressed in a suit and tie, still looked untidy, even scruffy. "This is Norrie. He is head of CM Security. He will give you your roles and explain the rules. Over to you, Norrie."

"Thanks, Veronica," he said. Norrie was only about five foot seven and he was probably in his fifties but could have been a bit younger as the years of smoking and drinking may well have taken their toll. I was in the second row of the bus and Norrie was standing in the aisle beside me. I could smell the smoke and his cheap aftershave wafting from him. There was dandruff on his collar that the thin strands of his greying brown hair didn't quite cover.

"Good morning everyone." No one answered. "I'll try again. Good morning."

This redcoat stuff was irritating. A few mumbled good mornings were offered, which fortunately was enough for Norrie to continue. "As Veronica says, I am Norrie and in charge of security. I work for Charles Moore Security and you are going to be working for Mr Moore today. He is a very important man and his daughter's wedding must be perfect. Understand?" A few people nodded, but no one said anything.

"I will tell you your jobs and introduce you to the people you will be working with. How many of you speak English? Put up your hands. That's good; all but one of you. How many people speak Scottish?" he said with a grin which showed his tiny little yellow teeth. I looked at my terms of contract in which Vicky had registered me as Grant Douglas. I thought that I may need him onside, so I put up my hand and said, "I'm from Birmingham, but my dad's Scottish."

"Good man!" he said. What's your name?"

"Grant," I replied.

"Sounds a bit Scottish," he replied.

"How many people are from here?" he continued. Norrie obviously had no communication skills, and I think he meant how many people were Scottish or British, but obviously a few misinterpreted and put their hands up. He shrugged and then continued. "OK, Grant, I'll start with you. You can speak the lingo, so you are going to work with matey over there." He pointed diagonally at a fellow passenger and indicated to that person to stand up and come down the bus. "That's it," he said, as if addressing a young child, "you come down here." Because the person couldn't speak English, Norrie was saying this very loudly and gesticulating.

"Name?" Norrie said. The young fair-haired man who appeared around twenty looked at Norrie but didn't say anything.

"What is your name?" Norrie asked again, this time with his face very close to the young man. It can't have been pleasant for him to smell Norrie's breath. "I am Norrie," he continued, pointing at himself. "This is Grant," he said, pointing at me. "What is your name?" he asked again.

"Me, Matis," the young man said, pointing at himself.

"At last. Thank you. Is that like the singer Johnny Mathis?" Norrie said with a grin.

Matis looked at him blankly. I stepped in. "I think his name is Matis," I said, emphasising the *t* in his name rather than a *th*.

"OK. Matis, you go there," Norrie said with a slight scowl aimed at me as he pointed to the side of the marquee. "Grant, you go there as well and wait for me."

He went through his registration procedure with everyone on the bus, and after twenty minutes we were all waiting in our designated spots and ready to go. As soon as he got off the bus, Norrie lit a cigarette in a flowing movement borne from years of experience. He came over and told me I was going to work on glass collection and that as Matis was to work with me, I would have to show him what to do. Matis was the other person who wasn't wearing a white shirt.

"Norrie, I'm sorry, but I forgot to bring a white shirt and I don't think he has one either," I said, pointing at Matis. I didn't mention my lack of black trousers either, hoping that my dark blue cargo trousers would suffice. Norrie didn't seem to notice.

"There's always a couple..." he said with a theatrical sigh. "Veronica's got a supply. I'll come round with them in a while. OK, let's go," he said, and we dutifully followed him. He had his fag cupped in his hand between puffs as we made our way to the back of the marquee. Norrie seemed the type who could make a roll-up out of three strands of tobacco and still get a good smoke out of it. "Wait there," he instructed, as he took a final couple of extremely long drags of his cigarette before throwing it to the ground and then going in. He re-emerged a couple of minutes later and told us to follow him. The bar was already set up and had its own staff on duty.

"Grant, you and him are working here. Now listen to me. You don't go behind the bar at any time. You and him collect the glasses and go to the side to deposit them and wash them. Maybe best that you collect and he washes." He pointed at Matis as if he was a dumb animal.

"Brian is the head barman. Brian!" he shouted. Brian came over.

"Hi Brian, you've struck gold, one of them speaks English," he said, pointing at me.

"What a result," Brian replied in a deadpan drawl.

"They're all yours," Norrie said, as he left with the remaining casual labour from the bus and took them around the marquee to assign them to their tasks. There was a hive of activity as a crew were setting out tables and chairs.

"What's your name?" Brian asked me.

"I'm Grant." I held out my hand and he shook it.

"What's your name?" he said to Matis.

Matis nodded. Brian sighed and shrugged.

"He's called Matis," I said.

"This is the biggest do of Clinkie's life. He is a very important man. We can't screw it up. Yet we get sent a bunch of muppets to help out."

I hadn't been called a muppet before...

"You, what's your name again?" Brian asked.

"Grant," I replied.

"Right, you, Grant, service has got to be perfect. You and your pal will not be serving behind the bar or at the tables." This pleased me, and I told him that I understood because Norrie had already told us that.

"You will be getting the glasses and cleaning and stacking them. We don't want empty glasses at any table, and we don't want the bar running out of glasses when the drink is flowing after the ceremony. This will go on to at least two in the morning and we need a constant supply of clean glasses. It's up to you two. You make sure that the bar staff always have enough glasses and that the plates and cutlery are taken out the back to be cleaned and stacked. Understand?" he asked, looking at me intently.

I nodded overenthusiastically. "Comprendo?" he said to Matis, who looked at him blankly. "Right, Grant, make it clear to your buddy what he has to do."

"OK, I will," I said.

"Where are your uniforms? You should be wearing white shirts and black bow ties."

"Norrie's coming round with them," I replied.

"OK, but I don't want any prick on duty that's not looking the part. Clinkie might do a spot check." They certainly knew how to treat their staff in these parts. First I was a muppet, then a prick. Perhaps I should have checked my contract. I decided to play the daft laddie, as they would say in these parts.

I replied, "You said that Clinkie is very important – what does he do?"

He laughed. "You never heard of Clinkie Moore?" I shook my head. "Where are you from?"

"Birmingham, but I've just started a course at Strathclyde Uni," I lied.

"Well, let's put it this way – Clinkie is a very successful businessman round here," he said with a bit of a catch in his voice.

"Well, if this do is so important—"

"It is," he interjected. "It's his daughter's wedding, for Christ's sake."

I sensed his nerves. "Yes, well obviously it's very important, so why does he bring in additional catering staff that in your mind are hopeless?"

"Easy," he said, lowering his voice and looking around. "That useless prick Norrie."

I looked at him waiting for him to go on. He didn't, so I asked, "What do you mean?"

"I shouldn't say this, but I'm so nervous about today and tried everything to get out of this gig, but my boss is pals with Clinkie and promised him his best bar staff. If anything goes wrong today we're mince."

"What's that got to do with Norrie?"

"That wee weasel is Clinkie's brother-in-law. Useless at anything he touches. But to keep the missus happy, Clinkie has made Norrie, who is her little runt of a brother, head of facility security at CMS. Which means that Norrie in theory looks after functions. Look at this, he uses a company that employs illegals who can't speak the lingo."

"Why does he do that?"

"Because the ugly little rat is shagging that fat cow Veronica and they are skimming from the wages budget and divvying it up. Norrie gets a budget and he's cutting costs to skim."

"Is that wise?" I asked rather unnecessarily.

"Of course not, but he thinks it's just catering and there is little that can be screwed up with menial labour. Tell you one thing, I wouldn't be fucking about with any arrangements for Clinkie's wedding."

I nodded. On the bus up from London, I had done an online search on Clinkie. It threw up many references to Charles Cameron Moore, aka Clinkie. He was of indeterminate age from the photos of him, but I worked it out as forty-seven from references to his age from reports over the years of his many dubious activities. Several reports from Scottish newspapers seemed almost deferential in the coverage of him. He was heavily involved in bookmaking and tax avoidance, it seemed. There were lots of references to his criminal associations, but he didn't appear to have spent any significant time inside, despite, I think, *clink* meaning prison in Scotland.

There was a sudden burst of bustling commotion and one of Brian's staff made a frantic hand signal. "Shit," Brian said quietly out of the side of his mouth.

"What is it?" I asked.

"Clinkie's on his way and he's agitated. You and him get out of the way. Get through the back and make sure you get your uniforms on."

105

I called on Matis and gestured for him to follow me. We went behind the curtains of the gantry of the bar into what effectively functioned as its cellar. It had numerous boxes of spirits, beer barrels and boxes of all types of glasses, and I drew the curtains across the opening just as I heard a gruff and almost indecipherable voice order people about. I peeked through the curtains and saw three men enter the marquee and make their way towards the bar. They were dressed casually, as if they were on their way to the golf club for a Sunday round. "Jonjo, get Brian," the smallest and oldest man instructed. He was wearing a pink woollen V-neck, and I guessed that this must be Clinkie giving the orders.

"Brian, get your arse over here," the man called Jonjo shouted. Jonjo was at least six inches taller than Clinkie and heavyset. He looked to be around sixteen stone, had a full head of black hair and appeared to be in his mid to late thirties. The other man was around the same age and height as Jonjo, but bald, with a close-cropped beard and looked far more athletic, as if he worked out regularly.

I once had a knife held at my throat thinking that I was going to die and also had a gun pointed at me by a desperate man, but neither of these people scared me like Clinkie Moore did. On those previous occasions these people were acting as they did because they felt they had no choice because circumstances had dictated their desperate actions. This was different. At first glance it was obvious that Clinkie Moore was one hundred per cent bad and that was his life. He wasn't tall – perhaps five foot nine at most and was powerfully built but not ripped. He spoke quietly and his voice was a low growl. He had small dark eyes that seemed to constantly scan and appraise a situation. He appeared calm, but ready to strike at any time.

"Brian!" Jonjo shouted again. Brian, who had been hiding in the back, ostensibly setting up the draft beers, walked over to the trio. His body language suggested he was trying to appear calm and in control.

"How's it going?" Jonjo asked.

"Fine," Brian replied, "everything is coming together." As he said this he gestured around the marquee and its surroundings with a wide spread of his arms. Clinkie said something, but I couldn't make it out. The group with Brian leading made its way towards the bar area. Jonjo and the other man were having some exchanges, and the way that bigger, louder people such as them skirted around Clinkie showed to me that he was a hard bastard who they were trying hard to impress. My heart skipped a beat as they approached the bar, and Clinkie said, "Let's have a look in the back. I want it set up like a proper bar, no short cuts."

"Of course," Brian said. I noticed that he didn't dare call him by name. My heart rate kept skipping as they walked up to the bar and then approached the curtains behind which I was standing with Matis. I quickly moved away and started moving some boxes of glasses just as they came through into the back. Matis just stood there. Clinkie looked at us both and surveyed the back of house area. "Are these yours?" he asked Brian.

"Nah, agency," Brian replied.

Clinkie looked at us both like we were something he had just trodden on. He turned to Brian and I could see he wasn't happy. "Look at the state of them. Where's their uniforms?" he asked in his low slow growl.

"Norrie's bringing the uniforms over," Brian replied nervously.

"Norrie..." Clinkie drawled as he walked over towards Matis and me. His small eyes were narrowed as he approached. I could feel my heart racing, and I wished that I was like Matis and blissfully unaware of the status of the man whose daughter was getting married today and for whom we were working. I didn't know what my voice would be like if he asked me a question and I had to reply.

He walked round me and I could smell his expensive aftershave. Despite this, I could also smell that he was a smoker, although he didn't have the overpowering smell of stale smoke that Norrie had, but there was just a trace not fully masked by his expensive cologne and soaps. Close up I could see that he had quite prominent acne scars as well as a small scar underneath and to the side of his left eye and that his short reddish hair had flecks of grey at the temples. He had a thick gold chain round his neck and wore a large signet ring as well as a wedding ring. Standing next to him I got a sense of the power that oozed out of him. The only people of any power or influence that I had met in the flesh had been my local MP and the head of the local council, both of whom had visited West London Action Group on different occasions. They had some sort of authority resonating off them which was compounded by the obsequious nature of their entourage. Clinkie had this aura but multiplied by ten.

"Look at the state of this," he said, gesturing to me. "Probably can't speak a word of English." I stood and tried to look like I didn't understand him as it meant he wouldn't ask me anything. Unfortunately, Brian enlightened him. "Nah, he is English, the other one is foreign."

My heart rate then went up further as Clinkie turned round and faced me. "This is my daughter's wedding and all my friends and family will be here," he said in a low controlled voice. "It better be perfect. If you or anyone fucks anything up then you will regret it." As he said this, he pointed his finger into my chest. "Understand?" he growled. Clinkie had barely touched me with his index finger but it felt like I had been clubbed. I nodded then looked to the floor. I didn't want to engage in eye contact with Clinkie or do anything that would make him remember me.

"Jonjo, get Norrie round here now," he said quietly but intently. Jonjo hurried away as Clinkie walked past me and out the back of the marquee. Brian and the other man followed. I didn't know what to do so I made a show of stacking the boxes of beer. Matis just stood there. I tried to use subtle mime, body language and eye signals to indicate to Matis that we had to be good and be seen to be good. However, Matis just continued to stand there. It was going to be a long day, I thought.

Clinkie and his group returned from their inspection outside. "Where the hell is Norrie?" Clinkie asked no one in particular. No sooner had he said that, when Jonjo and Norrie appeared. It looked like Norrie had had an accident in his trousers. His tiny dark hamster eyes darted around furtively, and unlike Clinkie's economic use of words, Norrie couldn't shut up.

"Hi Clinkie, how's it going? All's coming together. I am just about to get the uniforms and then I will—"

"Shut up," Clinkie said, and Norrie did as he was told.

"Look at what you've hired," he said, as he gesticulated towards me. I seemed to be the main object of his derision. "If these muppets fuck up, you're a goner." With that, he walked out from the back, through the bar and into the main part of the marquee. Jonjo and the other man followed him. Clinkie then took a call on his mobile and his group departed.

"You hear that?" Norrie said to me and Matis loudly. "No fuck-ups." He then handed me a white shirt and elasticated bow tie and did the same for Matis, whose demeanour had not changed at all. I, in contrast, was shaking, sweating and having palpitations. Brian had left to get on with his work and was, I'm sure, pleased that it had been made quite clear who was to blame if any of the agency staff *fucked up*.

Norrie was desperately trying to act authoritatively, but his problem was that he had no stature or presence apart from that of a nervous ferret. He quickly took a roll-up out of his pocket, lit it and, pointing at our shirts with his cigarette hand, said, "Right, get them on and do exactly what Brian asks you. Brian, come over here a minute." Brian looked up and carried on with the job he was doing before heading over several minutes later. All I think designed to show to Norrie that he didn't care a jot about him. Brian explained our roles again, which was a rehash of what Norrie had told me earlier.

Norrie listened to all of this then said, "So that's it, boys – do as Brian has told you. When the function starts you get no breaks until it finishes. Comprendo?"

I nodded. "What about you?" he asked, looking at Matis. "OK?" he asked.

"OK," Matis replied.

"Right, lads, get on with it." And with that he relit his fag and made his way out of the marquee.

"Wee prick," Brian said.

"Who are the other two guys with Clinkie?" I asked.

"Jonjo Laxton and Davie Heeps," he replied. "Hard bastards, Clinkie's right-hand men." He changed the subject, and looking at me he said, "Right, you know the script, let's do this and do it right. The first guests will be arriving in under three hours."

He explained that it was going to be a church wedding in the local kirk, as he called it, at one o'clock, and then from two o'clock all the guests would arrive in the marquee for drinks, speeches and the meal, followed by a ceilidh and a disco. I asked what a ceilidh was, and he explained that it was basically Scottish country dancing. The band that had been hired would play the ceilidh music then some pop and rock, which would be followed by a disco for the last couple of hours.

Matis and I had by now put on our uniforms and got to work, which initially was moving the stock and glasses into the bar area. There had been quite a transformation in the marquee in the short time we had been in the back now that the flower arrangements for the tables had arrived and were in place and all of the tables had their settings on them.

I looked at my watch, just under two hours to go, and wondered at what point I should try and steal Vicky's documents. Having now met Clinkie, I also wondered what fool would have the bottle to go into his house and steal from his desk in his office.

Chapter Fifteen

Clinkie and his entourage had left, presumably to get changed and then head to the kirk for the wedding.

Matis and I spent the next ninety minutes fetching and carrying. We were mainly moving boxes of glasses to designated spots throughout the marquee. We weren't even trusted to open any boxes and take the glasses out. That was a role for those further up the food chain. There was no sign of Norrie during this time, so I supposed that he had been allowed to attend the marriage ceremony. Clinkie's wife must hold some sway, I thought, because if Clinkie had his way then I am sure that Norrie would have been out on his arse, to use Jonjo's vernacular.

The waiting staff had arrived, and they were from the same agency I was with, but they were several levels up from Matis and me. They were already in their uniforms and had their names on lapel badges. They all appeared to be aged between twenty and thirty, were attractive and had the gender split eighty/twenty female to male.

Despite the waiting staff having brilliant white smiles that they could crack at a moment's notice if required, their attitude to colleagues such as Matis and me was one of barely concealed disdain. We were seen as the lowest of the low, which actually suited me as we were faceless mute accessories wheeled in to do a job and then we would be gone. I kept my head down and got on with any duties as directed by Brian or any of the head waiting staff, trying to blend in as much as possible.

There was a temporary store at the back of the marquee used for boxes and empty barrels of rubbish which I regularly visited to deposit some more crap. I was therefore aware of wedding-related activity outside the marquee as I looked out from behind the store towards the house. Several large cars had arrived and were disgorging what appeared to be hired muscle that I supposed were there to act as security. I counted at least twelve gorillas, which when added to Clinkie and his team and the security already in place at the house, seemed rather excessive. This made me additionally nervous as I considered the logistics of stealing documents from this man. I returned to the bar area and waited on instructions for my next task. Brian and a head waiter were deep in discussion for several minutes before the head waiter hurried over to me and hissed, "Get through the back and stay out of sight, as the guests are arriving soon. Keep out the way and wait for your instructions." I nodded, as I didn't expect he thought I could speak, and signalled for Matis to follow me, which he did.

For the next thirty minutes or so a variety of expensive cars arrived, crunching the gravel. There were numerous Mercedes sport and saloons, as well as a variety of Audis, with 4x4s also proving to be very popular with the Scottish criminal aristocracy. Clinkie appeared and was wearing what seemed to me like full Highland dress. He had a kilt, sash and even a small knife in his sock. Jonjo, Davie and several others appeared, all wearing exactly the same outfit. There were also several children similarly attired who were no doubt from Clinkie's family or offspring from his inner crew.

Finally, following Clinkie's car, the car with Hannah, his youngest daughter and radiant bride, along with her groom, appeared. All the guests lined the driveway and clapped and cheered when they got out. I was surprised at how attractive she was. Because of the criminal connections in the family and Clinkie's background that I had gleaned both from Vicky and in my online searches, I had expected her to be a hard-looking bitch with dyed blonde hair and the roots showing, nose piercings, tattoos and a screw you attitude. Instead, she appeared a vision of perfection. She was blonde, had a perfect body, lovely light golden tan and a bewitching smile. Not what I expected at all. Her husband was, I suppose, the male equivalent. I had asked Brian earlier what Hannah's husband did and was told that he was in business. Well, he was either brave or stupid, I felt, as it wouldn't be me marrying into that family. The thought of Clinkie being my father-in-law made me feel nauseous.

I caught sight of someone I assumed was Suzi Moore getting out from the car in front of Clinkie's. She was blonde, shorter and plumper than her younger sister. She was attractive, but in a hard sort of way. She didn't appear to have a partner with her and strolled about milking the attention she was receiving as one of Clinkie's daughters. Vicky hadn't mentioned any brothers, so presumably Suzi would be heir to her father's business.

The waiting staff were now in full on-duty mode, floating around the guests with trays of champagne, whisky, red and white wine along with canapes and other nibbles. They were very good at their job, I had to concede, and just seemed to know when to approach a group or individual, when to speak, when to stay quiet and when to flash their brilliant snow-white smiles. They were also very good at removing any empties and waste food. These trays were left at the side of the marquee on a table hidden behind a screen from where Matis and I were based. Our job was to take the trays, empty the rubbish and any glasses with unfinished drinks, then clean the glasses and dry and return them to a collection point at the side of the bar.

Doing this role gave me the time to observe the guests, most of whom appeared to have money and liked to display it. The majority of men seemed to be over forty, and they all displayed bling to a greater or lesser degree. Their aftershave could be picked up from a hundred paces away. Almost all of them smoked and had no qualms about stubbing out their fags on Clinkie's drive or patio, as indeed neither did Clinkie. No doubt some flunky in Clinkie's employ would be on hand to clear them up later. The men who weren't in kilts seemed slightly nervous or in awe of their surroundings and definitely gave Clinkie and his cohorts all due respect.

The women, as is normally the case at weddings, I suppose, had a greater freedom in their choice of what to wear. This resulted in a few stunning dresses, but the majority had chosen garish designs with unsuitable low necklines that didn't suit the wearer. Some of their voices carried quite far and I could pick up snatches of conversation and high-pitched laughter. There were a few couples together, but mostly the men were in their groups and the women in theirs. I was glad I wasn't a waiter, as some seemed to be getting a lot more close and personal attention from over-made-up middle-aged women than seemed decent. My muppet status was of comfort to me, as I could keep out of sight and away from such attention. I was interrupted from my thoughts by the shout of, "Hey, you two, over here."

I gestured to Matis and we made our way over to the head waiter, who told us that the catering vans had arrived and we were to unload them and take everything to the kitchen, which was housed in a large canvas structure attached to the main marquee. There were six transit vans whose insides were set up to maximise storage space. Matis, me and a few other muppets chosen to help unload the vans, were not allowed into them and we were handed something and went to the kitchen, where someone there collected our cargo from us without a word and took it to its designated place. We were unloading what seemed like endless amounts of stainless steel containers which held the starters and main courses along with trays with transparent covers that contained chocolate cakes, carrot cake and other desserts. As we were doing this, a van bearing the name *Great Cakes* on its back and sides, along with a logo of a cake with a cheeky grinning face, arrived. Jonjo assigned three of his gorillas to escort the two people from the wedding cake company as they took the three-tiered work of art into the marquee to be displayed in pride of place at the top table. I shuddered at the thought of what would happen if anyone tripped and it fell to the ground in a broken chocolaty mess with a few fag stubs stuck to it.

Jonjo, Davie and a third man called Mikey hovered around most of the time while us muppets unloaded and transported the meal. Occasionally Jonjo would shout, "Hey you, shift your arse," to one of us, which his two mates found disproportionally funny. They had very strong accents that I found difficult to understand at times, but I picked up snippets of their conversations, which mostly seemed to revolve around violence with a bit of sex thrown in. I had no doubt they were indulging in a level of bragging amongst themselves, but I didn't doubt that they were hard bastards and responsible for administering justice on behalf of Clinkie as and when required without a second thought. Being on the wrong side of them, which I would soon be if I got caught trying to steal Vicky's papers or when the theft was subsequently discovered, as of course it would be, heightened my already extremely anxious state. I just hoped I would be long gone and that no one would associate the muppet glass collector with the theft.

Jonjo and his colleagues were constantly on their mobile phones and reacting to messages. I couldn't work out what they were doing but figured that it would be concerned with keeping Clinkie's business ticking over. They had access to two Ford Kas, and on a couple of occasions they summoned an underling to jump in one of the cars and run a message. The cars were also used by them to drive from the marquee to the house or other buildings around the steading. I supposed that they were too important to walk. When they weren't being used, the cars were parked near to the marquee with the keys left in them. I don't suppose car crime was very high in this neighbourhood.

After our unloading jobs were done, we were ushered back to our positions back of house to stay quiet and out of the way. I heard an MC announce that it was time for all wedding guests to make their way to the marquee. The weather had been kind all day and so far no guests had felt the need to go inside.

I felt a rush of adrenaline as I considered that I was getting nearer to the task in hand. After my initial shock at being given this duty and Vicky talking me through it, I had considered that the best time to do it would be when all the guests were eating and therefore occupied. Now, however, it occurred to me that there would breaks in the meal, and serving as many people as this would result in some tables being served before others and that these breaks would be used by guests to leave the table to smoke, visit the toilet or speak to friends at other tables. Whereas during the speeches, everyone would be present as no one would dare disrespect Clinkie's father-of-the-bride speech by being outside when it was on. With a fluttering stomach, I made my decision that would be when I would do it. My stomach fluttered even more when I heard the same MC voice announce, "It is now time to take your seats as the speeches will be starting shortly."

There was a hum of voices mixed with laughter as the waiting staff effortlessly filled and refilled everyone's glasses in preparation for the toasts that would soon follow. After a few minutes there was thunderous applause. I sneaked a look and saw Hannah and her groom being piped to their seats at the top table watched by the proud father of the bride who was standing up and making a show of applauding them. I was surprised at how loud bagpipes were close up. The guests certainly seemed to enjoy them, and knowing their place they had followed Clinkie's lead and were continuing to clap as enthusiastically as possible. There was a middle-aged lady sitting next to Clinkie who wasn't clapping and was sitting calmly and smiling benignly. Mrs Moore, I guessed: Clinkie's better half and sister of Norrie. She was attractive in a natural way and I could see where the daughter got her looks from but couldn't understand how she and Norrie could possibly be related. Clinkie gave his daughter a kiss and shook the hand of her rather nervous-looking groom. Suzi Moore looked radiant as she sat with her family. There was no sign of Norrie in the marquee and no place set for him at the top table.

I suddenly realised that there didn't appear to be a best man. Not having attended a Scottish wedding, I thought perhaps that wasn't part of the custom, or more likely who from outwith the Clinkie Moore fraternity would have the balls to stand up there and try and entertain, or more importantly not offend or annoy any of the guests. I noticed that the waiting staff had withdrawn from serving and had retreated to designated spots along the walls of the marquee. Suddenly I felt a tug as Brian pulled me back behind the bar.

"Get out of sight," he hissed. "It's only me allowed on show at the bar while the speeches are on. Get back there and stay put until you get called on." I nodded and made my way beside Matis and three more of my fellow muppets. I felt in my pocket, extracted two of my tablets and quickly slipped them into my mouth. Only four left, I took a small bottle of mineral water from a pack of twenty-four and had a large gulp from it and swallowed them down.

Time to go.

Chapter Sixteen

Clinkie was in full flow. His accent sounded even stronger when amplified, and that added to the local references meant that I couldn't make out or understand large parts of what he was saying. His audience had no such problem, however, and laughed, cheered and clapped almost constantly. Clinkie would put his hands up occasionally in a bashful way, but I could tell that he was loving this.

I walked slowly past Matis, gave him a pat, carried on past the other staff and out the back of the marquee as if I was going for a smoke. I picked up one of the trays that we used for glass collecting and headed to the kitchen. Obviously, it wasn't my job to leave the marquee and go to the house, but I hoped that my prop would look convincing. On my way, one of Jonjo's henchmen stepped out of the shadows and asked, "Where you off to?"

"Must get glasses," I said in a ropey Eastern European accent. He looked slightly quizzical and then nodded and pointed at the kitchen in the house with his thumb. I nodded a greeting to the two people who had delivered the cake and were sitting in their van. The one in the driving seat was on his mobile. I got to the kitchen and shouted *Hi* to no one in particular and put the tray down. I heard a scurrying noise and my heart sank. Norrie was hovering about. Seeing him gave me a start, as even though there wasn't a place for him at the top table, I still expected him to be in the marquee at the speeches. His little eyes flickered nervously and moved slightly from side to side.

"Hi," I said.

"Hi," he replied loudly. "What are you doing over here?"

"Norrie – the portable bog is blocked, and I need a shite. Can I use the house toilet?" I asked robustly.

He shook his head and again very loudly said, "No. Hired staff use the portable. You shouldn't be near here." As he said this, I got the feeling that someone else was in our presence, hence the loud voice. The penny dropped. Norrie was family, albeit reluctantly from Clinkie's point of view, and he should be at the marquee listening to the speeches at his niece's wedding. The reason he was in the kitchen of the house was that he was probably shagging Veronica. I realised that I now had the upper hand and he needed rid of me.

"Look, I'm cleaning and drying hundreds of glasses and dishes and we need good food hygiene. The toilet's blocked, there's no water or soap. Do you want me to be distributing glasses with shite on my hands? What if the wedding party get food poisoning? Do you want me using the wedding guests' toilet? You heard what Clinkie said – no fuck-ups. What do you think Clinkie would say if half the guests got the runs after attending his daughter's wedding? Who would get the blame? I think it would be the person who hired the catering company," I stated aggressively, and was proud of my performance.

He shuddered and his little eyes looked quizzical. "All right, there's a cludgie down there under the stairs. Be quick, coz I'll get shot if anyone finds out," he added unnecessarily.

I didn't know what a *cludgie* was but assumed it must be a Scottish term for toilet. "Thanks, Norrie, won't be long," I said, as I scurried on in the manner of someone bursting for a crap as I went round the corner. I went into the toilet under the stairs, put the light on and then quickly and furtively re-emerged. I padded up the stairs, going slowly, taking them two at a time with very deliberate steps.

The office was located where it had been described by Vicky. I went in and made my way straight to the desk and was grateful for the thick carpet, which absorbed my footsteps. The desk was positioned exactly as Vicky had described. It was tidy, with only a large blotter, pen holder and three framed photographs on it. The photos were of Clinkie's wife and his two daughters. I sensed his presence in the room, and with a shaking hand I tried the top left-hand drawer, which had a key in it but was unlocked. I pulled it open and there were the documents. I was surprised that something that was so important to Vicky, and therefore I supposed to Clinkie, as it was his way of controlling her, was so easily accessible. However, I decided that security was lax because no one would be stupid enough to break into Clinkie's house and steal anything from him. That thought gave me a shudder.

The documents were in a transparent light green plastic A4-size wallet. I quickly opened it and leafed through the contents. There was a passport that had Vicky's photograph, which was made out in the name of Valerie Sykes, a driving licence, international driving licence and various other papers all made out in the same name. I loosened my belt and put the folder underneath my trousers and shirt against my back then tightened my belt to secure the package. Luckily, my shirt was baggy and concealed the folder without its shape being too obvious. I walked around the room to see if the package shifted in transit and was pleased that it didn't. I padded out of the room and made my way slowly and carefully down the stairs. I was acutely conscious of the package against my back and could feel sweat accumulating there. I nipped into the toilet under the stairs, gave it a flush and headed back outside where Norrie was having a smoke.

"Better?" he asked with a glint in his eye.

"Too right. I was touching cloth!" I replied, trying very hard to appear natural.

He laughed with his smoker's cough and said, "Hope you used air freshener. I don't want Clinkie tasting it!" Needless to say, toilet humour appealed to Norrie.

"Fresh as a daisy!" I replied, and kept walking as I didn't want Norrie near me. The guys in the wedding cake van were speaking to the same gorilla that had stopped me, but their conversation seemed more convivial. He was leaning against the van with his head nearly through the open window. His buddy was standing next to him and appeared relaxed. This gave me the opportunity to nip round the back of the van to skirt the treeline and then head over to the back of the marquee unobserved. I didn't enter the big tent though. Instead, I scurried over to the nearest Ka, slowly opened the door and climbed in. I sat in the driver's seat and could hear the wedding cake van start up and pull away. The two gorillas seemed to be reacting to a message and were making their way to the house but didn't appear to be in any hurry to get there.

I started up the car, resisting the urge to go careering down the drive, and drove very slowly as I approached the gate. The cake van ahead of me had just been let through and the gate was closed. It took me several seconds to work out how to get the car window to go down to allow me to press the buzzer for the guard. A metallic voice asked, "Who are you? What you up to with the work car?"

He must be watching me on CCTV from somewhere, I thought. I took a deep breath and said, "Jonjo sent me. I'm from the catering company and we urgently need more port. We need an extra couple of cases in the next hour, so I'm heading into town for them. He says I've got to get my arse down there right away."

The guard grunted with what sounded like a slight laugh of recognition at the Jonjo reference and sent me on my way. When the gate opened I nearly stalled and was unsure what gear I was in. However, I got to the junction at the bottom of the lane and then tried to remember what direction we had come from in the minibus that morning. I thought that if I tried to retrace my steps at least some of the way then I could get to a bus station or somewhere that would propel me as far away as possible from this place.

With the package containing Vicky's documents sticking to my back and my hands slipping on the steering wheel, I headed towards the main road. I vaguely recognised some of the landmarks and place names that I had seen from the minibus earlier on, but the road I was driving on was narrower and more undulating than I remembered. There were a couple of signs that warned of oncoming traffic in the middle of the road, but nothing to advise me how to deal with that. I then saw road signs for Glasgow and the M74 and followed them. Despite my age and having had a driving licence for over twenty years I am an inexperienced driver and dislike motorways intensely. I joined the slip road and was lucky that as it merged with the motorway there was nothing behind me in the lane I joined because I hadn't even looked in my mirrors. Before long, my inside lane had become a middle lane and I was enveloped by traffic. I was panicking big style and driving in a rigid fashion, as if a broom handle was up my shirt, as I concentrated intently. Then I had some hope as I saw the rear of the cake van up ahead and latched onto it. The company name, phone number and "Glasgow" were written on the back of it. Wherever it went, I decided, I was going. At this stage, Clinkie had dropped out of my mind and all I could think about was reaching a destination, any destination, and getting out of the car.

The van was definitely heading to Glasgow and I continued to follow it. As we approached the outskirts of the city, I was glad I was following something because I wouldn't have known what sign to look for or what lane to be in. It meant that to keep on its tail I had to run a couple of red lights and pull out in front of vehicles, which resulted in some annoyed hoots, but I avoided any bumps and kept the van in sight. I was fixed on the cheeky grinning cake logo on the back of the van and I think that flight or fight had kicked in and flight was guiding me. It didn't take long to be approaching what appeared to be the city centre. I saw signs for the High Street and Glasgow Green so guessed that I couldn't be too far away from the city centre and a train station or the bus station that I had arrived at that morning.

The van went past what I think was the main entrance to Glasgow Green and then took a sudden right turn, which took me by surprise. I followed it and narrowly avoided being hit by a car heading straight on in the opposite direction. I could see the van up ahead. It had stopped and was again indicating right. There were a number of railway arches converted into business units and that Great Cakes was based there.

End of the road for them. I carried on a bit further and saw signs for the railway station. Time to go, I thought, and I tried to see where I could abandon the car. I had travelled through several sets of traffic lights and had ended up in a lane for turning right. I therefore did so and saw on my left that there was a large area of cleared land that was about to be developed. It had security fencing around it and contractor's details on signs on the fence. There was a wide pavement and gravel path in front of two locked gates at the entrance to the site. I drove up to the gates, left the car unlocked with the key in it and got out. The road I had turned onto didn't look too promising, so I turned back towards the main road I had just left and continued walking in the direction I had previously been driving in as I was sure I had seen signs for a railway. I walked briskly as if I knew where I was going.

There were very few directional signs, but from one of them I realised that I was on what was called the Broomielaw, which was alongside the River Clyde and was a mixture of yuppie-looking flats, hotels, cafes/bars and pockets of waste ground. My heart sank as the railway sign appeared to be for a local station rather than one that could get me south. However, I decided to carry on my way in the same direction as there were lots of pedestrians around going in the same direction as me, which made me think that I must be heading towards the city centre.

It was now after five thirty, and as I continued along the Broomielaw, I suddenly felt that I was being followed. I'm not sure why, but perhaps this was as a result of the massive adrenaline surge that I had recently experienced now dipping and irrational fears replacing it. I stopped for a bottle of water at a burger van to give me a chance to surreptitiously see if I could check if my fears were real or imagined. I definitely got a feeling that a middle-aged man on the other side of the road was a bit too exaggerated in his nonchalance as he checked his watch when I glanced round. He seemed to then take a particular interest in a poster stuck to the hoarding around a gap site advertising a circus that had long since come and gone.

As I continued on my way the walkway was getting busier and more boisterous and I was unsure why. There were lots of people; men in particular in fancy dress, and there seemed like a stag party feel in the air. There were adults dressed in all sorts of outfits including; minions, smurfs, sailors, doctors ready for the operating theatre, people in gorilla suits and cavemen. The crowd was making its way towards an area which contained a concert venue, exhibition centre and a strange-looking building that seemed a bit familiar. I had seen this building before used as a backdrop when news correspondents report from Glasgow and remembered that it was called the Armadillo due to its resemblance to that animal. These random thoughts tumbled through my head as I tried to make my way briskly towards what I hoped was a quick exit from the city.

As I passed a modern hotel whose frontage was entirely glass, I glanced from the corner of my eye to look at the reflections in it, and the person I had seen earlier checking his watch and reading the circus poster was still there and was putting his phone back into his jacket pocket. I had the feeling that he must have a partner who was also on my tail or waiting for me to reach a certain point from where I could be intercepted. This position was bad enough for me, but being in a place that I had never visited before made my anxiety go through the roof. In an attempt to deal with this, I tried to carry out the mental exercises to deal with stress/panic attacks whilst in public places that my therapist had taught me. I focussed on my goal, which I decided was to keep walking until I found a bus or train station, slowed my pace, which went against my current animal instincts of *flight,* and controlled my breathing. I imagined sitting in the carriage of a train with a coffee and looking contentedly out of the window as the train chugged south.

It was hard to fully focus on this ideal scenario because there was a constant line of taxis disgorging excited passengers who enthusiastically and loudly pushed into the line of pedestrians and joined the throng. This slowed my progress as they barged in front of me. I nearly got knocked over by someone wearing a large dartboard-style hat and suddenly the penny dropped. There must be a darts match on. My thoughts immediately veered away from mental relaxation and coping strategies to *flight* mode and how I could use this situation to my advantage.

I worked my way into the crowd, which was on the pavement and spreading on to the carriageway as we neared the venue, and nearly tripped over a dog on a lead whose owners, a man and woman, walked in the opposite direction to the crowd. I raised my hand by way of apology and then pushed ahead into the crowd, which annoyed a few punters. The width of the mass of darts punters was then reduced because in the vista between the conference and concert venues there was work underway replacing kerbstones and installing a mini roundabout.

Instinct kicked in, and I decided that it was time to make my move. There was a white transit van with the name of the construction company on its side which was parked behind some pedestrian barriers and had its back door open. There were three construction workers kneeling down with their backs to the van as they placed kerbstones in the ground. As the throng of people, of which I was a part of, neared the van, I made my way up to it and quickly grabbed a hi-vis jacket and hard hat from inside. A couple of punters saw me, but instead of telling me to stop, they were laughing at my antics. I gave them the thumbs up and a cheeky jack the lad grin, put the jacket and hat on and continued with the flow. I rolled my sleeves up, as that seemed a bit more workmanlike.

After around ten minutes of high-spirited pushing and shoving, the queue made its way into the arena, which was a large exhibition centre with numerous halls. Now that I was in costume, I felt marginally more in control. There were lots of bar areas and food outlets in the expansive foyer, and tickets weren't checked until the audience went into the auditorium. I tried to attach myself to various groups with little success because they all knew each other and were obviously out together on an occasion that had been arranged for some time and eagerly anticipated. Although I had good-natured banter with some of them, I didn't manage to become part of any group. I got a beer from one of the numerous serving points after queuing for a while in a raucous line and then promptly had half of it spilled over me – which I suppose helped me blend in more.

The nonchalant middle-aged man with the Marks & Spencer light blue jacket, last seen lighting a cigarette on the Broomielaw, was not quite so calm now. I had tipped my hard hat down so the small peak was covering my eyes. I tilted my head to scan the scene and could see him displaying agitated body language as he paced up and down, took out his mobile and called someone.

I got in stride with a couple of guys who were both carrying enormous Munich Beer Festival-type beer glasses and had red and white felt stripy traffic cones on their heads. It seemed like a natural fit, so as they made their way back to their mates, I surreptitiously got in step with them. I put my pint on a circular table around a pillar at which about seven others were drinking and speaking animatedly. From here, I got a good view of most of the foyer, and the man at M&S, as I had come to think of him, was nowhere to be seen. Then, all of a sudden, I saw him with the man who had been walking the dog with his wife. Well, I didn't expect that. Perhaps the burger van operative was in on the act as well. My heart rate was increasing incrementally. I tried to keep calm as I imagined that my crime must have been discovered almost immediately and the Ka probably had a tracking device fitted. As the reality of this sank in, I actually wanted, and felt, I needed another beer, but I didn't want to leave such a good vantage point, so I reluctantly nursed my pint while frantically trying to work out what to do next. The thought of being dragged back to Clinkie's had to act as a spur for me to be creative and come up with a way to get me out of this shit.

There were announcements over the PA system stating that it was getting close to the time to go into the auditorium, so naturally everyone was getting prepared and delegated members of groups were dutifully queuing up for double rounds. I had to think fast. Clinkie had people on my tail who at this stage may not have spotted me in my disguise but were pretty sure I was using the event as cover. Fair enough, but when the crowd made its way into the auditorium then I would be left exposed, as there would be little or no chance of sneaking in without a ticket. I had to think fast.

M&S man and dog walking man had split up and were on either side of the foyer at the far end from me but coming in my direction. I pulled the hard hat down and walked in the opposite direction to my two pursuers and dived into the nearest toilet block. It was full of people queuing to use the urinals or cubicles but also with a number of people having a sly vape. Donald Trump came into the toilets quickly and banged into me as I stood in line. "Sorry pal," he said, "it's roasting with this on," he added, as he removed the rubber mask and immediately went into his pocket for his vape. He dropped the Trump mask while doing this.

"No bother," I replied, as my *flight* instinct kicked in and I picked up the mask from the wet floor and pushed my way back out of the toilets, hoping that his relief at satisfying his cravings would take priority over noticing that his mask had vanished. I pulled the mask on and became *The Donald*. It was wet against my face, presumably from the previous owner's sweat, and uncomfortable to wear as the latex stuck to my skin and moved with my heavy breathing. However, needs must. I was in full-on flight mode. I discarded my hi-vis jacket in a bin and only had my shirt on as my jacket was in the bus that had taken me to Clinkie's house that morning. My mind was racing and I realised that I needed a jacket to be dressed more in character for the part, and as I headed back towards where I had been sitting earlier, I noticed one hanging over the back of a bar stool. I swiftly took it, put it on in a flowing motion, then grabbed a couple of beers from a table and walked towards the main exit.

"Hey you, you thieving bastard, that's our drinks!" Super Mario shouted in a strong Glaswegian accent. Luigi beside him seemed particularly annoyed and gesticulated angrily.

I ignored them and kept walking making out that my legs were rubber as I approached the exit towards one of the many bouncers. I went up to him, pointed at the people shouting at me and said in my best growl, "Tell them to fuck off." The two disgruntled drinkers were getting nearer, and Super Mario, like his computer counterpart, was not giving up easily.

I swept around quickly, which made some of my beer swirl up, leave the glasses and splash the bouncer. He wasn't pleased. "Right, give me those," he barked, as he took my beer glasses, "time to go." He put the pint glasses on the floor and grabbed me forcibly by the collar and frogmarched me out of the building. "Now piss off. If you come back here I'll get the polis," he said in a deep growl.

I staggered back in an overacting drunken pose and gave him the thumbs up. "OK pal, but there's nothing wrong with me," I said in true drunk man's delusional patter. He turned and went back inside, reported in on his radio and then spoke with one of his colleagues while Super Mario and Luigi stomped off towards the auditorium. I don't think Luigi had quite got over it. The foyer was now almost completely clear as the crowds made their way excitedly into the auditorium. I could make out the figures of man at M&S and his dog walking accomplice pacing about in an increasingly anxious manner.

Job done.

Chapter Seventeen

I hurried away from the building and followed the sweep of the road, which went left and appeared to be heading towards a motorway. As soon as I got round the corner I took off my mask and threw it in a bin. *The Donald* grinned at me from his resting place amongst the litter. It was the first time that I had ever been grateful to or for Donald Trump.

I was wearing the loose-fitting black jacket that I had stolen and it fitted me well. I felt in the pockets and had a result. Nestling in the inside pocket was a wallet which was slim and only contained money; there were no credit cards, membership cards or any other paraphernalia. The owner had probably felt that at such a big place with all the crowds jostling about, it would be safer not to take his everyday wallet and instead had taken this one. There was just over £200 worth of notes in it, which would certainly help. The jacket's previous owner was obviously looking forward to a good night out, of which the darts would probably be round one. A few years ago I would have felt monumentally guilty at doing such a thing, but now I didn't give a toss. It was the lucky break I needed.

The whole time when considering stealing Vicky's papers from Clinkie's I had constantly been thinking of my escape home as being by either train or bus. Suddenly, as yet another taxi sped by, I had a better thought. I held out my arm and within seconds a taxi stopped.

"Airport please," I said.

"Glasgow or Prestwick," the driver replied. I didn't know there was another one. "Oh, Glasgow please."

"Nae bother, pal, where you off to?"

"London," I answered automatically. Then I mentally kicked myself for giving any information about me away. For all I knew, Clinkie probably had half of the Glasgow taxi drivers in his back pocket.

"You live there, pal?" he then asked.

"No," I replied, "just visiting." I didn't want to continue the conversation and give away anything else about me, so I said, "Sorry, but I've got to check in." I then made a great show of getting my phone out. I quickly googled flights and was relieved to see that there were still three flights for London that had availability. I didn't book them online; I was going to use jacket man's money to pay for the taxi and flight when I got to the airport.

It dawned on me that it might look strange going to the airport without any bags, so I made a pretend call to continue to avoid having to speak to the driver. However, fortunately, the taxi ride was short, and we were soon on the approach to Glasgow Airport. I gave the driver a £10 tip and bid him goodnight. I made my way to the booking desks and secured a single flight to Heathrow for £189. I couldn't believe the cost but didn't want to waste time or draw attention to myself by complaining, so I threw the money across the counter and the assistant gave me my ticket with a tight smile.

The flight was due to take off at eight thirty and I made my way to security. Having hardly ever flown before, each step that I had to do required asking someone and getting in the way of people who obviously knew the ropes and would brush past me with a certain level of disdain as I studied my ticket or looked for information on the electronic noticeboards. It was becoming difficult to throw off my muppet status gained earlier in the day.

I saw people taking out their passports at some stages and was suddenly nervous about the requirement to have mine. I didn't think I would need one as it was a UK flight, but asked someone after I had passed through the security checks and he told me that you don't need a passport, but you still need to prove your identity for a domestic flight. I panicked because I had left my driving licence at home under Vicky's instructions so that my real name would not be revealed if I was caught at

Clinkie's. I was so close to escape; I had my ticket and the plane was leaving in an hour. I didn't know what to do so in time-honoured fashion went for a drink.

I found a bar in the departure lounge, got a beer and, as most of the tables were occupied, I had to take one that still had empty glasses, spilled drink and crisp packets on it. I sat drinking my cold lager, staring at my ticket, wondering what to do next.

"You look nervous. Afraid of flying?"

"Sorry?" I said as I looked up.

"You look worried. Are you scared of flying?" The person asking this was an attractive female in her mid-twenties, I would guess. She was with two other similar-looking friends.

"Oh. Well, my problem is that I have forgotten to bring my driving licence and I don't know if they will let me on the plane." I tried not to sound pathetic, but the thought of not being able to board the plane and having to go back to Glasgow to make my escape scared the shit out of me.

"Where you flying to?"

"Heathrow."

"Who with?"

"I'm on my own."

She giggled. "No, what I mean is what airline are you going with?"

"Oh. British Airways." I held up my ticket.

"No worries. You don't need proof of ID to board with BA. Most other airlines require ID for domestic flights, but not BA."

"Really?" I said with a thankful gasp.

"Yep."

"Wow!" was all that I could say. I swigged down my pint in one. "How do you know this?" I asked in admiration.

"If you fly regularly then you get to know these things," she replied.

"And you fly a lot?" I asked

"A bit," she replied.

"Where are you off to?"

"Same as you – London."

"OK. Would you like a drink, girls?" I asked breezily, and made my way to the bar with a slight spring in my step. I had an enjoyable half hour or so with Becky, Sam and Christina. They were good fun, and while obviously quite posh, they were down to earth and naturally engaging. I was so pleased for Becky's intervention and enjoyed her and her friends' company. It turned out that they were involved in marketing and had been on a flying visit to Glasgow as part of an exhibition at the Scottish Exhibition and Conference Centre (SECC), which I realised was the name of the building where the darts match was held. They had been in one of the other halls of this very large building working at a skiing and winter sports travel fair and Becky gave me a flier for the event. They told me about when they had finished at their event how they had seen some of the pissed punters in fancy dress who arrived early for the darts. I nearly let it slip that I too had been there, but managed to check myself in time before revealing anything about the events that led to me being at the darts match and now the airport. I was disappointed when it was time to board and was also disappointed that when we did board I was nowhere near them on the plane. For a brief while I hadn't actually forgotten about my hellish two days that had culminated in me stealing from Clinkie's house, but I had had a welcome diversion from them.

Considering how many flights there were from Glasgow to London, I was surprised at the size of the plane and how full it was. I was in a middle seat, which was a bit uncomfortable. The drinks at the airport and the relief of getting away from Clinkie's house had made me feel mildly euphoric and chatty. I attempted some small talk with the passengers on either side of me to no avail and so buried my head in the in-flight magazine and then, after we had taken off, I ordered a small bottle of wine to see me though the flight.

I have never enjoyed the prospect of flying, but in the scheme of things, any nervousness at being in a plane was way down my list of anxieties. As I sipped my wine, I thought of what I had just done and the possible repercussions coming from it. I surmised that the theft must have been discovered almost right away, because, if as I strongly suspected, I was followed along the Broomielaw and into the SECC, then Clinkie or Jonjo had put the word out. Perhaps the two gorillas had been summoned to the house as a result of the discovery of the theft when I had jumped in the Ka.

I cast my mind back to entering Clinkie's office and the sequence of actions that I carried out and concluded that there must have been sensors or CCTV which alerted the security system to my presence. What my conclusion didn't explain was how I managed to get through the gate, as I was speaking to a guard who was presumably watching the car on CCTV and linked with the rest of the security system. All a bit embarrassing for CM Security, which would make Clinkie even more angry.

My thoughts returned to Norrie, and I wondered if Jonjo or one of his mates would have given him a doing when my theft was discovered, or if being family was enough to save his bacon. To be honest, I didn't care about him. He was knowingly part of a criminal gang and stupid and reckless enough to be cheating his brother-in-law who happened to be a major criminal boss as well. Thinking of Norrie got me thinking about the minibus that took us to Clinkie's house from the bus station, and my heart sank when I thought about leaving my jacket in the vehicle. No doubt the minibus would have been torn apart and my jacket found. I tried to think if there were any identifiable objects or papers in the garment that would give away my contact details but didn't think that there were. The contract that Vicky had set up with Catering Solutions had a fake address on it, or at least an address that wasn't connected to me, and there was no phone number listed. So at least my home address and contact details weren't known to them as far as I could work out. However, by stealing the papers that gave Vicky a new identity, I had now no doubt become embroiled with her in Clinkie's eyes. What a thought.

My drinking rate had increased and I ordered another small bottle of wine. My companion in the aisle seat gave an almost imperceptible snort of derision at the uncouth passenger next to him as he glanced at me out of the corner of his eye. I was just finishing the last of my drink when the captain gave us notice that we were landing in ten minutes. As we made our descent and I caught glimpses of the lights of West London behind the head of the silent passenger in the window seat, I had mixed feelings. I was amazed and massively relieved at actually carrying out the act that I had been tasked with. However, it occurred to me that when Vicky got her new identity courtesy of the documents that I had stolen for her, she would be off, never to be seen again by Clinkie or his associates. I would now be considered by Clinkie as part of her team, so where was I to go now, what should I do? I realised that while thinking and worrying about this, the plane had landed and most of the passengers were standing up and trying to retrieve their bags from the overhead lockers. The passenger in the window seat next to me was trying to stand up and get out, which seemed pointless as the aisle was full. He had a slightly annoyed expression on his face, which I blanked. Given my present troubles, not being able to get straight out of my seat and into a packed aisle was not a major concern.

We duly disembarked and I followed the herd into the arrivals area in Terminal Five. Becky and her friends had told me they were taking the Heathrow Express into town. I was getting the Tube from the airport and had hoped that I would perhaps see my new friends before they boarded their train, but unfortunately I didn't catch sight of them and made my way to the Tube, found a seat and looked at my phone.

I had received a text from an unknown number which started with *Ealing,* so it was obviously Vicky asking about my progress. This had been sent when I was flying. I hadn't sent anything to her since my text in the morning as I wanted to be sure that I was safely away before contacting her. I replied to her message, simply saying: *Job done – back in L.* I received a reply immediately: *Really?* To which I replied: *Yes.* The next message said *Good* and informed me to *make the donation to WLAG tonight.* I presumed that meant I had to post the documents through the letterbox of West London Action Group. I noted the complete lack of thanks or recognition for what I had just done on her behalf. She couldn't have expected me to have done the task so quickly and already be back home. I remembered that she had told me to steal the documents and go back to work, which would have meant me carrying out my duties for the rest of the night hoping that the theft wasn't discovered, then being dropped off in Glasgow in the early hours of Saturday morning after all forms of transport back south had ceased. As ever, it was all about Vicky.

My text alert went again. The message said: *Ealing*. Yet another new number to contact Vicky on. I looked up from my phone, worked out my bearings and realised that we were approaching Acton. I got off the train, waited a few minutes for the District Line to Ealing and boarded it.

West London Action Group was based towards the far end of Uxbridge Road, which was about a twenty-minute walk from the station, and I made my way there with no sense of urgency. It shared a building with two other organisations and was set back from the busy main road by way of a small car park. WLAG was based on the ground floor and could be accessed during office hours through the main door by using an intercom system. There was no communal reception and the other two organisations operated in the same way. WLAG also had a store which could be accessed via a rollover door in the car park. I wondered if Vicky or an accomplice were watching the building, or even inside it holding Maggie. It felt odd going to my place of work at such a time on a Friday night, and I dutifully posted the papers, which were still in the clear green plastic folder, through the WLAG letter box as instructed and then sent a text starting with the agreed word – *delivered* – to the new number that I had been told to send it to. Job done. It was finally time to go home. I didn't receive a reply to my text and at this stage I didn't expect one and didn't care. I also wasn't even thinking of Maggie or Di or anyone else, to be honest. I didn't hang about to see if there was any form of reaction as I just wanted to get home. When I was back on familiar territory I could then regroup and decide on my next best course of action.

I finally arrived back at the flat after my eventful two days. Tired from my travels and mental stress, but with a feeling of elation and relief at what I had achieved. The concerns about any follow-up action from Clinkie had gone temporarily to the back of my mind. I went into the kitchen and opened a bottle of wine that I had bought from an off licence after I had left WLAG. It cost way more than I usually pay for a bottle but, under the circumstances, I felt that I deserved to treat myself.

I poured a large glass, returned to the living room and automatically switched the television on, sat back and watched the images on screen as I recounted the events of the past forty-eight hours in my mind. I noticed out of the corner of my eye that the answer phone light was flashing. As I had been communicating with Vicky by text to a variety of numbers it was highly unlikely she would have called the landline. Brygida didn't know that number and always communicated by text so it wouldn't be her. That got me thinking of her and Ania, and despite the stresses of the past two days, I felt guilty at not contacting Brygida all day and resolved that I wouldn't text her now but would contact her first thing in the morning and suggest having breakfast with her and Ania. That feeling of normality, which I realised would be fleeting as they were leaving in under a week, made me feel better. I couldn't think of any of my few friends or acquaintances who would call the landline and therefore assumed that my attempts at Aunt Isa's funeral to have some form of reconciliation with my parents and my sister may have borne fruit and that one of them had left a message. However, I couldn't be bothered listening to any messages straight away so remained in my seat and enjoyed my drink.

I was halfway through the large glass of wine and suddenly felt very tired. The voices on the television were drifting off and I was beginning to slouch in my chair. The adrenaline and heightened sense of preparedness couldn't continue for ever and it was time for bed and hopefully some much-needed sleep. I sat up straight and glugged down the rest of the wine in my glass, even though I didn't really want or need it, then got up and put the empty glass in the sink in the kitchen. On my way to the bathroom, I flicked the switch on my answer phone. There was only one message. After listening to it, I decided to go back into the kitchen, retrieve my wine glass and pour another large drink. I also instinctively felt in my pocket for my pills. The message was from someone with a thick Scottish accent.

It simply said, "Get your arse back up the road..."

PART TWO

Chapter Eighteen

Morningside, Edinburgh 1985

The murmur of conversation from downstairs came against a backdrop of clinking cutlery and was occasionally punctuated by loud spontaneous laughter from her parents and their guests. She hated it when her parents had a dinner party, because she had to dress up and make polite conversation with the guests, who were invariably the same four couples. She was then banished upstairs to her cold bedroom and waited to be molested.

It was the waiting that she hated the most. As soon as he arrived with his wife and went through the opening pleasantries with Vicky's parents while they removed their outer garments, she knew that at some point that evening he would visit her room. It was usually after a couple of hours, when the main meal had been consumed and there was a pause until the cheese trolley was introduced and the coffees and ports were being arranged. He would leave the dining room ostensibly for a comfort break, pad up the stairs and enter her cold room without knocking.

She must have been dozing and awoke with a start. He was standing in the room looking at her with a benign smile. He always spoke softly, as if they were friends who had a secret, and he asked her to come over to him so he could give her a cuddle. She knew that he only ever had a few minutes so she lay stock still on the bed, hoping this would use up valuable time, although she should have realised that this ploy had never worked before. He moved nearer and whispered, "It's our little secret – remember, you led me on. You don't want Mum and Dad to know what you have done and what you have been up to, do you? Do you want Uncle's favourite finger?" He held up his right hand, which had a large ring on his second finger.

"Come close, let me comfort you," he said as he pressed against her. She could smell his breath, which later she would realise was from whisky and cigars, and feel his hardness against her trembling leg. Afterwards, he always gave a slight tremor as he adjusted himself before leaving the room. Vicky lay crumpled in the foetal position on her bed and within minutes she could make out his voice and laughter below. Her mother seemed to find something that he had just said particularly amusing.

Vicky longed to get away from home to escape his visits. She believed she would be able to leave home when she was eighteen and so would have to wait for another twelve years.

She fell into a fitful doze which was interrupted by her mother calling, "Victoria, Victoria, come down darling and say goodbye to our guests."

Vicky hauled herself up, checked herself in the mirror to ensure that her party face was on and made her way downstairs.

Chapter Nineteen

Vicky returned to her bedroom, curled up and stared at her wall. She lay unmoving in a dreamlike state and thought back to when it had all started.

It was all because of Linus. A tear formed in her eye as she thought of him. Linus was the family pet: a beautiful tiny cocker spaniel puppy. Vicky had wanted a puppy from as long as she could remember. She kept asking her parents but was always told to be patient and she could get one when she was ten. Vicky didn't give up though and she kept at them on a daily basis. On the morning of her sixth birthday, she was led downstairs to the kitchen and told to close her eyes. When she opened them, there he was: a delightful little chestnut brown bundle of fun with a diamond of white on his chest. He was so happy to see her, his little tail wagging, and he seemed to be smiling at her. He licked her face and hands as she picked him up and cuddled him. Linus was so excited that he made a little puddle on the kitchen floor, which Vicky found funny.

"Oh, thank you, thank you so much." She almost cried with excitement. Her mum picked her up and cuddled her as her dad smiled kindly.

"Remember he is your puppy, Vicky," Dad said. "You need to look after him."

"I will, I will!" Vicky gushed.

Vicky's birthday was in May, and over the next few weeks she would rush home from school to be with Linus. During the day, her mum, or more usually Mrs Prentice, who was both the cleaner and nanny, would see to him. If the weather was nice, Vicky would take him out into the garden. She loved everything about him. He was so cute and friendly, always wagging his tail and always delighted to see her. She played with him a bit like she did with her toys, which was quite roughly, grabbing and rolling around with him. She liked to try and put some of her dolls' clothes on him. He seemed to like it.

"Vicky, remember he's a dog and not a toy," her mum would often tell her.

"He likes it," she would reply.

At last the school holidays arrived and Vicky was out playing in the back garden with Linus. Her mum had gone shopping and Mrs Prentice was inside cleaning and looking after Vicky's younger sister, Samantha, who was two. Vicky was playing houses with Linus. He was chewing a blanket and she was trying to wrap it around him so that she could pretend that he was going to bed. She finally got the blanket around Linus while he struggled to get out from it. "Let's go to bed, Linus," she said, picking up her writhing bundle and trying to get him on her shoulder as she walked slowly to her Wendy house. Linus got out of the blanket and scrambled up past Vicky's face and on to her shoulder. She tried to hold him, but he scrambled even more, and his little claws scratched her. She instinctively let go and Linus went over her shoulder and fell down on to the ground head first. He landed directly with a thump on to a concrete slab which was part of a pathway in the garden. He let out a small yelp and then lay whimpering; his breathing was light and he was barely moving. "Linus, Linus..." Vicky screamed. He seemed to look at her with a sad quizzical expression. She bent and rested her face against his. "Linus, Linus..." she shrieked desperately as she tickled the white bit on his chest. He still didn't move, apart from his chest going up and down very slightly. She lay for several minutes with her best friend, trying to cuddle him, her face against his tiny body breathing in his puppy smell, not knowing what to do. Linus had his eyes open but he wasn't looking at Vicky – he seemed to be staring into space. All of a sudden she was startled by a familiar voice.

"What's wrong, Vicky?" She looked up. It was her uncle.

"He's had an accident. He's not well. Make him better," she blurted, and burst into more floods of tears.

"Let's have a look at him." He stroked Linus and spoke gently to him and then tried to pick him up. Linus let out a high-pitched whimper, which further traumatised Vicky and she collapsed in more tears. "Vicky, you are a bad girl. You have hurt Linus very much and he is going to die. You caused this. I will take Linus away and I won't tell your mum and dad what you did. You must tell them that he has run away and you can't find him. It will be our little secret." Then he gently picked up Linus and put the blanket round him. Small whimpers came from beneath it and Vicky caught a glimpse of Linus's little face as the blanket moved. Linus looked sad.

"I'll take him away to a better place. When Mum comes back tell her that you have lost him. I'll be back in a while and help pretend to find him. Mum and Dad were so good to get you Linus, you can't tell them what you have done to him. It would break their heart. And when Samantha gets older, she won't want to hear what her big sister did to Linus. Remember, Vicky, it is our little secret."

With that, he left, and Vicky stared at his back with his arms slightly spread out carrying Linus, who was looking back at her. Her world collapsed. She kept seeing his little brown eyes and sad expression every time she closed her eyes.

Eventually Mrs Prentice found Vicky in the garden sobbing uncontrollably, but she wouldn't tell her what was wrong. Vicky was told to sit at the kitchen table until her mother returned. She told her mother that Linus had somehow run away and went through the lie and pretence. Her mother was genuinely upset and distraught at losing Linus. Over the following days, she made posters and put them in all the shops in the neighbourhood, but of course nobody had seen him.

Vicky endured the worst school holidays ever in a tempest of howling, writhing, fitful memories and thoughts of Linus. The blanket that she and Linus had played with was a blue and white check one, and she couldn't bear to see anything that vaguely matched it as it brought back those terrible thoughts.

Her father appeared somewhat concerned, but her mother was taking it very badly and sacked Mrs Prentice because she blamed her for not looking after Vicky and Linus better on that fateful afternoon. That made Vicky even more upset because everything was all her fault and she definitely couldn't ever tell her parents the truth now.

They cancelled the family holiday just in case Linus was found and they wanted to be at home if he was. Her father made it plain that he was not happy missing their two weeks in Normandy and emphasised the sacrifice he was making on behalf of the family.

At the end of the dreadful school holidays her parents held a dinner party. They did this on the last Saturday in August every year and it was one of several that they hosted on set points throughout the year with the same four couples. Vicky asked not to have to eat with them. Her mother seemed to understand her pain and said, "That's all right, but you have to get dressed up and meet them darling, then you can go to your room."

Vicky did her best trying to speak to her parents' guests, but she was still so broken-hearted that she just wanted to lie in her bedroom alone. After she was excused, she trudged wearily upstairs and could hear the new nanny reading to her little sister as she passed by her room. She went into her room and lay curled up on the bed crying for Linus. She could hear laughter downstairs, and after a while she heard the new nanny slowly make her way there as she was going to be helping serve the meal and clearing up. Not long afterwards she heard her door opening. She thought it would be the new nanny and didn't want to talk to her. The new nanny seemed nice, but Vicky missed Mrs Prentice, and it was all her fault that Mrs Prentice wasn't here any more. She was surprised when her uncle came into the room. She sat up and just looked at him.

"You have been so brave, my darling. How are you?"

She thought that maybe he had somehow saved Linus and that Linus would be coming home. He again softly asked her how she was and then asked her to come over for a little cuddle. She had been feeling so lonely and upset as she lay in the room and so she went over to him. She found the cuddle nice and hoped so much that he would give her good news. He held her gently and stroked her hair. She felt warm and secure and put her arms around his legs. She must have been cuddling him for over five minutes and he said little or nothing. Then he said softly, "You will get over this, but remember it is our little secret and you can't ever tell Mum and Dad what you did to Linus."

He continued to stroke her hair, and she realised that Linus was not coming back as he then slid his hand underneath her party dress.

And so it began.

Chapter Twenty

After about nine months, Mum and Dad asked Vicky if she would like another puppy, but she didn't. She missed Linus so much and didn't ever want another puppy to take his place. Time was not a healer because she was subject to bedroom visits every time there was a dinner party. Each time he visited he reminded her that it was all her fault and that he would comfort her. Any time she saw a blue check pattern on anything she remembered the puppy blanket and Linus's little sad eyes.

During her school years in the 1990s, as her peers grew up and became interested in the Brownies, school plays and sleepovers, Vicky retreated into herself. By the age of ten she had torn up all the photos of Linus. This included a framed picture that had sat on the mantlepiece in the living room. Her parents had been aware of Vicky systematically getting rid of any picture of Linus that she could find but chose to ignore this behaviour until the mantlepiece incident. This prompted a visit to a child psychologist, where Vicky stayed mute and the matter was brushed under the carpet and no more was said.

She became a good actress, could hide much of her pain, control her outbursts and appeared to function almost normally. Her mother would often chastise her for not joining in more with school and extracurricular activities but made little effort to bond with or understand her daughter. Her father left her mother to deal with things like that.

With adolescence, her red hair, gawkiness and apparent shyness were seized upon by some of her fellow pupils at the Mary Erskine School, Edinburgh. She hated having to travel across the city in a bus with lots of her fellow posh pupils. She didn't care what holidays they had had or what their dad did. She hated hockey, she hated rugby and having to stand on the touchlines and support the school team. She hated being picked on, but by the time she reached the second year at high school, Vicky realised that the confidence of the leaders of the group when picking on someone was all a front and required a bravado that they got from being in that group. She sensed that when they were alone these girls were as confused and directionless as she was. She used her hurt at Linus's death to channel a genuine rage that was directed at the bullies one by one. Thereafter, they kept a wary distance from her. Vicky was aware that she was considered *weird*, which suited her fine, and she got through school relatively unscathed. All her teachers remarked that she could do better, and some pointed out that there appeared to be noticeable mood swings and signs of depression that would go on for days. None of them, nor her parents, looked closely enough to see that these signs occurred at the same point in every year: just after her parents had hosted a dinner party.

As the years passed, the bedroom visits that she so dreaded became less frequent as Vicky would find ways of not being in her room when the dinner parties were on. When she was fourteen, she even offered to help with the serving at one of them, which delighted her mother, who thought that Vicky was finally coming out of her shell and growing up. However, that only happened once because she was so nervous and uptight at being in the same room as that bastard that she kept spilling things, not hearing instructions from her mother and unable to respond to any chat from the guests with nothing better than a weak scowl. Samantha was growing up as well and becoming much more aware of things around her, so it became more difficult for him to carry on as normal. Like many abusers though, he was resourceful and would find ways of being alone with her. He was good at DIY, whilst her father was useless, and, on several occasions, this involved him suggesting to her parents that he could help, to which they were effusively grateful. On one terrible occasion this involved him arriving early with his wife for a dinner party. While his wife sat downstairs indulging in conversation with her parents, Vicky endured him hanging a new mirror in her bedroom followed by his attentions and a reminder that they shared a secret. When he left, she tore the mirror from the wall and threw it down. The next day, as the mirror lay smashed on her floor, Vicky said that he must be crap at jobs like that and she didn't want him doing any more in her room. Her mother told her to mind her language and to stop being so nasty as he was only trying to help.

She liked English, history and art but really struggled with maths and science. However, this was enough for her to make it through school with sufficient qualifications to get to university. Her lack of sciences restricted her choice, and that, coupled with her wish to get well away from Edinburgh, prompted her to choose the University of Leicester. Naturally, her parents were not happy at her choice. They wanted her to go to either an established Scottish university or a college abroad.

Vicky could see that her choice would not go down well as a subject matter when her parents hosted their next dinner party, as Leicester didn't have the same status as Edinburgh, Aberdeen or Glasgow. Too bad, she was going to Leicester. Her parents' displeasure was evident, but to Vicky this demonstrated everything that she hated about her upbringing. There was a lack of warmth, empathy and love. Her welfare or happiness wasn't the issue for her parents, it was how Vicky's activities and achievements were seen by their friends and how they reflected on them which was their main concern.

Her resolve held. After all, they had let that bastard into their house for all those years and warmly greeted him each time he arrived. She was going to Leicester and to her own room on campus. She would pick and choose when she returned home and hoped to find friends who could become her shield from the torment that constantly bubbled away inside her.

At the start of her first term, her father drove her to Leicester. The long drive was done mainly in silence; it was a Saturday and they had started early. Vicky tried to sleep but couldn't; her stomach was churning from nerves and excitement at her new direction in life. On the trip, she realised that she had no real bond with her father. She was fond of him up to a point, but she couldn't remember him saying that he loved her or just giving her a hug. He appeared to fulfil his role of being a father through a sense of duty rather than love for his children and wanting to do it.

Finally, they arrived, and after a couple of missed turns on the campus they found Vicky's accommodation block where they were met by a cheery young man with long hair and a purple fringe. He enthusiastically welcomed them to Leicester, told them that he was called Den and shook their hands. Vicky's dad greeted him rather less enthusiastically. They were led into the accommodation block and greeted by other student representatives who provided details of where to register to pick up a welcome pack and the accommodation keys. She didn't suggest that they get a coffee in the refectory on the ground floor. She sensed that he wanted out of this alien environment as soon as possible and was wishing that it was tomorrow and he was on the golf course for his Sunday morning four-ball. He kissed her perfunctorily on the cheek and wished her well. "This might come in useful," he said with a weak smile as he gave her a £20 note. She thanked him but didn't give him a second thought later on when she used it to buy a bottle of wine and a packet of cigarettes to get her in the mood for the welcome disco that night. It was one of a multitude of events that took place in freshers' week and introduced her to the social side of life at university. By the time of the freshers' ball at the end of the first week, she had perfected her act of cool detachment and had actually enjoyed herself at times.

She met Greg on her first day as he was staying on the same floor as her. He seemed shy and a bit overawed by the sudden change in his life from being at home under his parents' wing to being independent and able to make his own choices. Vicky bonded with him immediately. She didn't feel a sexual attraction, but more of a bonding of kindred spirits. She got the feeling that Greg would have loved Linus.

After a few weeks a group of friends developed, of which Greg was the catalyst despite his apparent shyness and nervousness with the opposite sex. This included her future husband John, along with the other guys, Jamie, Brad and Scott. Apart from Vicky, the females were two girls who were both called Rachel. They all lived in the same accommodation block and, apart from John and one of the Rachels, were studying for arts degrees. She enjoyed her social life, which revolved almost entirely around this group. Other people would dip in and out, but those eight were the ones who went to the student union and hung out every Thursday to Sunday and then often went elsewhere after chucking-out time.

Vicky didn't embrace the many extracurricular opportunities that were available. Concentrating on her social life and reinventing herself took priority. She treated her look and persona as a project and devoured fashion and art magazines and related articles in newspapers as she worked to perfect the image that she hoped would shape her future. She spent hours in the library, but this was seldom on course work. Instead, much more of her time was used researching hard, strong, cunning, resourceful and successful women in history and literature. This covered Boadicea, Lady Macbeth, Joan of Arc, Florence Nightingale and Edith Piaf through to Patti Smith and the Spice Girls. She sought to find any common ground amongst their traits and looked to see what appeared to make them successful. It appeared that the key elements were: looks, attitude, a definite goal or mission in life and drive to achieve this. It seemed to her that most didn't appear to require the regular support of a man. There were notable exceptions, of course, but she preferred to concentrate on those who could do it on their own. As she was studying for a BA in English, her course work could combine at times with her *project* and, when it did, so her marks would improve.

Vicky also regularly visited the psychology and psychiatry sections of the library to explore what made people tick, to learn what influenced human behaviour, and to use this understanding to help in creating a persona that would be believable and successful. She felt this would help lessen thoughts of her abuser and reduce his impact on her. Thoughts of that bastard did still occur, and her way of coping was to be hard, confident, alluring and domineering. She experimented with drugs, tried to keep up with the guys' drinking habits and embraced the party culture in general. Vicky often initiated sex and would periodically pick up someone at a party and force the pace. The next day she would discuss her conquest with the group as if she was one of the lads.

Contact with her parents was minimal, and at most, she would phone once a week for a brief catch-up, paying little attention to what her parents were up to and feeling a freeze in the pit of her stomach if the next dinner party was mentioned. She kept her return visits to a few days over Christmas and New Year when she had little choice. For the Christmas break in her second year, she invited the group up to Edinburgh to experience the famous New Year celebrations. This was for two reasons: to show her parents who her friends were and that she could make decisions without their influence, and also to ensure that her abuser would not come anywhere near her. Greg, Jamie, Brad and both Rachels came up. The girls stayed at Vicky's house, with the boys staying in a youth hostel in the city centre.

It was not until the start of her third year that she and John became an item. He accepted her eccentricities, was reliable and made her feel safe. As there was no way she was going to return to Edinburgh, Vicky decided that with university life soon to come to an end she needed a solid support to ensure she didn't have to rely on her parents. She calculated the need to get the relationship underway by the autumn so that it was well established by the time of graduation. One Friday afternoon towards the end of October, Vicky decided that it was time to initiate a relationship. Of the guys in the group only Greg and John were still single. It was a toss-up between them and Greg was her slight favourite as he was more on her level, had been the gel in the group forming in the first place and for it staying loosely together over more than two years. Her plan was really quite simple. She would go to the student union, then when much drink had been consumed, along with a few puffs, she would corner her prey, take him home and screw his brains out. Greg or John – to be decided.

The group made its way to the student union and the drinking got underway. They split into two groups of four for the rounds and Vicky was having a great laugh with Greg, who was sitting next to her. John and one of the Rachels were also in the round. She was keeping an eye on John, but by the time they got to the fifth drink of the evening, she had decided that Greg was the one. Even though he hated dancing, their type of music was booming out of the PA and so she would persuade him to share a tab then get up for a dance. He had gone to the bar with John as he was getting the next round and John was helping. When Greg came back she would whisper in his ear and get the party started.

Finally, Greg and John got served and started to pick their way through the crowd back to the table. On their way there, a very drunk and distressed female blocked their path. John, who was in front and carrying his and Vicky's drink, managed to sidestep her and continued to pick his way through the throng and back to the table. Greg put his drinks down on a nearby table and stopped to ask her what the matter was. It took almost fifteen minutes before Greg could extricate himself and return to the table. Rachel was grateful to finally see him as she was gagging for a drink and acknowledged his return with sarcastic applause.

John and Vicky didn't notice his return because they were now dancing. Greg and the rest of the group didn't see much of them for the rest of the night.

Chapter Twenty-One

Vicky got through university in a similar vein to her academic progress at school. Her natural intelligence meant that she did enough to get her BA second class degree. John was going for a BSc (Hons) in Biomedical Science. When it was time to leave university, Vicky had no idea what she was going to do apart from not go back to Edinburgh. John had another year of study to go and they decided to get a flat together. Vicky got a job in a doctors' surgery as a temporary receptionist providing maternity cover. She hated it. However, it gave her access to job opportunities within NHS East Midlands and she soon secured a permanent role as a programme administrator. She managed the administrative and clerical support of consultancy teams delivering a variety of health-related programmes across the East Midlands. This provided a reasonable salary and job security, but she had no real interest in what the teams were doing and little personal connection with the medical professionals delivering the programmes.

After a year, John graduated and got a job as a pharmacology technician in an NHS pathology centre at Leicester Royal Infirmary. John's grandmother died, leaving a significant sum to her only grandchild. They used this as a deposit to help secure their foot on the first rung of the property ladder and bought a small two-bedroomed house in Hinckley, not far from Leicester.

Vicky's life became routine and depressing. She had managed to escape the need to be with her parents and consequently the attention of that bastard at their dinner parties. She didn't particularly miss her parents, but she really missed her little sister Samantha and over the past four years had only seen her during infrequent visits to Edinburgh. Sam was now studying law at Edinburgh University and staying at home. She obviously had a good relationship with her parents, which was so different from Vicky, but of course Sam hadn't been subject to the regular visits from *him* that Vicky had had to endure for many years.

Vicky liked John, but he had become boring and uninspiring and the job that he did was of no interest to her. She realised that now he was out of the group, John had little to offer socially and, when she thought about it, over the years he had never instigated any of the fun and was always the follower. John had settled into the middle-class routines that he had been brought up to expect. Now that they were a couple and their close friends had dispersed, the routine of work and quiet weekends was beginning to bore her, and the thought of their future together was depressing.

One time, John had an interview for a promoted post at work. The day before the interview he bought a new tie and proudly showed it to Vicky when he got home that evening. It was a light blue check design, which Vicky grabbed off him in a rage and became almost hysterical as she thought of Linus and the pain that she had endured over the years. It took several hours for her to revert to normal. To his credit, John dealt with this and offered as much support as he could to Vicky, which was difficult because she wouldn't tell him why a new tie could have caused her to react in such a way. He didn't get the promoted post.

After about two years together, Vicky could barely stand being touched sexually or even affectionately by John. It wasn't him; it was her demons. To her, sex was for control, and she needed that and an element of danger, or at least intrigue. Regular sex with John just didn't provide that and her encounters with him were sporadic. John didn't complain, which at first suited Vicky, but after a while this annoyed her as it showed what a wimp he was. She started looking for quick, frantic sex which she would instigate and then lead with no expectation or requirement for future contact. Staff training courses, particularly if they involved an away day with an overnight stay, were ideal opportunities for this. Ironically, her keenness to volunteer for so many training courses was noted on her

179

record with approval by her senior management and HR department, and her career in NHS East Midlands appeared destined to flourish.

Vicky kept in touch with some of the group from university, but as ever with people moving around the country in the next chapter of their lives, this became more difficult, and arranging catch-ups became more of a hassle than a pleasure. Greg was working as a barman in the student union. This didn't surprise Vicky because it meant that he didn't have to completely cut his ties with student life. Several years after leaving university, and out of the blue, she got a call from Greg asking her and John if they wanted to meet for a drink the following week. The reason for the invitation was that he was moving to London. Only four of the original group; Jamie and one of the Rachels along with Vicky were able to meet up. John couldn't make it, which suited Vicky absolutely fine.

They met at a pub that had been one of their regular haunts for several years, and it was a good night despite there being lots of career-orientated and house chat, which Rachel led on describing the wonderful property that she and her new partner had bought and were doing up. Greg was going to London because someone who he had chatted to at the student union while he was serving in the bar had told him about a room in a flat in West London in which two of Greg's acquaintances were staying. Therefore he had decided it was time to move as he could always get a bar job down there.

Vicky admired Greg's independence and ability to make off-the-cuff decisions without having to think about them or consult anyone else. She kept in touch with Greg and after about a year started to visit him in London on a few occasions. She knew that John would be unhappy at her going to Greg's flat in London but that was easily dealt with. Using her admin skills that were constantly evolving, she would produce a course programme and fictitious details of a training course and tell John that she had to attend it that weekend. With that, she would be off.

The first time she stayed at Greg's flat she was given his room and he was going to sleep on the sofa in the living room. They had gone out for a few drinks at the local bar and had had a good catch-up. There was a level of awkwardness from Greg when they got back to the flat as she could sense that he was going to give it a go. There was no chance of that being successful and she offered no encouragement. They sat with wine then coffee and chatted until the early hours. Mike, one of Greg's flatmates, came in at around midnight, said a brief hello to Vicky, had a quick chat with Greg and then left them to it. Dave, Greg's other flatmate, was in his room with his girlfriend. It was about two before Vicky retired to Greg's room. Greg was putting a brave face on not being encouraged to join her and settled down for the night on the sofa. Vicky dozed for a couple of hours then very slowly and quietly opened the bedroom door, tiptoed past the lightly snoring figure of Greg in the living room and then slowly and quietly opened Mike's door. She took off her pyjama T-shirt and shorts and slipped into Mike's bed. He stirred but didn't wake up. He was lying in the foetal position and she snuggled in behind him and started to gently stroke his neck. Her hands then moved over and onto his chest. Mike groggily woke up and Vicky quietly shooshed him. She ran her hands down his body and into his shorts. As he was beginning to realise what was happening, Vicky smoothly turned him onto his back and took one of his hands and placed it on her breast, then she let go of his hand and let it roam. She leaned forward and quietly shooshed him again. She whispered seductively into his ear, "Mike, my darling, I need you, but please be very quiet – let's not wake Greg." Mike nodded and smiled.

When Mike was spent, she cooed into his ear for a few minutes then told him not to say a word because she and Greg might become an item. Mike nodded understandingly and Vicky returned silently to her room. The next day Greg took her for lunch before she got on her train back to Leicester. She made several more visits to Greg's flat over the next couple of years, which involved a couple more visits to Mike's bedroom. Then when Mike moved flats, she introduced herself to Ryan, who was Greg and Dave's new flatmate.

Vicky's look was developing. She appeared far more sophisticated and glamorous than during her student days, while Greg pretty much still had the permanent student look, feel and attitude. As far as she could tell, Greg was blissfully unaware of her night-time excursions when she stayed at his place. She could see him almost exploding with desire and need, but she wanted others who offered danger and no further requirement after the act. She knew if she slept with Greg he would follow her like a favourite puppy, and if she ended up in a relationship with him it would soon replicate the one she was in with John.

Vicky spent seven uneventful years in Hinckley staying in the same house, unchanging routines at home and avoiding Edinburgh as much as possible. The dull routine was occasionally broken by visits to London, her sister coming to stay or visiting a swingers' club for quick uninhibited sex. In between times she could be visited by her demons at any time. She sometimes went months without thinking of it or him. On other occasions, it could happen several times over a short period. At these times she welcomed the cloying familiarity and routines of John and their relationship. It was all that kept her with him.

John secured a job at St Bartholomew's Hospital in London. He was delighted and Vicky couldn't believe her luck. At work she had risen to become a popular member of the senior management team. However, she didn't hesitate to hand in her notice to her disappointed colleagues and set about arranging their move to London. The day after John confirmed the job offer, Vicky had the house on the market. However, they had done little work on it, and despite being in an area that was being gentrified, it wasn't a particularly enticing product and it took what felt like a lifetime to sell.

John had to move into accommodation provided by the hospital while Vicky stayed in Hinckley. Her three-month notice expired, and after she left the NHS she funded herself by a succession of temporary administration posts in the East Midlands. John's salary had increased significantly, she was comfortable financially and had an empty house and lots of extra time to meet her urges if required.

Finally, the house was sold, and Vicky and John secured a furnished rented property in North London. It was well positioned for the Northern Line for John to commute to work. John had wanted to try and buy something to get a foothold on the London property ladder, but Vicky managed to persuade him to wait for a year or so until he saw how his job was progressing. She now felt that opportunities would be presenting themselves to her and wanted as few commitments as possible as she weighed up her future. When it was time to go, as she knew it would be soon, the quicker and easier to get away from him the better.

There was little point hanging around their new house when there was no chance of bringing someone back, so Vicky got a temporary job. She had been working for a month in an administration role in an estate agent called Armfield's near Wembley when she met *him*. He turned up at her office out of the blue ten minutes before her shift finished.

Chapter Twenty-Two

She hadn't seen him for at least three years and had not been alone with him for over five. Her scream shook the office. There were four customers and her three colleagues in the shop. He stood and looked at Vicky in shock. She sat at her desk transfixed, staring at him and quietly mumbling unintelligibly. Nick, the manager, reacted first and rushed over. "What is it, Vicky, are you OK? What happened?"

She said nothing.

"I just came in and was going to ask for details on a house shown in the window," he said, pointing at the front window, "and she just screamed." He hadn't sat down at any point and was standing several feet away from Vicky, unsure how to react.

"And you said or did nothing else?" Nick asked.

"No, nothing, I swear I did nothing."

"Fiona, come and help Vicky to the staffroom and put the kettle on," Nick said to one of Vicky's colleagues. Fiona came over and gently coaxed Vicky to her feet and led her away from the public area. Whilst she was doing this, the third colleague was diplomatically removing the remaining customers from the shop and putting up the closed sign.

Nick asked the man to sit down. He appeared genuinely shocked and bemused by what had happened and had nothing to add to what he had already said. Nick asked him where he was from and established that he lived locally, he and his wife had bought their previous house through Armfield's and were looking to downsize now that their children had grown up and moved out.

Fiona gave Vicky a cup of sweet tea, which she cradled in her hands but didn't drink. "Are you OK, love," she asked. Vicky just sat holding the tea and gently rocked backwards and forwards. At this point Nick came in.

"Vicky, can you help explain what happened?" he asked sympathetically. She looked at him blankly.

"Mr Reynolds doesn't know what he has done. He has told me that he didn't even speak to you and that he was going to ask about a house shown in the window but didn't get the chance." Vicky still remained silent. Nick carried on, "Him and his wife bought their last house through us twenty years ago and are now looking to downsize." Vicky looked up at this but still said nothing. Nick continued, "They live in Chesington Crescent and are looking for something smaller in the same area."

"What's his name?" Vicky asked very quietly.

"Sorry, Vicky, what did you say?" Nick asked.

"What's his name?"

"It's Gordon Reynolds," Nick replied.

"Where does he live?"

"I just told you, Vicky, he lives in Chesington Crescent," Nick replied softly. He could tell that something was wrong with Vicky but didn't know what.

"Does he come from Edinburgh?" she then asked.

"No, Vicky, he doesn't come from Edinburgh. He is English and lives here in London. In Chesington Crescent."

"Not from Edinburgh?"

"No, definitely not from Edinburgh," Nick affirmed.

Vicky looked down at her feet and mumbled.

"Sorry, Vicky, what did you say?" Nick asked.

"Tell him I'm sorry. Please tell him that I'm so sorry." With that she burst into tears. Nick went to speak to Mr Reynolds and Fiona stayed with Vicky.

Nick and the team at Armfield's Estate Agents couldn't have been more helpful and supportive in the immediate aftermath of Vicky's outburst. Nick asked if she wanted to talk about it with him or any of her colleagues. Fiona suggested that they go to the nearby pub for something stronger than tea if she wanted and Nick chipped in to reassure her that the company would pay her taxi home. Vicky thanked them very much, but she just wanted to be on her own. She assured them she would be all right and would see them the next day. Nick and Fiona emphasised their support and Nick told her to take a couple of days off if she wanted to. Fiona gave Vicky her mobile number and told her to phone anytime if she needed to.

Vicky didn't go into work the following day or the day after that. In fact, she didn't return at all. She felt three overriding emotions: shock, embarrassment and anger. She was shocked at how someone who bore a resemblance to *him* had caused such a reaction within her and how she had been unable to control her emotions. She was embarrassed at her outburst and angry that she could not reveal the reasons for it to anyone.

For several weeks after the scene at Armfield's she experienced extremely vivid dreams involving bumping into *him* in some urban environment. They were always very similar: she had a new flat and he asked to see it. She would refuse, but then somehow he was in it and threatening to tell her parents about Linus. The next thing would be him violating her with his *favourite finger* before trying to go further. At which point she would wake up screaming with a shaken John trying his best to calm her down and reassure her. After about an hour, calmness would descend, but sleep would be impossible as Vicky lay with her demons and John lay beside her feeling helpless and unappreciated.

However, the episode at work had helped focus her. She looked back to her past and how he had used her puppy to start his abuse; well, Linus was long gone; she was an adult and he had no control over her any more. She resolved that the bastard was indeed out of her life and it was now time to reclaim it. One night, as she lay on her sweat-soaked sheets and contemplated her future and her past, she told John that she would seek therapy for her demons and promised him that things would improve.

Therefore, and with John's blessing, she gave herself a two-month break from working. She decided that as part of her therapy it was time to get in touch with Greg and see if he could rekindle the spark that she had had at university and perhaps meet a couple of his mates. It was good meeting up with him again and she genuinely enjoyed seeing him. However, she couldn't commit herself to him beyond having a coffee and a catch-up and so her therapy of having numerous one-night stands, or more likely daytime liaisons with complete strangers, resumed.

Then she met Kevin Osborne, and everything changed.

Chapter Twenty-Three

Vicky sat at the back of the café on Saturday morning with a large Americano as she gathered her thoughts. Her hair was dyed black and she had her glasses on. Her backpack was sitting on the floor and contained the green A4-sized plastic wallet folder with the documents that Greg had got for her. They had not yet been put to practical use, but she had passed on the details he had got on Piotr.

As she nursed her coffee and considered her options, a thought struck her from out of the blue. *Why had they called the puppy Linus?* There was a Peanuts tea towel that was hung in the kitchen which showed Charlie Brown, Snoopy, Lucy and Linus, who were the key characters from that comic strip. She couldn't remember why they choose Linus as the puppy's name when Snoopy was the dog. Also, she thought it was odd that her mother had such a thing because her parents certainly never watched or read anything as frivolous as cartoons or comics.

Her thoughts then tumbled onto her marriage, and she regretted the breakup with John, but only in terms of committing all those years to her husband when it was obviously going to be a complete waste of time.

The regular meetings with Greg over the years had helped to a point, but when she met Kevin Osborne, she moved into a new environment and one in which her carefully constructed persona seemed a perfect fit. Kev had the confidence, looks, arrogance and style that she so admired, and meeting him was her turning point. Although from quite different backgrounds, they had immediately hit it off and their success together was instantaneous. She considered where it had got them though: him dead before he could stand trial and her getting locked up for eight years. Thinking about this caused her to cast her mind back to how she behaved and reacted when Greg got caught up in the whole polonium smuggling operation and his aunt being kidnapped. Vicky remembered that when she realised Greg had become unwittingly involved, she had felt guilty and sorry for him to an extent because she had always liked him. She had finally slept with Greg during this time and left him thinking they were going to become an item. However, now thinking about it, she used him simply as a commodity. He was useful to show her around town when she first arrived in London, and she treated him like a childhood toy or object that you kept for sentimental reasons to serve as a reminder of simpler, less complicated times. She now wondered how she could have been so callous. She had created an artificially hard outer skin to deal with the effects of her abuse, but she disregarded one of the nicest people she had ever met and truly one of her few good friends, and at the time it barely crossed her mind. And now she had done it again, but worse, far, far worse. She had got Greg to steal from Clinkie Moore. *Clinkie Moore*. Poor Greg, she had never bothered about the danger she was putting him in when giving him his instructions to go to Clinkie's and steal her false papers and passport. By successfully stealing from Clinkie, Greg had effectively written his own death warrant.

She asked herself what she had become. Not only was Maggie held captive, but she had trussed up Di and left her at Greg's without a second thought. Vicky decided with a tremor that made her spill her coffee that this had to stop now and that she must get Greg out of danger. This would inevitably mean that she would go back to prison, but it was worth it. It would save Greg and would give her time to deal with her demons and finally confront the bastard who abused her and ruined her life. Also, it was time to tell her family.

Vicky was unsure what had caused this epiphany, but on reflection she considered that the time she had held Maggie while Greg was at Clinkie's daughter's wedding may have been the trigger. She had tried to avoid speaking to Maggie or listening to her, but it was impossible to shut Maggie up without gagging her, which she did regularly. Inevitably, some of Maggie's chatter got through and Vicky sensed an overwhelming essence of her trust and respect for Greg. Vicky fought off her inner urge to feel sympathy for Greg as she waited for him to hopefully complete his task. When it was done, he had got what she wanted, and now as she looked at the backpack containing the documents that could lead to beginning a new life, instead of feeling elated at this opportunity, she felt quite the opposite and completely directionless.

Vicky suddenly felt overwhelmingly guilty that she had caused Greg to be in such grave danger, which gave her a clarity after all these years on what now had to be done. She took out her tablet and started typing:

Dear Greg

I expect that you will never forgive me for what I put you through and I understand that. I am massively sorry for the hurt caused to you and the role that I played in your aunt's kidnapping. I know that words from me will never suffice, but I want you to know that every day of my life I regret what I became involved in and the suffering that this caused.

Over the past two years in jail, I have had time to think, and it is only now when I am out and on the run that I have had some clarity in my thoughts and what I need to do.

I am going to hand myself in and give evidence against Clinkie and his associates if necessary.

I will ask for therapy to help alleviate the demons that have controlled my actions for so many years.

I hope you have continued reading and made it this far, and if so, I will give you a summary of my life leading up to the events of two years ago.

From the age of six, I was sexually abused, and I now realise that this has affected who I am and how I have behaved for more than thirty years.

I was brought up in a typically Scottish upper-middle-class Presbyterian household, where expressing your emotions was frowned upon and so many things went unsaid.

It sounds ridiculous, but I have blamed myself for what happened to me and what I endured, and by trying to deal with it myself instead of seeking professional help and by ignoring it and its effects, something has built inside me that exploded a few years ago causing my behaviour.

I thought that finally I was being strong. I thought that I was finally saying "fuck you" to the demons inside me. Of course I was wrong.

I am not strong. I have sometimes been a good actress, but I am weak. I have caused hurt to you and others that is wholly unjustifiable.

Two wrongs don't make a right. What I have put you through and what I am putting you through again is terrible and I have never once considered how you feel. Until now.

You helped make me a social person at uni. I was scared of my own shadow, and it was you, Greg, who started to give me confidence. You gave me unconditional support without looking to get anything back. You even introduced me to John. I shouldn't have married him, and I should have married you, Greg. Although, to be honest, any of my relationships were doomed to fail because of the harm my abuser has caused me.

Meeting Kev Osborne seemed to square the circle. I really, really thought I was getting somewhere and that I was happy and looking forward to the future. I just didn't think or know what I was doing.

It is only now when I have put you in grave danger again that I suddenly realise that my life is a pack of cards and I need to bring it tumbling down to be able to start again.

Looking back to when we had you searching for the code that Kev needed to get the polonium, I told Kev that you had found Cassie and that you seemed to know her role – I told him that we needed to get rid of her. What was I telling Kev? Obviously, I was asking him to kill her. He said, "Consider it done." All I thought was – good, that's that problem out the way. That's what I have become, thinking nothing of asking for someone to be killed. It has to change.

I am going to turn myself in. I know I'll get more time inside, but I am going to use that time to repair myself.

Prison has got all kinds of professionals who can and want to help, and all I've done is resist and try to hide behind my posh girl facade and be the prison bad bitch.

I am going to ask how I can report and confront the bastard who abused me over so many years (who is still alive BTW), how I tell my parents and how I try and move forward and repair myself.

I am not going to ask my parents for forgiveness. I am going to tell them what happened and ask that they believe me and deal with it. I want this bastard in the dock and for everyone to see what he has done to me (who knows there might be others that he as abused as well...). I clearly remember the large ring he wore, and even now, the sight of a signet ring sends shivers down my spine.

I am going to ask you for forgiveness though, Greg. I truly want you to believe me, please Greg. I want you to forgive me.

I am going to the police station today. I want you to answer me, Greg, even if it's a no.

I want to know that you have read this. That will make me feel better knowing that you know my secret.

One thing that I am already clinging on to is that when I am back in prison and hopefully getting professional help, that you may consider visiting me, Greg.

That is giving me some sort of hope for the future. That is giving me some sort of strength.

Please get in touch.

With all my love

Vicky xxx

She pressed send. She realised that tears had been streaming down her face and her coffee had long gone cold. She looked up and a couple in the opposite booth hurriedly turned away.

Vicky composed herself and then went up to the counter and ordered another coffee. She felt nervous but in an almost excited way. She felt lighter and more composed, almost clear about everything. In many ways she was ready to hand herself in right now but was wanting to give Greg a few hours at least to respond. Also, she had to decide how she would have Maggie released, who she had left incarcerated in the storeroom of West London Action Group while she had come to this café.

Suzi Moore had taken Maggie there and held her overnight before Vicky took over after having met Greg at the pub and giving him his bus ticket to Glasgow. Vicky had briefly seen Suzi when she took over watching Maggie before Suzi left for the airport and her flight to Scotland for the wedding. Vicky hoped she would never see Suzi again, although she accepted that there would be plenty more like her where she was returning to.

She ordered a third coffee and a slice of carrot cake. There had been no reply from Greg. Vicky realised that what she had told him was a lot to take in, to put it mildly, and after what he had just gone through she could understand why he hadn't replied instantly. However, there was a part of her that just wanted to know that he had read her message. She sent him a text which said *Check your emails* then checked her reflection using her smartphone as a mirror, took a deep breath and got up and slowly walked out of the shop. Yes, she thought, it will be a long haul, but it will be worth it. For the first time she could remember she wasn't dreading the future.

She walked out of the shop into the glare of the sunshine, and as she stepped onto the pavement, she felt her left then right elbow gripped very tightly, and she was directed forcibly, silently and very efficiently into the back passenger seat of a car whose door had opened seconds previously. The car took off smoothly and joined the flow of traffic. Somehow she was now in the middle seat with two large and strong men either side of her. Her heart rate, which had been pumping rapidly, increased further when the figure in the front passenger seat turned round. It was Jonjo Laxton. They had never met, but Vicky knew who it would be, having heard lots about him from Suzi Moore.

"Clinkie wants a word with you," was all that he said before he turned round and faced the front.

Chapter Twenty-Four

Vicky opened her eyes and checked her watch as the car doors opened. It was over an hour since she had left the coffee shop. She felt groggy, disorientated and floppy and realised that the bastards must have drugged her.

The car was parked in an alleyway and Vicky was hustled out of it and into a building through the fire exit. She was in the basement of the building, but couldn't tell if it was an office, hotel or warehouse. She didn't really care and just wanted out of there. She was then dragged into what seemed like a storeroom and shoved on to a hard back chair in the middle of the room. The room had one long table at the end of it in front of shelves packed with stationery. A laptop sat on the table and the two men from the back of the car went and sat at either end of the table after depositing Vicky in her seat. Jonjo remained on his feet and she sensed a female presence and a familiar scent behind her.

Jonjo went over and fiddled with the laptop and Clinkie appeared on the screen. She realised that he was watching her via Skype. Before he could speak, she got up, approached the screen and said pleadingly, "I'm sorry, Clinkie, I'm so sorry. I'm going to hand myself in, Clinkie. I don't want to go abroad. I don't want any money or drugs or the car or anything. I want to go back inside and get help."

He said slowly and quietly, "Sit down." One of the men got up to approach Vicky, but she returned to her seat and so he sat down. Clinkie continued quietly, "You fucked up my daughter's wedding. You thieving little bitch, you stole from me. Your boyfriend conned his way into my house, he even stole one of my motors..." He tailed off, then continued, "Where is he?"

"I, I don't know, Clinkie... I haven't seen him, but I know he came back to Ealing," she said.

"He's not at his flat, but we'll find him, which will be fun for Jonjo and the boys when we do. Jonjo, get the medicine." Clinkie appeared to be very calm.

"It's not Greg's fault, Clinkie, I made him do it. I kidnapped his boss and threatened his parents. It's all my fault. I was abused as a child. I'm going to nail the nonce bastard. I'm going to tell my mum and dad and I'm going to get better." She looked pleadingly at the screen. "Please, Clinkie."

Clinkie's expression did not change. "What a shame. You can tell all you want, but it will be St Peter that you answer to. Hope you're thirsty," he said evenly and quietly and then raised his voice. "Jonjo, bring her a drink." Jonjo walked past Vicky to the back of the room.

Jonjo returned with a full bottle of whisky and a decanter. Vicky could just catch sight of a female out of the corner of her eye who was hovering behind Jonjo. She handed something to him, but Vicky couldn't make out what it was. Jonjo dispensed half of the bottle of whisky into the decanter and then added to it whatever it was the woman had given him. "Looks like a good blend," Clinkie said, and Jonjo laughed. Jonjo approached Vicky with the decanter in his hand. He grabbed her hand and made her hold the decanter for a few seconds, then he made her hold a crystal glass.

"Open her mouth," Clinkie instructed, and Jonjo carefully took the glass from her. Vicky sat still and didn't try to offer much resistance; there was no point, she was spent. Her mouth was prised open and her head held back by one of the men from the car as the whisky was poured down her throat by Jonjo. She briefly caught sight of Clinkie on the screen impassively watching the spectacle. The woman who had handed something to Jonjo was Di, who now stood in front of Vicky and winked.

Vicky closed her eyes and thought of Linus in his blanket, the feel of his lovely soft fur, his own special puppy smell and his sad little eyes.

PART THREE

Chapter Twenty-Five

The message simply said, *Get your arse back up the road*. I panicked and finished my bottle of wine while considering my options. Obviously, there was no way I was returning to Clinkie's house or anywhere near it; going to my parents definitely wasn't an option, and as I wanted to get away as quickly as possible, I went online and booked the first available flight to Tenerife on Saturday morning. In this case, flight mode literally meant just that. I felt that I didn't have a moment to spare and booked a taxi which arrived at midnight.

I got to Gatwick Airport at one thirty on Saturday morning £90 lighter after the taxi fare, feeling rough and confused. I had hoped to fly from Heathrow, which was much quicker and easier for me to get to, but there wasn't a flight to Tenerife from there until nearly eleven o'clock in the morning. The taxi ride to the airport was unbearable as I had foolishly sat in the front passenger seat. The driver was a friendly young man from Afghanistan who had recently moved to the UK with his wife and two young children. He was very talkative, and he told me he was keen to improve his English, which was very limited. As a former teacher of English as a Foreign Language I should have been encouraging him, but because of my current predicament, I was too scared to make small talk and just wanted to keep my head down as I kept nervously looking in the wing mirror in the hope that we weren't being followed. About halfway into the trip he eventually gave up trying to converse with me and I was aware of him sneaking glances out of the corner of his eye at the strange passenger next to him.

When we finally arrived at Gatwick. The driver said something to me which I didn't catch. He repeated it, "Terminal?"

I nodded and said, "Terminal."

He looked at me quizzically and repeated, "Terminal?"

I nodded and asked how much. He told me the amount, which I paid using money from the wedge that Vicky gave me, gave him a £5 tip and got out of the car. He was still giving me an odd look. After a few minutes wandering around the car park trying to work out where to go, I discovered that there were two terminals and now realised that the taxi driver was asking me which one I had wanted to go to. I had no idea, so went in search of an information desk, which took quite a while and added to my anxiety.

I worked out that I was in the North Terminal and had to get to the South one. Having found the monorail that links the two terminals, it took a while to locate the airline check-in desk. My anxiety had reached a level where I felt somehow removed from everything and it was almost like I was playing a part in a film as I was guided by very patient staff. I had packed one backpack very quickly which wasn't particularly sturdy and the check-in operative made sure that my bag was securely fastened before she put a sticker on the handle and gave me my passport back.

Despite not having any hand luggage, I set off the alarms in security because I had a bottle of water in my jacket pocket. When I was asked to move to one side to be searched and then go through the electronic sensor again, there was a part of me that wanted to be apprehended because it would mean that I would be taken to a safe place and Clinkie Moore wouldn't be able to get to me.

It was after two in the morning when I passed through security and entered the large departure lounge feeling totally disorientated and unsure what to do next. A bit like Glasgow the previous night, the number of people around at that time surprised me. As ever in a crisis my first reaction is to go for a beer and again to my surprise there were plenty of bars open. I decided I would knock a few back, which would hopefully calm me down and perhaps would help me get some sleep later when I got on the plane.

As I headed towards the nearest bar, I realised that airports were a whole different world to what I was used to. I passed excited passengers dressed for the tropics, although it was October in the UK, overconfident salespeople trying to entice me to buy a ticket to win a luxury car that was beside their stand and shops bustling with free-spending customers.

The bar was quite busy, and if you ignored the screens displaying flight information, it resembled the type of local hostelry still found in most high streets. There were a number of groups of quite lively young people some of whom were in fancy dress, but not as imaginatively dressed as at the darts match in Glasgow the previous night, as well as several middle-aged to elderly couples, where in each case the man was drinking a beer and the woman was making do with a tea or coffee.

As I drank my first beer, I was raging at Vicky. I knew she was a cold heartless bitch, but even by her standards doing what she did after I had delivered everything that she wanted in under three days was incomprehensible to me. It had to be her that gave Clinkie my phone number and no doubt my address as she was the only person linked to me and Clinkie. I just didn't understand how anyone could be so cruel. I ignored the increasing noise levels coming from a bunch of lads two tables away from me as I considered this and mulled over a number of other factors. Vicky now had the fake passport, UK and International driving licences and other documents that would enable her to get out of the country and begin a new life, and I asked myself why she had given my contact details to Clinkie. I guessed she was using me as bait to divert Clinkie whilst she made good her escape. "Bitch," I said out loud as my anger levels increased. I was gripping my glass so tightly that I was lucky it hadn't shattered in my hand. I put my beer down, took several deep breaths and wiped the sweat from my brow.

It was very late, or early, and I had hardly slept for two nights, which may have affected my judgement, but I could come up with no other conclusion than that I had been sacrificed by Vicky, resulting in Clinkie Moore being on my tail. This worrying thought then led me on to my next question, which was why did Clinkie's people not go to my flat? Why did they phone and leave a message which let me know that they knew who I was and where I was? All I could think of was that they might tail me in the hope that I led them to Vicky or Piotr, and by leaving a message, that would spring me from my lair. That thought sent a shiver through my body and I looked at the drinkers in the bar around me wondering if any of them were in fact in the employ of Clinkie Moore. Judging by the noise levels and the speed of their drinking, they all seemed too preoccupied with the excitement of going on holiday to be undercover hitmen. However, when I cast my mind to last night and my walk towards the darts match, I considered who would have thought that man at M&S and dog walking man were part of Clinkie's outfit.

It was time for another beer. I was slightly unsteady on my feet as I made my way to the bar, down to tiredness more than anything else. Everyone seemed to be having a good time apart from me. No doubt there would be those hiding their demons behind a façade, but I doubted if anyone in this bar was in more serious shit than me. I returned to my seat and looked at one of the display screens and saw that my flight was still scheduled to leave at six am. I then considered why I was flying to Tenerife. My panic at the phone message in my flat sparked an instant reaction of wanting to get the hell out of there as soon as possible. I had narrowed down my few choices and flying away seemed the best option. Flying to Tenerife no doubt jumped out in my mind because I had just booked flights for Brygida and Ania to go there. I felt a chill in the pit of my stomach. In my tunnel vision as I carried out the acts on behalf of Vicky that she had forced me to do, I had not once contemplated the implications for them. I was so pleased with myself when I had got Brygida drunk and worked out Piotr's location so quickly. As soon as I had left Brygida's flat I had phoned Vicky. It had not crossed my mind for a second that I had put Piotr's life in jeopardy. The next day, I had booked flights so that Brygida and Ania could go and stay with him. The more I thought about it the worse it got. Vicky had mentioned something about double crossing Clinkie so that some major player several notches up the crime ladder would use him as the lead to Piotr then get the polonium and wipe out Clinkie. Piotr and Brygida and Ania would be caught up in this and no doubt would become collateral damage.

I was very scared and so ashamed at what I had done. I tried to reassure myself that Vicky had forced me into it, which she had. However, I could have levelled with Brygida and told her why Vicky had appeared at my door. If I had told her the truth, perhaps she would have changed her mind about going to Piotr's at this stage. Also she may have agreed to my suggestion that I went to the police and got them to search for both Vicky and Maggie. I had felt so responsible for Maggie that I hadn't considered the implications for those much closer to me. My feelings that were stirred when I realised that Brygida was leaving were genuine, and now as I contemplated what may happen as Clinkie and perhaps other criminal elements descended on Piotr, I had to work out a plan of action.

I took a moment to consider if I should contact Brygida. She was still in London for another five or six days. I tried to work out what day it was when I booked the flight tickets. It was on Thursday, and the flights were eight days later, so that made it this Friday. If I alerted Brygida then she could alert Piotr and no doubt he would be off. I felt it would be a better long-term plan for me to track him down and let him know what danger he was in to allow him to weigh up his options to make crucial decisions. I also needed to work out how I was going to get to the harbour unobserved by Clinkie and/or others.

I took out my phone to google details of Puerto Colón and noted that it was just a short taxi ride from the airport. I desperately needed sleep and decided that I should find somewhere to stay as soon as I got there and get my head down for some much-needed rest. After which I could scout out the harbour and start planning in detail. At the moment I had no plan other than to tell Piotr about Vicky. He already knew of course about Brygida and Ania coming to stay with him. I assumed that Piotr must have some kind of plan himself and had spent the last two years establishing a network of contacts with the long-term goal being to get Brygida and Ania back and then start their new lives together.

As I was finishing my second pint my stomach churned. It got me thinking to when I had last eaten, and I realised that it was something like eighteen hours since I had my greasy bacon roll at Buchanan Bus Station. Adrenaline and anxiety had numbed my hunger pangs up to now, but I knew that I had to eat. Also, I thought, much more beer on an empty stomach and I might not make it onto the plane. However, on looking at the state of some of my fellow travellers at other tables in the bar then perhaps I would still be in better nick than them.

It was now just after 4am, and as I got stuck into my cottage pie, another worry struck me. Money. I was on minimum wage and had just over £1,000 savings in the building society. Vicky had given me £250, of which £120 was left. I had also found the £200 in cash from the jacket I had stolen. Most of which had gone on my flight from Glasgow to London. I had put the flight to Tenerife on my card, which had a £5,000 overdraft limit. I would have to pay for accommodation, taxis, food and sundries, and from that point of view alone, the sooner I could reach Piotr the better. However, I didn't know what the consequences of that would be. At this point, I decided that I couldn't think too far ahead. I had to meet Piotr first and take it from there.

Finally, the flight was called. As I stood in line waiting to board, all I could think of was that I needed to sleep. Once I had got at least a couple of hours shut-eye on the plane then I would be able to think a bit straighter. I had to with Clinkie Moore on my tail; I needed to be rested and able to function to have any chance.

I got on the plane and my heart sank. The party that had started in the departure lounge had now transferred to the plane and had ratcheted up several notches.

Chapter Twenty-Six

I was in the middle seat in a row of three. On either side of me were two lads in football tops who looked around eighteen. Lots of their pals were dotted about the plane along with several other groups of raucous men. There was also one vociferous group of females, which I guessed was a hen party. From the moment that everyone had boarded, the party kicked off. The onboard announcements were ignored, as was the safety demonstration. Several people around me had brought their own booze on board and were surreptitiously scoffing it. The lads beside me acted as if I didn't exist as they leant across me and noisily exchanged high-spirited banter, mostly about drinking and sex. When we had taken off I suggested that we move seats so that they could sit together, which I hoped would improve matters. I was now in the aisle seat. However, one of them, then the other, would need the toilet and would have to get me to move. My row was around the middle of the plane and there were toilets front and back which had a constant flow of visitors to both. The cabin crew had great difficulty getting past the queues as they did their food and drink service. When they finally arrived at my row, I worked on the basis that under the circumstances it would be better to join in, so I bought two small bottles of red wine and a panini, which was so hot it took twenty minutes to eat. There was still one and a half hours to go after the trolley service had finished and I tried my best to engage with my companions next to me and across the aisle but found it very difficult as I had nothing in common with them. I was too tired and stressed to engage in inane banter, so I buried my head in the in-flight magazine as I knocked back my wine. This lasted for about ten minutes, when, to the amusement of many, someone three rows in front of us and sitting in the middle seat threw up. This raised lots of laughing and extremely loud comments mostly preceded by a few swear words. The poor cabin crew had to manoeuvre the drunken passenger into the aisle and then try their best to clean up his mess. I felt sorry for the passengers sitting either side of him who didn't appear to be part of his group and who had to endure this. I watched as you do a car crash, and for a while Clinkie Moore left my mind. The sick person returned to his seat and sat down on top of a clean dry towel that had been placed on it. This was done with a welter of "sorry, sorry," from him. When the people next to him ignored him and didn't respond to his fatuous apology, they were met with, "I said I'm sorry, what more do you want?" So that's all right then. I couldn't believe this was what going on a holiday meant to people. Having said that, I would rather have been in the sick person's shoes than mine. He would arrive in Tenerife with a sore head and a mouth tasting like the bottom of a parrot cage, I thought, but after a sleep, a shower and the encouragement of his mates, would be all set to head out in party mode, whereas for me I felt that the shit was about to hit the fan.

"Wake up, pal, wake up!" I opened my eyes as I heard someone speaking and shaking me. "You must have been pissed!" one of the young lads said to me with a laugh. I was disorientated, and it took a few seconds to understand my surroundings. "That's us landed, time to get off," the young guy added. I nodded then realised that I must have dropped off though exhaustion after the sick spectacular and we were now in Tenerife. Just like on the London flight the previous night, everyone was impatiently grabbing for baggage in the overhead lockers or trying to get past people still sitting down to get to the aisles.

I looked at my watch and it was quarter past eleven. I felt very groggy and took a deep breath before unclipping my seat belt and standing up. It was difficult to stand straight as I was being barged by impatient youths who couldn't wait to get off the plane and start their holiday. I stood my ground and finally the queue up the aisle began to make its way towards the front of the plane.

It was a shock to the system when I got on to the steps leading down from the plane and felt the heat. We had a short walk to a series of buses. They already looked very busy and I got on the nearest one. I squeezed into the bus past people standing right at the door who weren't prepared to move an inch and found a stainless steel pole to hang onto. I was dismayed to see that it was also being held onto by sick boy. He looked even more aggressive than an hour previously. I avoided eye contact and studied the floor as well as the safety instructions stuck on the window.

The bus lurched into life and we had a five-minute hop to the terminal building. Passport control was a thirty-minute wait and then finally I was able to go to retrieve my bag. The airport was vast, and I didn't have a clue where to go, but luckily I recognised the two lads who were next to me on the plane so got in tow with them. Despite it being their first holiday abroad without their parents, they were certainly more clued up than me. After an anxious wait, I finally recognised my backpack trundling along the conveyor belt, and as no one would stand aside to let me through, I pushed through the hen party and retrieved it. I followed the two lads, who had got their lurid-coloured sports holdalls and were off to security.

After passing through security, I was now at the point where I felt alone. All of my fellow passengers were being met and briefed by friendly brightly jacketed couriers on where to get the bus that would take them to their resort, or taxi drivers holding up signs with passenger surnames on and then following them eagerly to their cars. I inwardly kicked myself as I had had so much time in Gatwick to google a few possible cheap digs in Puerto Colón. Instead, I had sat and drunk and done nothing but worry.

I found a café beyond the taxi rank, bought a water, sat down and switched on my phone. It took a while and I was greeted by a welcome to Spain message before I could select a network and get going. My head hurt and I couldn't be bothered concentrating, and to compound my agitation, I had difficulty accessing the internet and had to settle for roaming, which would no doubt hit my budget. I finally got underway and eventually found three cheap-looking accommodation options where you could pay for a minimum of three days. I wrote down their addresses and phone numbers and, as I had forgotten to get any euros, I used the last of the cash from Vicky backed up by my debit card to get 300 euros from an exchange booth and went in search of a taxi. That was easy, there were dozens available, so I was in one in a few minutes.

It was now twelve thirty. I sat in the front and I tried to give my choices in Spanish, but the taxi driver replied in English. He saw that I was reading from a list, so he gestured for me to give it to him. I did so and he started laughing at the first choice, pointing at it and asking, "You want woman?"

I realised that this must be a brothel or similar. He pointed at the second one, shrugged his shoulders. "Maybe," he said. The third one he put his thumb up and indicated that this was the one.

We arrived at what was third on my list, but there were no rooms available at the price quoted online. We then went to the second one on my list with rooms available at under thirty euros a night, which my budget could just about cover. It appeared to be run by Russians primarily for Russians. After a long wait at reception, I finally got booked in. I remembered to check if there was a Wi-Fi code and there was, but at five euros per day, so I reluctantly handed over another fifteen euros. My apartment was on the second floor, and I took the stairs, having given up waiting on the lift. The rooms were clean, although they were dated, and looking out from the balcony straight onto other rooms made me feel enclosed. I had chosen self-catering as it was the cheapest option. In the kitchen there was a hob and an oven, both of which appeared to work.

The dishes, pans and cutlery were a mish-mash of styles and all very well used.

It was just after one o'clock. I threw my bag down onto the bed. I had been wearing my jacket all the time and took it off and lay on the bed beside my bag. The one hour of sleep on the plane wasn't enough and I needed a nap before I could regroup and decide on my course of action over the next couple of days. I took off my socks while lying on the bed. I couldn't be bothered removing any other clothes and I drifted off with the sounds from the pool and traffic noise in the background. I woke up, rolled over and drifted off again. Eventually, I stretched out, yawned several times and looked at my watch and was surprised to see that it was now just after four thirty.

I got up from the bed slowly. I had been wearing the same clothes since Thursday, apart from my white shirt, which Norrie had given me on Friday morning. I removed that damp garment and noticed the thick tide mark at the neck. I desperately needed a shower. I managed to get the water on, but it was cold. I stood to the side of the stream of water and waited for it to heat up, but nothing seemed to be happening. I had noticed a couple of switches just outside the bathroom that were off, so I put them on and went back into the shower. That seemed to work, and a minute or so later I was treated to some warm water. I had forgotten to pack any shower gel but there was a discarded plastic bottle of *Imperial Leather* sitting on a window ledge which I used and that did the trick. It took a mighty effort to drag myself out of the shower.

While I was towelling myself down there was an almighty bang and rumble, and I instinctively threw myself onto the hard ceramic floor tiles, which was very painful. Despite constantly worrying about being tailed on my way to Gatwick, when I got to Tenerife, I suppose because of my tiredness and alcohol consumed, I had completely forgotten about that until now. I thought that someone had kicked the door in or thrown something through the balcony window. I lay on the floor nervously expecting some kind of follow-up and then the sound changed and appeared to be coming from above me. I realised with huge relief that it was in fact the very old and poorly working air conditioning system causing the commotion. I tried switching it off and on and it appeared to have simmered down, but about ten minutes later it erupted again, and I made a mental note to report it when I went out. That had certainly woken me up. It was now just past five.

When I checked in, I had noticed a small bar beside the pool and decided to go there for a drink and perhaps pick up some local knowledge from the barman. I got a beer at the reasonable cost of two euros and sat at the bar on a tall stool. I was just about to start chatting to the barman when I noticed a text message on my phone. It was from Vicky telling me to check my emails. I sighed and went to my inbox. There was one email from Vicky, I opened it and read the first few words, which said, *I expect that you will never forgive me for what I put your through and I understand that. I am massively sorry for the hurt caused to you and the role that I played in your aunt's kidnapping...*

I scrolled down and could see it was a long message, no doubt full of more self-indulgent bullshit. I sighed and raged at her for sending me this crap after all the serious shit she had put me in previously and had now done so again. All about her as usual. I pressed delete, as I had urgent matters to attend to and no time for this.

I then thought of someone I did care about – Brygida – and decided to check her Facebook page, as I felt guilty about disappearing with no goodbye and was wondering what she was up to. I tried but couldn't log in. I thought in my fuddle that I had mistyped the password. I knew that I couldn't forget it. It was easy: *Brygida1Ania1*. I had made it up and logged in the first time for Brygida. I tried logging in again but still could get no access, which immediately set alarm bells buzzing. I tried to put that to the back of my mind for a minute and got chatting to the barman and asked about the harbour and how to get there. He told me it was five minutes away and very busy with both large charter boats and small dinghies, and that there were lots of bars and cafes. I thanked him and said I would head off for a visit.

It was now just after six, and on my way out of the apartment, I remembered to go to reception and reported my faulty air conditioning, then left and made my way to the harbour. The barman's directions had me at the harbour in minutes. It was definitely a working harbour. I walked round watching the comings and goings of vessels then decided to go into one of the many bars for a refreshment. I chose a seat outside, but as I didn't want to be a sitting target, I sat back from the pavement so that I wasn't too obvious and there were plenty of people in front of me. As I sipped my beer, I continued to watch the boats and associated activity and wondered where Piotr was. I decided that I would take a good look at the boats after my drink and see if I could spot *El Tiberon*.

I contemplated Brygida and my lack of access to her Facebook page and that worried me. She must have changed her login. I guessed that she was suspicious of my disappearance so soon after Vicky re-emerged. I had probably underestimated her. As I was thinking this, a pretty waitress appeared and asked if I wanted another drink, and I smiled and said that I would. She brought my beer along with a small bowl of olives. I love olives and ate them hungrily. They were very moreish and made me thirsty, so I beckoned her over and ordered another drink which I finished quickly. Having finished that, I decided that the food prices in this café were too expensive, as would be the case with most establishments here, so I went back to my apartment block and got a burger from the pool bar, had another couple of beers and went up to my room on the second floor. I felt settled to an extent and ready to get on with finding Piotr the next day.

I had an extremely restless night and tossed and turned, as I would have the air con on, then when I couldn't stand the noise any more I switched it off before I got too hot and switched it on again. I finally settled for off and lay naked on top of the sheets. I woke in a pool of sweat and realised that I had been woken by a gentle knock on the door. I looked at my watch and couldn't believe it as it told me that it was just after eleven. I checked my phone, and sure enough that was the right time. I was angry at myself for having done so little so far in my time in Tenerife but sleep. However, today, now that I was fully rested, and after I had a hearty brunch, I would be ready to go looking for Piotr and tell him my tale.

I got up, pulled on a pair of shorts and went to answer the door. I assumed it would be the maintenance man to have a look at my air conditioning. I opened the door.

"Hello, Mr Stewart."

The person at my door was Piotr.

Chapter Twenty-Seven

"It's Greg, Piotr." Because I had been his lecturer at West Thames College, Piotr still deferred to me. I didn't know what to say after that. I looked at him and he gave me a small smile. He looked just about the same as I remembered him. Roundish baby face and bowl haircut, although he now had a small blonde goatee. I didn't know what to do so I shook his hand and asked him to come in. The apartment was stifling and I put the air conditioning on.

"You have saved me a lot of time. I was going to start looking for you today. I have lots to tell you and it is serious shit. Do you mind if I have a quick shower then we can go to a café and talk? I don't have anything to eat or drink here," I added. I was speaking much quicker than normal, which was no doubt down to nerves.

Piotr gave another small smile and said, "Of course."

I went into the shower, which as well as reviving me, gave me time to get my story in order. I didn't want to miss any key points out, but on the other hand I didn't want to let him know how close to Brygida I had become either, so some bits would have to be edited. It was difficult to drag myself out of the shower, but I finally did and then had a shave. Feeling clean and fresh certainly helped me feel a bit more positive.

Luckily, despite packing so hastily on Friday night, I had included a pair of cargo shorts, and I put them on along with a clean polo shirt. As I was getting dressed in the bedroom, the air conditioning did its usual explosion and thundered into life. "Sorry, that's the AC," I shouted to Piotr.

"No worries, I will fix it for you later," Piotr shouted back. As a mechanic, fixing the air conditioning would pose him little problems. However, it was the least of my concerns. I was hoping that after my catch-up with Piotr I would be getting close to having a plan to dig myself out of the shit I was in.

I gathered up my wallet, phone, passport and keys and we left the apartment and made our way to the harbour front. Piotr acknowledged several people on the way, some in Spanish, some in English and others with just a nod. As we made small talk, I noticed that his English had improved considerably over the past couple of years. We chose a café next to the one I was in the previous night. Despite my nervous anticipation at what was going to transpire over the next couple of hours, I was very hungry and wanted to eat. There was a full English breakfast option and I chose that, while Piotr settled for a croissant and coffee. The harbour was getting busy and I wondered what it would be like in the height of summer. We continued our small talk as I devoured my breakfast, washed down with orange juice. I signalled for the waiter to replenish Piotr's coffee and bring me one as well. When they arrived, it was time to talk.

"Why did you leave me with the polonium two years ago? Where did you and Cassie go?" I asked.

"When I saw the polonium, I knew we were in serious shit. I didn't want to be around. I didn't want..." He was struggling for the right word.

"Associated?" I suggested.

"Yes, associated. I was building a good business stealing cars and bikes and my name was known by many gangs. I didn't want near big stuff like that."

"OK, what about Cassie? What happened to her? Where is she?"

"When you went to buy us lunch, we talked and she was in an even worse position. She wanted away."

"So, you both made the decision then? Yet you hardly knew each other," I stated, as I continued my gentle probing.

"Yes. We worked out that, with the Audi, and the other vehicles we had, we could sell two of them and then get away."

I remembered that Piotr had a BMW bike and another car in his lock-up. "Where did you go, and did you tell Brygida?" I asked him.

"We sold the other vehicles to one of my contacts. The Audi had all its paperwork in the car and we went to Portsmouth and took a ferry to Santander."

"Did you tell Brygida?" I repeated.

"No," he answered softly.

"Why?" I asked.

He ignored my question and continued, "After selling the other vehicles we each had about ten thousand pounds. I had no plan, and neither did Cassie, apart from heading south. Cassie thought that it would be a good idea to go to Tunisia."

"Were you and Cassie an item?" I asked. He looked quizzical. "You know – were you a couple?"

"Just good friends," he said, with a slight knowing grin. I couldn't let it go by.

"Were you sleeping with her?"

"Sometimes – needs must."

Strange, that was exactly how Brygida described our sexual relationship.

"So how did you end up in Tenerife and how long have you been here?"

"We got to Cadiz in the south-west of Spain. It has a port for passenger traffic, commercial traffic, fishing boats and ship repair facilities. We looked for work and I got a job on a boat. Cassie got a job as a cleaner. We couldn't speak Spanish then and it was difficult for her. After about two months, someone that I worked with told me about a friend of his who had bought a boat and was going to keep it in Tenerife, and he was looking for staff, asked if I was interested and I said yes. There is a ferry to Santa Cruz de Tenerife, so me and Cassie took the Audi on the ferry and drove here. It was much better for both of us because everyone speaks English here."

"Where is Cassie?" I asked

"She is around," he answered. His enigmatic reply didn't help, but I had more pressing matters to deal with.

"When did you get in touch with Brygida?" I asked.

"After about six months," he replied.

"Was she upset with you?" I asked.

"Of course," he said wistfully, "but she understood."

I waited for him to say more but he didn't. I racked my brain to see if I could remember any noticeable change in Brygida around eighteen months ago but couldn't think of anything.

"How did you find me?" I asked, changing tack.

"My wife told me you were coming," he replied. So, I was right, she had put two and two together and came up with four. Piotr continued, "I gave your description to waiters at some of these bars. You happened to be in one of my favourites last night. I got a text and came over here and followed you. You looked tired and stressed so I thought I would let you sleep, and I would come round today to see you."

I wondered what his description of me would be. Probably something like tall, pale, unshaven, scruffy paranoid-looking Brit. There can't be too many of them; so, an easy spot for the waiters.

"I didn't tell Brygida that I was coming over here, and in fact I only made my decision late on Friday night, so how can she have been sure?"

"She told me about Vicky. She told me that you were asking for where I stay and that you booked flight tickets for her and Ania. She thought that you might have been going into her Facebook."

I wondered how Brygida had worked that out but let it ride. Then I took a deep breath and started to tell Piotr about Vicky. "Vicky arrived unannounced at my flat a few days ago. She was sentenced to eight years in prison. She has been in for just two and has escaped. She has kidnapped my boss who is being held at knifepoint, has tied up another colleague of my mine and threated my parents. I was told to find your whereabouts so that the Audi can be located, and if I didn't then there would be consequences."

"Why?" was all that Piotr said.

"Because Vicky learned from criminal contacts inside prison that the Audi contained eight phials of polonium, not just the four that we found." Piotr looked startled, which was odd for him, and before he could say anything, I continued, "Also, she reckons there is a large wedge of cash hidden in it." He was wide-eyed now. "The problem is that Vicky knows this because a major crime lord who should have got the polonium originally from Kev Osborne is still looking for it. That is why Osborne was killed on remand. He thinks that Osborne deliberately held back on the other four phials and the cash, but he didn't know anything about them.

"To make matters worse, I think the reason Vicky wanted to give your contact details to a crook from Glasgow called Clinkie Moore, who sprang her from jail, was to tip off the other gang that Clinkie was on your tail. That way, she hoped that Clinkie would be followed and killed in his pursuit of the polonium. By the way, Clinkie made up a passport and false papers for Vicky to help her start a new life. She got me to steal them from Clinkie's house."

"What?" Piotr exclaimed and looked captivated by my tale and not as nervous or anxious as I expected.

"Do you understand the shit we are in, Piotr?" Before he could answer, I continued, "I should have added that is why Brygida hasn't seen me and I haven't been around to help her. I had to go to Glasgow to steal the documents. I got away, but when I got home there was a message on my phone from Clinkie's gang. Vicky must have told him about me. I am shitting myself, Piotr.

"I am truly sorry about finding your location and giving it to Vicky because someone will now be on your tail. I am so, so sorry," I said genuinely, and looked directly at Piotr as it all sunk in. Even if Clinkie got what he was after, there was no way he would let me or Piotr off the hook. Our only chance would be if Clinkie was taken out first.

"It's OK," Piotr said softly, and patted my hand. He called over to the waiter and ordered two coffees and two brandies. When they arrived, he picked up the brandy and said, "Salud." I did likewise.

"What do we do now?" I asked.

"Easy."

"Easy?"

"Yes, is easy. I sold the Audi, but it is still in Tenerife. You are going to steal it."

Chapter Twenty-Eight

Martin Stafford can be Tom Jones, Roy Orbison or Elvis. It depends on what time of day it is and the venue he is in. How do I know this? Well Piotr informed me that he had sold his car to Mr Stafford, who is a tribute act singer at several bars in Playa de las Americas. As I sat digesting this news, Piotr sprang up and went over to a tourist information booth at the harbour side and came back with a tourist map. He marked with an X where we currently were and showed me where Playa de las Americas was, which, although the map wasn't to scale, didn't look far. He then added several crosses to indicate some of the bars at which Stafford performed. He told me that he had seen the car around a fair bit and that Stafford needed to drive it to work because he kept his stage gear in it.

"How do I steal the car?" I asked nervously.

"Easy."

"Easy?"

"Yes, I have key. I had a copy made before I sold the car. We will get the key then you go and find him, watch his act for a few minutes and then find his car and take it. Easy. I will give you the address to take it to. After that I mend your AC. Deal?"

Piotr seemed so cool and wasn't fazed by me telling him about Clinkie Moore and even bigger fish probably being on his tail. I asked him about that, and he asked me to confirm that I had told Vicky that he was staying on a boat called *El Tiberon*. I nodded.

"I do stay on the boat sometimes, but it is away for two weeks just now," he told me.

"Where is it? What is it doing?" I asked. Piotr just smiled and shook his head. I assumed this meant something underhand.

"Did you give her my description?" he asked.

I hadn't thought of that. "No," I said with relief.

"See, they think I am living on a boat which isn't here, and they don't know what I look like, so that should give us some time to work out what we are going to do."

I didn't know if I felt reassured at being included or not. Piotr did make it sound all so easy. However, I guessed there would be more than one person being Elvis or Tom Jones in such a large resort and I could spend all day unsuccessfully traipsing around in my quest to find Stafford. He also hadn't allowed for my nervousness at driving, particularly in an expensive top-of-the-range model in a foreign country on unfamiliar roads; and he hadn't mentioned what we did if and when I managed to steal the car.

Despite all these concerns, an hour after having dispatched my second brandy, washed down with another coffee, I found myself on the main drag of Playa de las Americas systematically approaching every bar and checking the posters and blackboards which listed what acts were performing on the premises. I had expected that there wouldn't be much activity on a Sunday, at least until the evening, but I was wrong. It was now just after two in the afternoon and most of the bars had already got acts performing. Quite a few bars that had no live entertainment still had some form of loud music playing, and I wondered where people went for a quiet drink round here.

Piotr had given me a description of him, but I wasn't quite sure how I would recognise Mr Stafford if he was in costume, particularly as Piotr had described him as quite old, with grey hair and that he was a bit overweight.

My search process was based on looking at the display boards outside each bar I approached, and if there was an Elvis, Tom Jones or Roy Orbison performing, watching them for a few seconds from the pavement before moving on. I had checked out around ten bars before I found my first Elvis; up to then, Freddie Mercury and Cher were the most popular tribute acts. Unfortunately, I was sure this Elvis wasn't my man as he was quite young and in leathers. I had a feeling that Stafford would be Elvis in the Vegas years. I continued on my way, witnessing in the flesh the worst Rod Stewart that I could imagine, basically someone putting on a big blonde wig, dodgy leopard-skin trousers and singing "Do You Think I'm Sexy?" in bad karaoke style.

My throat was parched, and I was so thirsty I decided I would have a small drink at the next bar, being mindful that I may have to be driving soon. I crossed a busy intersection and approached *Temptation*, which was located on the corner of the junction and had two sides that bordered the pavement. Its set-up was similar to all the others: a small bar area at the back which had the toilets, an area of approximately ten metres square that had around fifteen tables with four chairs per table and a very small platform with an amplifier either side of the stage area. There was latticework surrounding the area with ivy plants cascading down them.

There were five or six people sitting drinking and the music was playing in the background. I sat down and a waitress appeared almost immediately. I asked for a small beer and she smiled and returned within seconds with a cold bottle and a frosted glass on her tray. I almost sighed with anticipation as she poured it. She smiled again and said in perfect English with almost no trace of an accent, "Looks like you need it!"

I nodded, smiled and said, "Yes." Then something strange happened. I constructed a persona for myself out of the blue, making it up as I went along. "Yes, I've been walking up and down the strip," I said, spreading my arms out in the general direction of the main road. "I've been looking for someone. He's an Elvis tribute act that is supposed to be very good and I want to find what bar he is in because I'm on holiday with my family and it's my parents' golden wedding and they both love Elvis. I've been told that the guy I'm looking for is the best and I would like them to come and watch him as part of the celebration."

She nodded understandingly and enthusiastically. "We have an Elvis play here. Wait a minute." With that, she scampered off and then reappeared a few moments later with an A5-sized flier that listed everyone who was playing in the bar that week starting from today.

"Look, there is Elvis," she said, pointing at a fat Vegas version with dodgy shades.

"Great, that's very helpful," I said. Mr Stafford would be playing in this bar at five o'clock tonight.

The poster was very handy as it gave the real names of the tribute act, so Martin Stafford was Elvis, Joe Bloggs was Freddie Mercury and so on. In most cases Stafford would be two different acts in the same day. Today, for example, he was Elvis at nine o'clock but at five he was Roy Orbison. This could be perfect, as I imagined he would play at this bar, go to another one and then return here for the Elvis show, which could be his last of the night. I could watch his first show then follow him discreetly to his car, see where he parked and then wait for him to go on stage at nine when he returned and then steal his wheels. As Piotr would say – *easy*.

Piotr had given me his phone number and told me to call him as and when required. I phoned and told him I had found Mr Stafford and gave him an outline of my plan. Not being an experienced car thief, I thought I may have missed or not thought of something, but Piotr assured me that it sounded good. That relieved me a bit, but I had the same gnawing sensation in my stomach that I had at Clinkie Moore's before I stole Vicky's documents. I tried to reassure myself that I was getting good at this type of thing. I reminded myself how convincing I had been when lying to the waitress and getting an instant result. I caught the waitresses' eye and asked for the bill. "By the way, thanks for the details on the acts – I will definitely bring my parents over here during the week," I said.

"You're welcome," she said. "I hope they enjoy him when they visit."

"I'm sure they will," I said with a smile.

"Where are you staying? Are you in an apartment?" she asked.

I lied so naturally. "No, we have two rooms in one of the big hotels over there," I said as I pointed generally in the area of lots of big hotels. "My parents are in one room and I'm in the other with my brother, who is five years younger than me, so it's a bit of a challenge but worth it to bring my parents here for their anniversary." I was almost believing the story myself.

"That is so kind of you," she said, returning my smile.

"Yes, I'm glad me and my brother have done it, but I don't really get on with him, so it is nice to get away from the hotel and be on my own for a while."

"Sure, I totally understand," she said.

I asked her where she came from and what brought her to Tenerife. She told me she was from Switzerland and a student. I told her I was going to watch Stafford as Roy O then go for something to eat and come back on my own later to scout him out as Elvis. "Will you still be here?" I asked.

"Oh yes, I get a break in an hour then I am on until two o'clock in the morning."

From nowhere I asked, "Do you fancy us having something to eat together on your break?"

"Yes, of course!" she answered.

"That's great," I replied. "Hi, I'm Greg," I said, and held out my hand.

"I'm Martina," she said as she shook my hand. I felt my heart flutter but in a good way. She was called over to another table and I looked forward to spending some time with her soon. It would be a pleasant distraction from my task in hand.

Talking about my imaginary parents to Martina got me thinking about my real ones. I wondered what they would think if only they knew what I was now involved in. With Isa gone, I felt that things might get worse for a while as they took stock. I still found it incomprehensible how they continued to hold me partly responsible for the trauma that Isa suffered that ultimately lead to her death, when it was a series of random *what ifs* that came together to embroil me and change my life forever. I resolved that if I somehow managed to get through the next few days unscathed then I would make it my mission to resolve our differences and try to resume a more normal relationship.

I had to put this to the back of my mind as I needed to be focussed if I was to successfully steal the Audi and get away. There was a loud boom from the speakers followed by some feedback then a voice drawling, "One, two, one two, one two, one two three, one two three." He then made clicking noises into the microphone. I hadn't noticed the appearance of Roy Orbison as I had been totally wrapped up in my own thoughts. He was already in costume and was wearing a leather jacket and trousers, dark red shirt and had thick black shades on. I assumed he had a wig on as his thick black hair didn't look authentic. It was warm here and I wondered what it must feel like doing an act in that costume.

Within five minutes of his soundcheck the owner of the Audi was underway. I'm not particularly familiar with the work of Roy Orbison and so it was hard to tell if Stafford was authentic or not. He seemed to sing out the side of his mouth and most of the words came out in an unintelligible drawl. He didn't say anything to the audience between songs apart from a curt thank you, until the fourth number, which he dedicated to a member of the audience called Ruby, who looked like the image I had created of my imaginary mother to Martina. The lady was sitting at a table with another three women who all looked like her. Apart from that table and mine, there were four more tables occupied. Most people gave a brief clap between songs and that was it.

I was watching Stafford closely because I didn't expect there would be an encore and that his exit would be briefer than the time it took to get set up. He played around ten songs, of which three were identifiable to me. Finally, he reached the last song. "Thank you very much," he said, in what I assumed was supposed to be an American accent. "See you all again soon." And then he launched into "I Drove All Night", with which I was familiar. When that song came to an end, he again thanked the audience very much and stood for several seconds, I assume to see if he was being called for an encore. None was forthcoming, and he was called over to the table containing Ruby the birthday girl for selfies. I could hear him speaking to them and he was still keeping with the phoney accent.

I got up as if I was going to the toilet and went out the side exit and scanned the street. The Audi was parked in the car park of a large pharmacy set back from the road two buildings away. I leant against a lamp post, took out my phone and pretended to make a call. I had been doing this for about two minutes when Stafford appeared and went to the Audi. I was right about the wig, because that was now off and he did have a head of thick grey hair. As he walked to the car, he pressed his remote and the lights flashed. He opened the doors, chucked his holdall on the passenger seat, jumped in the car and was off.

Hopefully in a few hours I would be doing the same, I thought. I felt the Audi A7 Sportback three-button remote smart key that Piotr had given me in my pocket to give me some reassurance and returned to the bar. I sat back down at my table and finished the last of my beer. Martina came over and I asked, "When will you be finished?"

"In about fifteen minutes," she replied. "Is it OK to wait?" I asked.

"Of course."

While I waited, I sent a text to Piotr confirming my plan. He asked me to text as soon as I was on my way with the car. I wondered how I was going to do that, because when I was driving, I wouldn't want to stop until I got to my destination. When I'd left the café with Piotr in the early afternoon, he had escorted me for a few hundred metres and pointed in the direction to walk to get to Playa de las Americas. He also pointed out a large boat workshop at the far end of the harbour. It was the first of three side by side. He had told me to take the car there. My walk into Playa de las Americas had passed quickly as I was trying to memorise landmarks and plot my route back for when I would be driving an unfamiliar car on the wrong side of the road.

"Greg, Greg, are you ready?" Martina said with a smile.

"Sorry, I was daydreaming," I replied. "I'll let you lead the way." We went to a restaurant that overlooked the sea and was set well back from the busy main road. The staff knew Martina and we were taken upstairs to a terrace with a nice dark decking and trendy thick glass tables. Martina only had forty-five minutes so we ordered quickly. She recommended the minute steak, so I went with that and we both chose sparkling water to drink.

"This is nice," I said, which was a bit a lame, and quickly followed it up with, "So tell me about yourself and how you ended up here." This set Martina off and she told me that she was twenty-two years old and was taking a year out before starting her fourth year of studying to be a vet. I asked why she had come to Tenerife and she told me that she was an only child and her parents, who she loved very much, were quite old, and life at home in the summer could get boring so she decided to come here, enjoy the sun, make some friends and have a good time.

Her smile was the most beautiful I had ever seen; it was so natural. Martina had medium-length brown hair, a lovely light tan and a very healthy-looking body. I was becoming smitten and had to give myself an imaginary shake as I had my business to do first before getting involved in any holiday romance. Plus, she was sixteen years younger than me. When

I was a college lecturer, I prided myself on being friendly and approachable to the students but had a line that I would not cross. I resolved to resurrect that line.

The meal was over all too quickly. We sat, looked at the sea, continued chatting for a few minutes and then it was time to go. I still had a couple of hours to kill, so I accompanied Martina back to the bar and ordered a coffee and drank it slowly. It was soon time for Cher, who was hopeless. I got up halfway through and waved to Martina as I made my way to the bar. "She's rubbish!" I said with a laugh, and she laughed back. "I'm going for a walk and will be back for Elvis. I probably won't be able to stay to the end because my family will want me back at the hotel," I said with a theatrical sigh. She nodded and smiled understandingly.

I left the bar and wandered around the block a couple of times and then went along the esplanade. Time was passing so slowly. Finally, it was just after eight forty-five and I returned to the bar. It was much busier now and a couple had taken my table, so I found another one and sat down. Martina was serving someone else and a waiter quickly arrived. I ordered a beer and waited for Elvis. He must be popular, I thought, as nearly all the tables were occupied and there was quite a hubbub of cheery talk and laughter.

At five to nine Elvis appeared in a white jumpsuit that didn't do his beer belly any favours. The jumpsuit had a red sash and he wore large tinted shades. He did the same warm-up as for Roy Orbison and then said good evening in a fake American accent that was a bit different from Roy Orbison's, before starting with "Blue Suede Shoes". When he finished, he got a good reaction and immediately went into a medley, after which he spoke to the crowd whilst mopping his brow with a hankie before launching into "Suspicious Minds". The audience were loving it and joining in.

All the time I had been nervously playing with the key fob in my pocket. It was time to go and I got up, waved to Martina as she was at the far end of the bar and I mouthed and signalled that I would be back tomorrow. She smiled and waved back.

I felt the sweat running down my temple and also in the small of my back. I visited the toilet, quickly dispatched a very loose stool, then left the premises and went looking for the Audi, still nervously playing with the key fob in my right hand. The car was in the same place as before and, like Stafford, I took the key fob out, pointed it at the car as I was approaching it and the lights flashed reassuringly. I could still hear Elvis. It sounded like he was singing *Route 66.*

I got in and played about with the controls to get a feel for what I was about to do, then started the car, and it lurched forward straight into a lamp post.

Chapter Twenty-Nine

The car had been left in first gear as it was parked on a slight upslope. I instinctively hit the brake, put the handbrake on and found neutral. The bump had shaken me, but despite the noise from the collision with the lamp post, no one seemed to have seen or heard my scrape, and if they had, they didn't appear to care. I had narrowly avoided hitting a tiny moped parked nearby and I gave myself thirty seconds, took a deep breath and then let the handbrake off, allowing gravity to take its course and for the car to slowly roll back down the slope avoiding the moped. I took another deep breath and looked in the rear-view mirror, only to see Elvis gesticulating wildly and running towards the car. He was joined by Freddie Mercury, who, despite a beer belly hanging out of his bright yellow tunic, was running faster than Elvis and soon overtook him.

Frantically, I spun the car in the direction that I hoped would take me to Puerto Colón and sped past my pursuers, who were coming towards me. They jumped out of the way, shouting angrily as I headed towards the junction with the strip. I looked back and they appeared to continue heading in the opposite direction. As I approached the junction, I was held up by a lorry in front. I stole another look in my mirrors and saw that Freddie had started up the small moped and Elvis was squeezing on to it as well. Meanwhile, the driver of the truck slowly got out of his cab and nonchalantly opened up the back of it and I realised that he was delivering supplies to one of the bars. With my heart racing, I pulled out and passed him and got to the junction, only to find a red light. Lots of tourists were crossing without a care in the world. Gripping the wheel tightly, I edged forward willing the lights to change and hoping that the moped would struggle under the combined weight of Elvis and Freddie. The lights changed, but I had to move forward slowly given the number of people still ambling across the road, some of whom had come out from the bars where Elvis and Freddie had been performing and no doubt would be wondering what had caused them to flee.

As I turned right, I could see Elvis and Freddie approach the junction. I followed the traffic driving along the very busy strip with all the bars, restaurants and hotels off from it, feeling conspicuous, as if I shouldn't be in such a car and, to compound that, being pursued by Elvis and Freddie. A few pedestrians waved at me thinking that I was a taxi; I ignored them and after a few minutes got to a roundabout, then someone stepped out in front of me and I slammed on the brakes. She glowered at me and gesticulated. I wondered why she was so angry when it was her fault. As soon as she was out of the way I continued, gripping the steering wheel even tighter. Just further up, a similar situation occurred again, at which point I realised with a sickening shudder that I didn't have the lights on. I held up my hand in apology and slowed down as I frantically tried to work out where the light switch was, and judging by the honking of horns, there were a few impatient drivers behind me. I couldn't see Elvis and Freddie and was desperate not to draw attention to myself as I continued on, feeling that soon all of the strip would be looking at the prick in the big black Audi. After a few failed attempts I saw the sweet sight of the lights reflecting off the car in front and I picked up speed. My shirt was stuck to me and, much like when driving to Glasgow, I was in a tunnel of nervous concentration.

I still couldn't see Elvis and Freddie in my mirrors and wondered where they could be. I had no idea if car crime was a priority in Tenerife. I hadn't seen any police in my walk around the resort as I waited for Elvis to come on and I hoped that would remain the same. I also hoped there were was no CCTV that could be used to track my journey when Elvis reported his car being stolen, as he obviously would. A top-of-the-range black Audi with British plates and right-hand drive being pursued by Elvis and Freddie would be pretty easy to spot I feared.

I noticed a bar that I had stopped by on my walk to the strip previously which confirmed that I was going in the correct direction. Again, a few people gesticulated and I thought that I had driven through a red light, but then I saw the moped behind me driving up the central reservation designated for pedestrians. It wasn't going that fast, but as it was on a walkway and had a much clearer run than me, it was catching up. Freddie's cap had blown off and Elvis's cape was billowing behind him, giving the impression that they were going faster than they actually were. They weaved between walkers, with some gesticulating and others laughing or clapping, perhaps thinking this was a publicity stunt. People moved out of the way, and as I approached another set of lights, the moped was almost alongside me. Freddie was grinning manically with half his false moustache flapping in the wind whilst Elvis was shouting and signalling for me to stop. The lights had just changed to red but I sped through on the tail of the car in front. There was a loud horn sounding repeatedly as I crossed the junction, and from the corner of my eye I saw the toytown tourist train come round the corner. In my mirrors I could see the passengers looking shocked and surprised and realised that the moped must have crashed into the train. Some passengers and pedestrians had rushed to the aid of Elvis and Freddie while others filmed it on their phones. Elvis was being held back by the train driver as he got up and tried to run after me. I could see that his shades had come off, his costume was torn and blood was oozing out of his right knee. I couldn't see Freddie but imagined he was posing for pictures after he had stuck his moustache back on.

I was watching this unfolding drama fade into the distance behind me as I continued to drive, feeling hugely relieved that I had shaken off my pursuers. However, I heard sirens in the distance so I tried to drive calmly and not attract any attention. After about five minutes of uneventful driving, I wasn't far from the harbour at Puerto Colón and relaxed slightly as I passed the familiar bars, cafes, restaurants, and ice cream stalls en route to my destination. However, my anxiety returned as I tried to negotiate the narrow streets approaching the harbour and the workshops near the water's edge. There was barely enough room for one car to get along and I dreaded meeting something approaching from the opposite direction.

Throughout my short eventful trip in the Audi, an English-speaking station had been playing on the car radio. Its crass banality, loudness and annoying adverts were grating and increasing my anxiety. I tried to switch it off while still focussing on making my way to the boat workshop but must have hit the CD player rather than the off button because Elvis suddenly boomed over the speakers singing *All Shook Up*.

I was nearly there; I successfully negotiated a bollard then turned right and approached the entrance to the workshop. The road slid away to my left as it formed the slipway into the harbour. I just wanted to turn right as quickly as possible and get into the workshop. However, a family of four walked in front of me as I was turning. I hit the brakes and waved them on as I tried to hold the car on the clutch. I failed miserably and it started going backwards as I over-revved. They looked at me strangely as they kept walking and the car then lurched forward. I tried to slow it down as I entered the workshop and caught the nearside wing on the entrance before stopping in a welter of scraping metal noise.

I sat in the car shaking, feeling my heartbeat in my neck and the sweat dripping off me. I could see in my mirrors that the family that I had let past were standing staring into the workshop. I didn't want to get out of the car until they went away as I expected they could be credible witnesses to my crime. After a few seconds I was pleased to see them depart.

I remembered that I was supposed to have let Piotr know when I was on my way, but of course in my extreme anxiousness I had forgotten.

There didn't appear to be anyone around, which suited me because I needed a few minutes to calm down and adjust. I noticed a bottle of water in the compartment on the passenger-side door and leant over and grabbed it. I took a large gulp, which felt like nectar. Then I instinctively felt in my wallet and retrieved two of my pills. I swallowed them with another gulp of water. That was me down to only two left, but I didn't care. I needed something to get me into a state where I could cope with whatever was to happen next. Also, I reckoned I would be able to get more from a pharmacy here, and if I couldn't then I was sure that Piotr would be able to do so. As I was thinking this, Piotr appeared.

"Well, Mr Stewart, where is your L-plate?" he said with a small smile as he looked at the side of the car. I got out of the car, walked over to Piotr and handed him the key fob, glad to be rid of it. I looked at the damage. The front left headlight was smashed, and the entire wing was heavily dented. A lot of the black paint was scraped off, revealing the original white, which was the colour of the car when I first encountered it.

"Sorry," I said. "I'm not an experienced driver and this car is out of my league. Also, Elvis chased me. And he had Freddie Mercury with him..."

Piotr looked at me incredulously and burst out laughing. With tears in his eyes, he then started to sing *We Are The Champions* very badly. When he finally settled down, he said, "No worry, we don't want to drive the car any more. We want what's inside it." With that, he jumped in the car, straightened it up and moved it into the back of the workshop. He went into a small office, opened a panel then inserted a key and suddenly the large up and over door started to come down. When it was fully down, Piotr padlocked it at either end. It was dark outside and gloomy in the workshop. "Is it light enough for you to work, Piotr?" I asked.

"I will use a torch," he said. "We don't want people to know we are working in here."

I hoped that the family who had watched my entrance were now in a café enjoying a meal or ice cream and my prang was a distant memory. Fortunately, there wasn't a boat in the building, because then room would have been scarce. Piotr brought a variety of tools over from a large bench and cabinet and lay them beside the car. It was now time to get down to work.

When I had worked out the code that had opened a secret hatch in this car, the hatch was in the passenger footwell. Piotr lifted the rubber mat and pointed at it. I nodded knowingly. He removed all of the rubber matting on the car floor and looked for any signs of other hidden compartments.

"I thought you might have done this before. You know, when you and Cassie ran off," I said. As soon as I said it, I realised how churlish this sounded coming from such an inexperienced car thief and international villain. He shrugged in his calm way.

"When we got to Portsmouth, we looked for anything worth keeping or selling and got rid of anything else. We didn't find any other compartments, but we didn't expect that there was any more polonium hidden," he explained, and I nodded in understanding.

We took out two holdalls which contained Stafford's stage costumes for Tom Jones and Roy Orbison and put them on the floor, then for the next ninety minutes Piotr systematically took the car apart panel by panel, expertly and carefully so that it could be put back together again. I played little part in any of this work apart from occasionally handing him something or taking something to a spot designated by Piotr. After a while my mind had started to drift and I was roused back into reality by Piotr saying quietly from underneath the car, "Got it."

I had been sitting on a stool with my back against the office wall and sprang up. Piotr emerged from underneath the car holding a black container which was around three foot by two foot and not very deep.

The container was made of a hard dark plastic that was moulded to fit into the shape of the undercarriage of a car.

"How was it fixed on?" I asked.

"Bonded with silicon," he answered. I nodded but didn't really know what he meant.

He took the container over to the workbench and fixed it in place with a vice. Then he got a small hacksaw and started cutting carefully along the edge. This took a few minutes before he pulled away the end piece and then repeated the process along the side. When he had done that, he pulled the container open. Inside was a dark plastic cover, which he removed to reveal a large plastic bag containing what looked like vacuum-sealed bags of cash in £50 notes. He took out the plastic bag, tore it open and picked up one of the sealed bags. He looked at me and raised his eyebrow. I acknowledged him and indicated with a nod to get on with it.

The cash was in sterling. "Let's count it," he said. We set about our task. It took some time. Well, Vicky was correct. There was certainly a *wedge* in the car – exactly £300,000.

Chapter Thirty

As ever, Piotr was at least outwardly very cool. My reaction had been, "Jesus Christ. What are we going to do with it?"

"Calm down," Piotr said. "Job only half done. Remember polonium?"

Of course, that was what had caused all this in the beginning – polonium. Secretly, I hoped we wouldn't find anything because it was serious shit and serious players wanted it. I just wanted to keep the money, return the car to Mr Stafford and be done. We could somehow get a message to Vicky that the car was at his flat, give her the address and be gone. A few years ago, I would never have considered sacrificing someone as I was thinking of doing now, but I was in a different world and had to react that way to survive.

We searched for another hour and the car was in bits. Suddenly a thought occurred to me. The whole time I was searching for the code to unlock the first box it was against the clock. My aunt was being held and they gave me twenty-four hours. The work that Eustace Barrington did in making the security box was intricate and skilled, definitely not something you could do in a few hours. "I bet the polonium is still in Doug's garage," I said.

"What?" Piotr asked.

"Doug's garage. Eustace would have made a proper hiding place. There obviously isn't one on this car and I bet Eustace had hidden the polonium somewhere so that when he had completed the second security box in the car, he could put the polonium in it and job done. Unfortunately, he never got the chance because Kev Osborne killed him.

"Piotr, this could be good news – we don't want to be anywhere near the polonium. Let's work out what to do from now. We need to get Clinkie and any other gangsters off our back. Where's Cassie? We need to get her involved." Piotr looked at me but didn't say anything. "We can split the money – that's a hundred thousand each – and get out of here," I blurted.

"Where would we go?" Piotr asked calmly.

"I don't know, but just get someplace else where we don't get caught," I spluttered.

Piotr sighed then said, "You have got to have a plan. I know that it is not easy to disappear. You are always looking over shoulder. We don't know who is looking for us."

"We do," I said impatiently. "It's Clinkie Moore and his team."

"But you keep going on about a bigger player," Piotr interjected. "Someone who is more dangerous than Clinkie Moore and we don't know who he is. You have given Clinkie details of Brygida and Ania and so they are going to be followed. I can't just run without a plan; I need to keep them safe."

He looked angry now, and the way he looked at me made me feel guilty. No wonder, because after all, I had given their travel details to Vicky, who no doubt had passed them onto Clinkie.

"Yes, yes, I am very sorry, Piotr. It's my fault they have details of her flights. I was put in a position that gave me no wriggle room. They have kidnapped my boss and threatened me and my family. I am so sorry. I really didn't want to be any part of this."

"Not your fault," Piotr said forcibly. "We need to think what we do and how we do it. We have what you call a…"

"A code," I interjected. "Yes, we don't want her and Ania coming here with Clinkie on our tails. Where would you go instead?"

"I don't know yet. Need to think. But I won't tell you or Cassie. Must be a secret."

I couldn't argue with that. I was desperately trying to weigh up my options in how I was going to proceed. I had run desperately from my flat and Clinkie knew where it was. Vicky would be on my tail as well if I returned to London, so that seemed a no-go. My boss was tied up somewhere, and would I be seen as an accomplice? Also, I had just stolen a car here, so another felony to add to my list. What about my parents? What about my sister? Should I go to DI Stevenson?

Despite me cracking a code originally and finding what now turned out to be half the cache of polonium, international crime, or crime of any level, was not my scene. How I yearned for a simple uneventful life. Although not getting on with my parents, I still felt I couldn't just cut and run and never see them again. I wasn't one for being on the run, constantly looking over my shoulder and living on my nerves. Piotr was far more able than me in that department, but I could see that it would be difficult for him with his wife and child in tow.

As I saw it, there were two elements to deal with. Clinkie Moore and the original big player who had expected the polonium. I was clear that Vicky's plan was to somehow convince this head honcho that Clinkie had what he wanted and then lure Clinkie and his men into a trap which would see them eliminated and the big shot get what he wanted. Presumably Clinkie's men would be on their way as they knew of Piotr's location and his wife's travel plans. I expected that someone would arrive before Brygida's flight to check the lie of the land and that someone would also follow her and Ania as they made their flight from London.

It was hard to work out what part Cassie played in all of this. I hadn't given any details of her to Vicky, so presumably Clinkie wasn't concerned with her. From what little Piotr had told me of their escape from England to mainland Spain and then Tenerife, she appeared to have few connections to the UK and would settle easily into a transient life, particularly in a resort with lots of ex-pats. My worry was if she could keep her mouth shut.

Another issue to consider was how would we transport the money when we split it. Cash is so obvious and electronically is so traceable.

I also wondered what I should do about my boss. My instinct was to contact DI Stevenson and get his guys on the case, as the thought of Maggie trussed up in some shithole was hard to bear. However, my worry about that course of action was that it may re-establish me with Vicky and her cohorts in the eyes of the police. I had desperately hoped after her trial that I could just get on with my low-level unaspiring life.

"Piotr, can we put the car back together and leave it so that Clinkie or his men will find it, then we tip off the Mr Big who could top Clinkie?"

"Only one problem, Greg, we don't know who that is, so how can we tip him off?"

"Shit, I hadn't thought of that…" Perhaps that was why I wasn't suited to international crime.

"Well, if he is aware of Clinkie then surely he will have him, or his men, followed. If he is aware of them going to Tenerife, then they will surmise that they are coming for the car and the polonium."

"Perhaps," Piotr acknowledged.

"And he probably doesn't know or care about the money. That's small change to him but for us it could be life-changing.

"How long will it take to put the car together?"

"Easy," Piotr replied with his stock answer.

"Yes, it might be easy, but how long?" I replied tetchily.

"Will have it done by end of tonight."

"What does that mean?" I asked. "What time will we be finished?"

"By breakfast."

Phew. "Shall we contact Cassie?" I asked.

"Not yet. We build car then contact her. No point just now."

"OK. We can think of our plan while we are putting the car together."

"I have the first part of the plan," Piotr replied.

"Already? What is it?"

"We split the money like you say, Greg. A third each. At least one of Clinkie's men should be here already. I will get followed by him and lead him away. You and Cassie go your own way."

"Where?" I asked.

"Up to you. Not me."

"Where are you going?" There was a slight tremor in my voice.

"Not telling. I've already said that."

"So that's the plan?"

"Yes. If I can get Clinkie's men away somewhere then the other gang can kill them then and job done. Then I'll meet Brygida and deal with anyone on their tail."

"OK," I said. "Where will you drive to?"

"Don't know yet. I will think while we are building the car."

"OK. Remind me where Cassie works."

"She works at an English bar in Costa Adeje."

"Where's that? Does she live there?"

"You have walked past it. She has an apartment near the bar."

"How often do you see her?"

"Not much now. She has her own life, which suits us both. Especially now that Brygida is coming," he said with a slight smile.

I never liked Cassie, who had been the first person I saw back when all this shit first started. It had been her that opened the door when I arrived at Eustace Barrington's house to return his driving licence. She had watched as my flat was ripped apart by her accomplice Kev Osborne and had never expressed any sympathy or empathy towards me despite being heavily involved in screwing up my life. For these reasons I said, "Do we even need Cassie to know that we have the car and have found this money? Why don't we just leave her out of it? It's one less element to think about."

Piotr suddenly looked very angry and said, "Mr Stewart—"

"Greg," I interrupted.

"Mr Stewart," he repeated, "I always trust you. How can you say that?"

"She screwed up my life, Piotr. She doesn't care about what damage she caused to me and others. Why help her?"

"She is a victim too, Mr Stewart."

I wasn't sure why Piotr was speaking to me in formal tones, but I expected it was because of his anger at me and a sign that our relationship had changed.

"Cassie helped me, and she was good partner to help me get here."

"OK, I am sorry, Piotr."

"That's all I hear from you – *sorry*," Piotr said, softly but with feeling.

"I shouldn't have thought like that, and I cancel that suggestion," I replied. "Shall we start on the car?"

Piotr nodded and walked over to the car, which was still on the ramp.

"OK, we don't need to put everything back together, just to make it look acceptable and for it to run. I will tell you what parts I need and you bring them to me and hold them in place when I tell you."

I nodded and we got to work. Piotr was absolutely focussed, and we hardly stopped as we worked through the night. We also barely spoke; he would point or occasionally grunt an instruction and I would dutifully respond. I felt guilty at suggesting that we leave Cassie out, and after several hours of labour in a period of reflective contrition suggested that Piotr's cut of the cash should be £150,000 as he had Brygida and Ania to care for, and I would take *only 50k*, with Cassie getting the rest. He angrily refused and stated, "No we split three ways."

I accepted with no argument and we continued our work. By 7am we were finished. As Piotr had said at the beginning, we didn't put the car fully back together, particularly the furnishings, but from a distance of a few metres it looked as good as new, apart from the damaged nearside and headlight of course.

"We go for breakfast then we finish our plan," he said tersely. I nodded in agreement and we made our way to Piotr's usual café, which was just coming to life. We chose a table that was right next to the pavement looking on to the harbour.

"Hopefully Clinkie sees us," Piotr said with a small smile.

I smiled and nodded back. Despite my nerves I was hungry, and I had the cooked breakfast with Piotr settling for his usual croissant and coffee.

"When we have finished breakfast, we go back to the workshop and split the money. We then go for a drive to see if anyone is on our tail," he told me.

"How will we know?" I asked.

"I will know," he answered confidently. "When we are sure that we are being tailed we go to Cassie's. I will call and let her know we are coming. I will drop you off at her place and you will take her and your money. I say goodbye and we never see each other again."

"Is it wise that we are seen going to Cassie's?" I asked Piotr.

"Of course. They don't know me, but they know I left UK with a girl. They need to see me with you so they know that I am Piotr and they put two and two together. Then they will follow me, and I will deal with them."

Well, he had it all worked out. He seemed calm. I, in contrast, was a welter of emotions at what we were contemplating and sadness at never seeing Piotr or Brygida and Ania again and wondering what sort of life they would have. It also stuck me that in a few hours, that was it. "Can I go back to my apartment before we go to the workshop, please?" I asked Piotr nervously. I wanted to get my bag and some clothes and toiletries to take with me. My mind was racing – what the hell do I do in a few hours? Piotr no doubt was clear what he was going to do. Cassie would have an almighty shock, but having £100,000 would help her get over it and she would be able to react accordingly, but me, what was I going to do?

We finished our breakfast, which I tried to take as long as possible over, paid the bill and made our way to my apartment. Piotr became catlike as he walked beside me, alert to any imminent danger. We went into my apartment; I picked up the stuff I needed and left. I didn't check out as there wasn't anyone at reception and I didn't want to spend another second there. I was now in flight mode. We went back to the workshop, locked the door behind us and started splitting up the money. We used our backpacks for each of our share and put Cassie's in a large grubby holdall from the office.

"OK, time to go," said Piotr. I nodded. "Open up."

I went to the big door, unlocked it and rolled it up. Piotr reversed the car out, turned it and took the workshop keys off me and locked up. He looked so relaxed. We left in the direction I had taken the previous night and headed for Playa de las Americas. Despite it having been taken apart and put back together, the car was running smoothly. Piotr drove very slowly, but we were soon along the roads I had nervously traversed not so long ago. After Costa Adeje, we went to Playa de las Americas, did a loop and returned to Playa de las Americas, before heading for Los Cristianos. All the time I was unaware of anyone on our tail despite repeatedly looking in the wing mirror.

"OK. Time to go," Piotr said. He put his Bluetooth on and called Cassie. She answered on the second ring.

"Hi, Piotr, you're up early."

"Cassie, I am coming to meet you. Are you at the flat or the bar?"

"What's the hurry? I'm on breakfasts, so at the bar. Do you want anything? I'll put an order in to chef."

"No. I need to see you."

"Can't it wait?"

"No."

"Why not?"

"Eustace," Piotr said firmly.

That must have been a code warning word. I think I heard a sharp intake of breath before she said, "OK."

"See you in five."

"OK," she said again.

We were in Playa de las Americas heading back along the strip towards Costa Adeje. Piotr still seemed calm and was driving slowly. The roads and pavements were quiet. A man in a Liverpool top and his heavily sunburnt wife who was pushing a pram were walking towards us on the pavement. They were having a good laugh about something and, maybe because of that, they weren't paying attention, because they suddenly stepped out on to the road right into our path. Despite driving slowly, Piotr had to brake suddenly and swerve simultaneously. We manged to stop just in time. My heart was pounding. I had seen the wife go down and was hoping that we hadn't hit and crushed the pram.

"Don't move," Piotr ordered.

I ignored him and got out to attend to the victims. As I did so I was grabbed from behind and yanked heavily to the ground, which I hit with a thud. This momentarily dazed me, and when I regathered my breath, my instinct took me to the front of the car to check the casualties. The pram lay on its side with a broken baby doll beside it. I suddenly had to dive out of the way as the car exploded into life and accelerated towards me.

As I got up, the car sped past and I saw the man in the Liverpool strip in the driver's seat with his wife in the back alongside Piotr. She appeared to be holding something against his neck. It was hard to tell, but it looked like a gun.

Chapter Thirty-One

I rubbed my elbow, which was badly grazed, my heart was thumping and I was breathless. The Audi was now out of sight. There were a few people on the pavements, but nobody seemed aware of what had happened.

Fight or flight? Flight definitely. My first decision to be made was should I get Cassie or not? I was walking in the direction of her bar and felt that this was my subconscious telling me something. I walked slowly as I tried to piece things together. Piotr, the money and the car had been snatched, but by whom: Clinkie Moore or some other gang? The very first part of the plan had fallen apart. They had the car so would soon discover that there was no polonium in it. Piotr would have to try and convince them that he had hidden it somewhere to buy some time, but there was every chance he could be killed. Also, there was now no money for me and Cassie to use to get away. I decided that I had to see Cassie to let her know what sort of danger she could be in and so kept walking towards the bar. I hoped that a plan would formulate in my head by the time I got there.

I brushed against or nearly collided with several people as I headed towards Cassie's bar, as I was totally wrapped up in my predicament. I was shocked at what had happened and the main thing that distressed me was that Piotr had been blindsided so easily. From my previous involvement with Piotr, I had built up a perception of him being one step ahead of those he was dealing with. However, here he had been taken so easily. Piotr drove around the area that morning to attract attention, he hoped, from Clinkie's men, and I assumed that at some point, despite me not seeing anything, they had made that tail and that was why when we were heading to Cassie's bar he got snatched.

I picked up pace and worried that if I was being followed it would be unlikely that I could shake them off my tail. It then struck me that I didn't know where the bar was. Piotr had told me that it was called the *King George*. I searched for it on my phone and discovered that I was minutes away. I carried on walking along a narrow strip of pavement then turned left into a large car park area which had a line of shops and restaurants on one side. At first, I couldn't see the *King George* and rechecked my phone as I stopped outside what looked like a mobility scooter hire facility. The phone told me I was in the correct place and I looked again and then saw the sign for the pub. There were at least twenty pavement mobility scooters parked outside and I made my way past them and into the bar. I chose to sit inside and found a corner table. As I sat down, I clocked Cassie immediately. She had hardly changed since I last saw her – very good-looking with beautiful brown eyes, amazing figure and her naturally sallow complexion was a bit darker. Cassie didn't see me as she made her way to a table outside where she took an order. The bar was very busy, and I could see that this was because they did a breakfast special at a knock-down price with a further discount for pensioners, which would explain the number of mobility scooters outside.

I didn't know what I would say to Cassie, but I was given breathing space because a waiter approached my table and asked for my order. I had no desire for a big breakfast and ordered a large beer. It arrived quickly and I took a gulp and started preparing my story for Cassie. Whilst doing this, I tried to work out if there was anyone watching me, but being an amateur at this type of thing I couldn't tell. I decided that I just needed to tell Cassie what had happened chapter and verse and see where that took us. I finished my beer in minutes and decided to order another before trying to attract Cassie's attention. Three boisterous middle-aged English guys entered the bar, but fortunately the waiter came to my table first and I ordered another beer. I was grateful for that because he then went to their table and had to endure lots of bad taste laddish banter as the three of them decided what they wanted. They then asked for the TV, which was showing Sky Sports, to be turned up so that they could indulge their football centric banter further.

Having sunk a pint and a half of lager on an empty stomach, I was beginning to feel lightheaded and decided that I needed to speak with Cassie straight away and get some sort of plan moving. She was clearly assigned to the outside tables and only came into the bar to place her orders or pick them up and was then straight back out again. I decided that despite the risk of being seen I needed to go outside in order to make contact with her. I went to the toilet and emptied my full bladder then returned to my table and told the waiter that I was going outside to finish my drink. He nodded and made a note in his pad.

Most of the pensioners were outside and appeared to be having a great time. How I wished that I was them. I found a seat in the shade on the right-hand side of the terrace. Cassie was serving a table which had two elderly, but sprightly looking couples. She had some chat with them and told them that she hoped they enjoyed the meal then turned looking for any customers needing to place an order. I gave a small wave, which she acknowledged, and she made her way towards me. I had my shades on and she hadn't recognised me.

"Hi! What can I get you, love?" she asked.

"Cassie, it's me," I said.

"Who?" she replied.

I lifted up my glasses. "Greg."

"Fuck sake," she gasped, "what are you doing here?" She was trembling as she said this.

"Didn't Piotr tell you?"

"He just said that he was coming to see me this morning – no mention of you. Have you come to screw things up just as it was all coming together?" She almost spat these words at me. I was worried that someone in the bar might notice her behaviour.

"Look, Cassie, we are in serious shit. Piotr's been grabbed by some people and I don't know who. I'm going to order another beer and a big breakfast; when you bring the beer, I will give you the basics and when you bring the breakfast, I will give you further details. Please smile and look like everything is OK, because I am sure we are being watched. You got that?"

She gave a small nod, a big smile and rather loudly said, "A large beer and a breakfast, love."

I said, "Yes," and smiled back.

When she brought the beer, she took her notebook out as if she was adding something to my order. I told her briefly about Vicky and Clinkie and how Brygida and Ania were coming to Piotr, and of course about the additional polonium. She smiled and went back to the bar. After her initial shock, she was playing this well and was a good actress.

Just over five minutes later she arrived with my food. As she was placing it on the table and giving me my cutlery, I told her about stealing the car, not finding the additional polonium, but finding the stash of cash. I asked for a jug of water, so when Cassie returned with it, I told her about Piotr's plans, which involved giving her a share of the money before us being left to our own devices. I told her that he had just been snatched and that there must be a few people involved. I didn't have time to tell her about some crime lord possibly tailing Clinkie's men.

There didn't appear to be anyone watching our conversation. The pensioners were tucking in and one of the three football banter guys from inside was making his way back into the bar clutching a Barcelona top that he had presumably just bought from the gift shop next door. Cassie smiled, made some small talk quite loudly then said softly as she wiped the table, "In a couple of minutes, before you have finished your food, get up and go into the bar as if you are going to the toilet. Go past it to the end of the corridor and open the fire door. There's no alarm. I'll be outside. Let's get out of here."

I smiled and thanked her.

Two minutes later and with half a pint remaining and most of my breakfast untouched, I got up and went into the bar. The same three guys were there speaking loudly to one another while staring at the TV. Another couple of tables were now occupied. I walked past the bar, turned the corner, went along the corridor and pushed the fire door open and went out the back.

"Quick!" Cassie hissed. She was standing amongst the empty cooking fat containers in the yard of the pub. I went towards her, she pointed, and I followed. We went into a small lane that ran between the pub and the gift shop. Cassie took something from her pocket, which I realised was a key fob, and quickly made her way to a two-seater mobility scooter. We jumped on, she started it up and we passed the gift shop and headed towards the esplanade. I looked back and saw one of the three guys standing in the car park looking for something. As we made our way along the now busy esplanade, I glanced back and caught sight of another of the football guys making his way on foot along the pavement that ran parallel with the esplanade, separated by a public garden.

"It's them," I shouted to Cassie. "Those three from the bar. The football banter guys. It's them that's following us." She nodded and was expertly manoeuvring us along the esplanade. We were doing the maximum speed of eight mph, which was hardly startling but better than walking pace and easier than running. Also, I didn't think our pursuers would have expected us to flee in this way and hadn't actually spotted us yet.

"Slow down," I said to Cassie. She turned her head and looked at me. "Slow down for just a second please." She looked quizzical but did so. I then leant over and snatched a cap and straw hat from a display outside a gift shop. I put the straw hat on and told her to get the cap on. We continued on our way with Cassie driving in a way so as to not attract attention.

"Where are we heading?" I asked her.

"We need to get someplace to get our heads down to give us time to think and work out what we do next," she said. "Let's hide in plain sight. Get a couple of towels," she instructed. She slowed down and said with a smile, "Pay for them!" I nodded with a slight smile and grabbed two towels and some sunscreen and went into the shop. Luckily it was empty, and I was greeted with a pleasant smile by the middle-aged woman serving. It came to around eighteen euros and I handed her a twenty, declined the offer of a bag and my change, picked up the goods and left the shop. I couldn't see the scooter. "Here!" Cassie called as she walked towards me eating a large lolly. "Let's get on the beach." We walked quickly across the hot sand and went to an area where sunbeds were for hire. There were the traditional foldaway beds along with ones which were similar in style to a four-poster bed. Cassie called the attendant over and had a conversation in a combination of broken Spanish and English. After what felt a while, she indicated for me to follow and we went towards the four-posters. The attendant indicated which one was ours and Cassie thanked him again with her beautiful smile.

"Give him a hundred, Greg," she told me.

I looked at her. "What?"

"Just do it."

I did. The attendant left with a grateful nod and we laid out our towels on the bed. "What was all that about?" I asked.

"This bed is reserved but won't be used until the afternoon. He didn't want anyone to use it because he is worried we will still be here when the hirers turn up or we will leave it in a state. I assured him that we would be clean and not stay long and make it worth his while."

I suddenly realised how good a hiding place this was as Cassie unclipped the curtains from each side of the bed and drew them closed. We had to keep this level of creative thought up as it was now time to start a plan.

Chapter Thirty-Two

"Get your shirt and shorts off," Cassie told me.

"What?"

"Come on, we have to look the part and blend in. Look like tourists, OK?"

"Yeah, of course," I replied, and took off my sweaty shirt and dirty baggy shorts.

Luckily, I was wearing a pair of dark grey boxers that could pass for swimming trunks. Cassie quickly stripped off down to her pants. I tried not to stare but it was difficult not to gawp at her beautiful near-naked body.

"Right, let's get some lotion on," she instructed, and handed me the bottle. I did my front and arms and legs then she took the bottle and did my back, which felt nice.

"OK, do my back," she said, and handed the bottle to me. Despite the urgency of our plight, I didn't want to rush this task as I may never have got the chance again. I slowly rubbed the lotion into her back from the top and worked my way down. I noticed that her pert breasts were the same lovely shade as the rest of her body.

"Do you want your legs done?" I asked.

"You enjoying this?" she asked.

"Of course."

"Well be quick, because you may have forgotten that we are in deep shit."

"OK."

She had a pair of black tanga briefs, which complemented her bottom perfectly. I worked the backs and inner thighs and gave them a more than adequate covering, all the while conscious of trying to contain any excitement in my boxers. As soon as I was finished, she pulled the curtains back.

"Why did you do that?" I asked. "Now anyone can see us."

"Hide in plain sight, Greg. Look around, how many of these beds have their curtains drawn? The guys chasing us will be professionals and will look for anything suspicious. It's best to look like any other sunbathing couple."

She was right, and I could only see one other bed with its curtains drawn.

"Right, let's act the part and sunbathe," she said.

We both lay on our fronts.

"Have you told me everything?" she asked.

"Just about," I replied. "The only other thing was that Piotr was hoping to get tailed because he thought he could lead the real big players to Clinkie's people and that one would wipe out the other and we would get away."

"Great plan," she said sarcastically, and I must admit when describing it to her it did sound flimsy to say the least.

"I couldn't see anyone on our tail, but I think Piotr did. However, it wasn't them that jumped us, it was a couple with a pram."

"A pram?"

"Yes. They looked like typical English tourists – a young couple and their child. We weren't far from your bar when they walked out in front of the car. Piotr braked and swerved but we hit the pram. I was getting out to see what I could do when I was thrown to the ground. When I looked up, the guy was driving the car and his wife had Piotr in the back with something held against his neck. The baby was a doll. It happened in seconds."

"Shit, and then you came straight to the bar?"

"Yes, I was sure I would be followed but I didn't know what else I could do."

"So, you led them straight to me...?"

"What else could I do?"

"You could have gone in the other direction."

"Yes, I could, but Piotr and you are or were a team. There's a hundred grand of your money in the back of that car."

It was strange having this conversation as we lay face down with our heads resting on our arms and talking sideways to each other. She turned her head to look at me and said, "I'm sorry, and yes, you did the right thing."

"OK," was all that I could come up with.

"So nothing was said by the people that took Piotr?"

"Nothing that I could hear."

"What direction did the car go off in?"

"It was heading in the direction of your bar and Adeje."

"I've got to know Piotr very well over the past two years and he's a cool customer. He won't have panicked and would have instantly realised there was no point resisting and would have already started thinking about the next step," she said firmly.

"I get all of that," I said, "but what would he have been able to do about any next step?"

"Well, I think they would have wanted to get the car somewhere quick and discreet to search it. They would have found the money of course, and when they couldn't find the polonium, they would have started working on Piotr."

"But we didn't find any polonium, so what could he tell them?"

"That's in his favour. If they had found the polonium, then Piotr would be dead by now."

I always knew that we were in deep shit, but hearing it said so matter of factly suddenly made it sink in.

"They will know that Piotr took that car apart and I think they will have taken him to the workshop at the harbour. Piotr may have planned for this and might have a few surprises waiting for them there," she said.

"Really?" I said. "I didn't see him doing anything like that."

"Do you really think he would have let you?" she replied.

"I suppose not. So we make our way to the workshop. What do we do when we get there?" I asked nervously.

"Well, we need to get an idea of who is there or around it. Maybe we do something like call the cops, tell them there has been a kidnapping and let them deal with it. Hopefully that will save Piotr, get some of these bastards arrested and get the others off our backs for long enough for us to get out of here."

Cassie was no doubt determined and resourceful, as her life over the past few years demonstrated, but she was more of a doer than a thinker and so that was it. That was our plan. However, it was better than anything I could come up with and so I agreed.

"Time to go," she said.

"Where to?"

"Follow me."

Cassie had pointed out that I shouldn't wear my shirt as they would have my description and details of what I was wearing. We walked hand in hand, me in my boxers with my straw hat on and towel draped over my neck, Cassie in her little briefs, still topless and headed for the shore. We had bundled our clothing into her shirt and made it look like a bag, which I gathered up and carried.

"Here we are. We're going to hire a jet ski. Let's stop here so you get the money without fumbling about in front of the guy," she told me.

"How much do I need?"

"Fifty."

Luckily, I had a fifty in my wallet. I wished I had taken a few notes from the money we found in the Audi because I was rapidly running out. I handed the note to Cassie and she carried out the transaction.

The guy led us to our machine, rattled something off in Spanish, which Cassie responded to, and he smiled, gave us the thumbs up and turned to return to his hut.

"What was he asking?"

"Just if we needed a demo of how it works."

"Are you an old hand on these?"

"Yeah."

"You were pretty good on the mobility scooter, by the way. How did you get the keys?"

"Aggie and Des from Peterborough come over for a month at a time. They have breakfast every day and she doesn't like keeping the keys in her purse, so she gives them to me to look after."

"So, they'll be stuck at the bar?"

"Yeah, but I don't have time to feel guilty – it got us away. Anyway, most of the people who use these scooters here can walk, they're just too lazy. I parked it with the keys in so it might get reported and returned. Forget that; we need to get going."

We had walked into the sea up to calf level and Cassie held the machine and told me to get on. I did and then held my hand out to help her on. As I was doing this, I became aware of a commotion quite near to where our sunbed was. I saw that one of the football guys from the pub was in a scene and apologising profusely for pulling open the curtains on a four-poster sunbed that contained a copulating couple who were not impressed at being interrupted. He backed off and was joined by the oldest-looking of the three and they made their way back up the beach towards the esplanade. So, they were on our tail and being thorough.

Cassie kicked the jet ski into life, and we headed out to sea. She was an excellent driver, and for a few seconds I forgot our troubles and enjoyed the exhilarating ride and holding on to her with my arms wrapped around her waist. She made a right turn and we were closing in on Puerto Colón. I could make out the harbour and the outline of Piotr's workshop. Reality struck and the butterflies in my stomach seemed to draw out any strength I had, making my arms feel limp.

"Keep holding on," Cassie instructed me, and I did my best to comply. She cut down the speed as we approached Puerto Colón. We didn't go into the harbour but went past it, round a corner and carried on for another couple of minutes before heading on to a small bay where a few families were playing or relaxing. She cut the engine as soon as we were in water shallow enough to let us get off the machine. We did so and dragged it onto the beach. A few people looked at us momentarily, but our arrival attracted little interest.

"What do we do now?" I asked as we walked up the beach.

"Let's get some other clothes," she said, pointing to a gift shop straight ahead while putting her bra on. I got a plain grey T-shirt that had *Tenerife* written on the front and Cassie chose a bright yellow Brazil football top. When I questioned the wisdom of something so striking, she replied, "Hide in plain sight. I was wearing a white T-shirt now I've got something quite different." I didn't really agree with her logic but nodded and we continued on our way to the harbour.

"What do we do when we get there?" I asked nervously.

"Let's observe," she replied. I waited for more, but she didn't add anything, and we walked hand in hand hoping to blend in. Some of the landmarks were familiar and I realised that we had come from a different direction and were now approaching the street where my apartment was. We walked slowly, looking in shop windows, and whilst we were doing this, my heart sank. In the reflection of the shop window that I was looking in I saw the guy in the Liverpool strip who had kidnapped Piotr coming out of the front entrance of my apartment block and heading towards the harbour.

"Don't turn around," I whispered out of the side of my mouth, "but the guy in the football top heading for the harbour has just come out of my apartment block. He's the one who kidnapped Piotr."

"OK," she said tersely, "let's follow him." She then put her arms around my neck and snogged me. "Got to look the part," she said with a smile. Despite the stress, I was enjoying the method acting.

We could clearly see the Liverpool man approach the workshop. We went to the first café and sat outside and were careful to position ourselves in such a way as to be partially hidden by the large blackboard with the various menus on. I then saw his partner. "That's his wife," I told Cassie.

"They're just the grunts," she said. "The main ones will be inside."

The waiter approached and Cassie ordered us both a coffee and two bottles of water. I wanted a beer and she could tell that. "No beer until this is done," she told me, to which I reluctantly agreed.

Chapter Thirty-Three

The waiter was soon back with our drinks and I went straight for a bottle of water, but my nerves caused me to fumble and nearly drop it as I attempted to unscrew the cap.

"Try and calm down," Cassie said quietly and with a smile. She was playing her role of loving partner so well, whereas my agitation, despite my best efforts, was showing. Cassie picked up her coffee cup with a steady hand, took a sip and said, "Lovely coffee." All I could do was nod. We could see Liverpool top and his wife walking in opposite directions and patrolling the area around the boat workshop.

"They are definitely in there," Cassie said.

"Yeah, what next?" I asked.

"Let's give it a few more minutes to see if anything happens. There might be some more people to turn up, maybe even a head honcho," she said. "When you think about it, it's under two hours since Piotr was taken, so after they searched the car, they will have needed to get the message over to the person in charge where they have gone to try and find the polonium."

I agreed with that and we sat in silence for a few minutes drinking our coffees and observing the harbour and surrounding area. I wondered where the three guys from the bar were, still back in Playa de la Americas I hoped. It was getting progressively busier as tourists arrived to either book excursions or queue to board a couple of large boats that were doing day trips, which made it harder to observe the workshop, but there didn't appear to be anyone else in it apart from the two who we had already spotted.

"This might be the cavalry," Cassie said quietly and shifted in her seat. A medium-sized pleasure boat was making its way into the harbour. Someone on deck was going through the procedures for docking and was getting the rope ready. At this stage we couldn't see who else was on the boat apart from the person in the front steering it in. As soon as the boat reached its berth, the crewman slung his rope round a cleat and pulled it tight to bring the boat to rest against the wooden dock. He then waited as a crewman came over and tied the knot. The crewman had the small walkway unfolded and in place in seconds and stood beside it as his passengers prepared to disembark. My heart rate went through the roof. "I know them," I said to Cassie.

First off the boat was someone who I recognised but didn't know the name of, followed by the unmistakable features of Jonjo Laxton and his sidekick, Davie Heeps.

"Who are they?" she asked.

"Don't know the first one, but the one in the middle is Clinkie Moore's number two, Jonjo Laxton, and the one behind is called Davie Heeps. They are hard Glaswegian bastards," I added.

"Good," she said.

"What?"

"Good. Piotr's plan has worked in that he has lured Clinkie's top guys to him. If his and Vicky's plans work then there should be some bigshot's operation watching all of this and ready to take out the lot of them."

"You seem to have forgotten about Piotr," I said accusingly.

"No, I haven't, but he will see that the first part has worked, apart from him getting caught obviously, and he will be working out his options. This is like a battle, Greg, and people get lost in war. I really like Piotr – we've been through a lot together and I don't want him to get hurt – but we are messing about with the big boys here and we have got to look after our own backs first."

I totally got what she was saying, but I desperately wanted to help Piotr. I had always liked him from when I knew him originally as a student of EFL and part-time cleaner in my local sports centre before I knew of his double life. I was so fond of Brygida and Ania; for Piotr to be killed now just as it looked like they were going to be able to resume life as a family was too much to bear.

"I get that," was all I could say in response as we continued to observe the workshop. Clinkie's guys made their way purposefully there and the crewman and captain stayed on the boat. On their way they passed Liverpool top's wife, but with no acknowledgements from either side. From the angle where we were sitting, we couldn't see if there was anyone at the front door, but as soon as they got there, they went straight in and I imagined that the door was swiftly closed behind them.

"OK, my usual question," I said. "What do we do now?"

"I don't know. We have two choices as I see it. One, try and get near and see what is going on inside, or two, sit here and observe what is going on and then give the details of that boat to the police and hope that some of these bastards get lifted," she said as she pointed to the one that Clinkie's guys had got off.

Well option two was the safer one for us no doubt, but even for an inherent coward such as me, that was not an option I could go with. "It has to be option one," I said. "Option two is certain death for Piotr and I can't sit back and do nothing."

"Agreed," she replied, which surprised me after she had just used a collateral damage analogy when discussing Piotr's plight.

"OK. How do we do it?"

"You know the workshop better than me, so what is the layout inside?"

"Well, it's mainly a big workshop with a crane and slipway for picking up boats and then putting them back in the water after they have been seen to. Apart from that, there is a small office to the left as you walk in, a storage yard behind the building which can be accessed from a door at the back and a toilet to the right, and that's it.

"I guess the Audi will be in bits in the middle and Piotr will be held in the office. They may have torn the office and storage area apart looking for the polonium. How do we get near? Those two are patrolling. There are no doubt a few more as well as Jonjo and his mates. Their boat isn't guarded, but what use is that to us, as by the time they get back to it, Piotr will probably be dead."

"We have to cause some kind of distraction and snatch him," she said.

"Oh, come off it, Cassie, this isn't a film. There are two of us and God knows how many of them who are probably all armed. And we don't even know where Piotr is." She accepted this with a nod and a sigh.

I had noticed another small boat arrive and berth alongside Jonjo's boat. The person getting off had to step on and walk across Jonjo's boat to get to the harbour. He stopped and talked to the pilot and crewman and it all seemed very convivial with lots of handshakes and laughter before he made his way onto the quayside. His boat then slowly started to back out and left the harbour. The man, who I guess would be early fifties, was dressed in the stock casual wear of the rich: chinos, pink polo shirt and tan loafers. He walked towards our café and took a seat a few tables along from us and checked his very expensive-looking watch before picking up the menu. Not a care in the world I thought, wishing I was him.

Cassie and I looked at each other and we saw the panic in each other's eyes. We were out of our league and knew it. How could we possibly execute plan one? We couldn't even get close enough to the workshop, far less get in it. Even if we did, we would be caught long before we got anywhere near to Piotr. As I looked at Cassie, I could see the man in the polo shirt on the phone laughing heartily. "Plan two?" I asked with a sigh. There was quite a pause as Cassie gulped, dabbed at her eyes and nodded. She then said very quietly "We've no choice…"

I summoned the waiter and ordered two brandies; Cassie didn't complain. She knew it was over. We sat in silence until our drinks arrived, and I surreptitiously swallowed my last two pills.

"Piotr," she said, with tears slowly running down her cheeks as she raised her glass.

"Piotr," I repeated croakily. We clinked our glasses together then drank the brandy quickly.

Cassie took out her phone and said, "OK, let's do this," as she prepared to make the call.

Just then we became aware of something happening at the workshop. It was hard to see clearly because pink polo shirt was joshing with the waiter, who was standing in our line of sight. There was no sudden noise or shouting, but suddenly, Jonjo, Davie and their mate were running quickly to the boat and jumped on it while signalling to the crewman and pilot to get going. It reversed out much quicker than the previous one and may have banged against a couple of other vessels. It turned around and hastily headed for the open sea. Within seconds it was becoming a dot on the horizon. Suddenly there was a bright orange flash and the speck was no more. I looked at Cassie and she at me, our mouths were open. *What now?* we asked each other with our eyes.

That question was answered immediately by a man standing directly behind us. He was wearing expensive cologne. It was the man with the pink polo shirt. "Get up nice and casually," he said quietly and with a smile. "Let's go this way," he said, as he shook us both by the hands, employing the Cassie school of method acting. We walked alongside him offering no resistance. We were walking away from the workshop and towards the street that my apartment block was in. When we got up from the table at the café, I had looked over again at the workshop, but there appeared to be no further action there. My stomach heaved at the thought of what might have gone on inside that building and what collateral damage had ensued.

"Where are we going?" I asked.

"Shoosh!" he said quietly with a smile. Just then, a dark blue SUV with local plates pulled up and someone inside opened the doors. "Get in," Pink Shirt said, and we did as we were told. It was nice and cool inside and the windows were tinted. Pink Shirt sat in the front and the driver started up as soon as he nodded. There was a black man wearing dark shades and dressed in smart but casual clothes already in the back seat and Cassie sat next to him, with me against the other window.

"What the fuck has just happened?" Cassie blurted out.

"All in good time," Pink Shirt answered. Then followed it up with,

"Don't worry, you're with the good guys now."

Chapter Thirty-Four

We drove in silence for a few minutes. I took Cassie's hand in mine and held it. She didn't resist. The man next to her looked straight ahead. I tried the door handle but of course the child locks were on. I looked out of the window and felt numb, unable to fully take in what had just happened and what might happen next. Pink Shirt had told us that we were with the *good guys*. Given the world that we had become embroiled in, I had my doubts as to how reassuring that was, as the level of good was perhaps relative. After a few minutes we turned on to a main road with lots of signs for a water park and headed along it for a while before turning off on to a dusty road that led inland. We slowly passed what looked like a bottling plant before stopping outside a nondescript unit next to it which had no company name and appeared to be a small disused factory. The driver got out and opened my door. I stiffly climbed down and held my hand out to help Cassie. "This way," Pink Shirt said breezily, and we dutifully followed with both the driver and the other man following behind us. We went round the back of the building and entered it from an unlocked door. I didn't know what to expect as we made our way in and were directed to a large empty space that was stripped of any tools or equipment. However, I was massively surprised to see Piotr there and so was Cassie.

"Piotr! Piotr!" She shrieked in delight as soon as she saw him and tried to give him a hug, at which point the driver held her back. She tried to resist. Piotr was dishevelled and it looked like his nose was broken.

"Calm down." the other man said in a deep Caribbean lilt. She stopped instantly.

"OK, OK," Pink Shirt said. "You've had, shall we say, an interesting morning. I want to tie up a few loose ends. If you behave then things are going to look a whole lot better for you than they did an hour or so ago." He seemed so urbane and middle class, the type you would meet at a cheese and wine or the local tennis club, but not here wrapped up in all of this. There was a table with about ten foldaway metal chairs next to it. "Sit down," Pink Shirt ordered, and we walked over to the chairs and did as he instructed. Piotr, Cassie and I sat in a line, while our captors remained standing. I felt a bit threatened by this but then realised that no one was brandishing a gun at us at least. Cassie started asking Piotr how he was, but he just gave a small enigmatic smile and before he could answer, Pink Shirt told her to be quiet. He then looked at me and said, "You've been tailed since you left London." I just looked at him because I didn't know what to say and it looked like he wanted to tell us something. "You two," he said, pointing at Piotr and me, "and of course Vicky, were right that by getting Clinkie on the trail it would attract bigger fish. Appropriate we should end it at a harbour." He smiled at his perceived witticism.

"Your Scottish friends," he said, looking at me, "were doing some serious damage to him," as he nodded towards Piotr. "They have been dealt with. Now we need to speak to each of you and get this matter tidied up. Greg, come with me." We walked back out to the SUV. "Hop in," he said lightly. I did so and was followed by Pink Shirt and one of his henchmen and we sat in a line.

"It's a bit cramped," Pink Shirt said, "but walls have ears and we need each story told individually to see what cross references. I don't care how long it takes, but this all started with you and I want to hear everything from the start, OK?"

I nodded. "What do you mean the start?" I asked. "Is it from Vicky being sent to jail or after that?" "Before that," he replied, and his voice had suddenly developed a bit of an edge, "from the very beginning."

I nodded again, took a deep breath and started giving them the history of the whole ridiculous, dangerous, unexpected and life-changing situation that I had been thrown into. I missed out nothing, from sleeping with Vicky and Brygida, even though Piotr was nearby, Vicky's unexpected return, my boss being kidnapped and still held as far as I knew, breaking Piotr and Brygida's code right up to stealing from Clinkie and then stealing the Audi. I wanted him to see that I was laying it all out and that I was telling the truth. I emphasised that I had been set up and double-crossed on several occasions and that I needed to be trusted. I told them about my theory regarding the polonium and their body language registered a definite interest.

"Have you anything to add?" he asked. I told him I didn't. "Thank you, Greg, you have been very helpful."

"Sorry, there is something," I quickly added.

"Yes."

"What happened to Clinkie's guys?"

"All dead. Now come on, we need to speak to your friends," he said breezily.

I was taken to the same big room as before and now only Piotr was there. The man behind his chair nudged him and he got up. "Over here, Piotr," Pink Shirt said, and I went to the seat that he had been sitting in. We gave each other rueful smiles as we passed, and I noted the extent of the swelling on his nose and under his eyes. There was no sign of Cassie, and I imagined she must be in what looked like a staff area just off from the big room.

I don't know how long I sat for before Piotr returned. I was then called back again and returned to the SUV. I hadn't been given anything to drink in all this time and was feeling parched. "Any chance of a drink before we start again?" I asked.

"Yes of course," Pink Shirt said as he went to the boot of the vehicle and brought out a cold box. "Fancy a cold one?" he asked, holding up a bottle of chilled Heineken. I should have refused and asked for a water, but by now I was in a don't-give-a-shit mentality and accepted his kind offer.

We both got in the vehicle and the questioning resumed. "Tell me what you meant about your theory on the polonium," he asked.

"Not much to add," I replied as I took a swig of the amber nectar. It felt good and instantly relaxed me. Perhaps not a good idea given my current company.

"As you say, it's a theory and I don't have any proof that this is what Eustace did."

"But I do," the other man said. It was only the second time he had spoken. Suddenly the penny dropped. He was the man who approached me at the Old Bailey two years ago after Vicky's trial. This was David, Eustace's brother. He could see the flicker of recognition grow and said, "You know me now, don't you, man?

"Yes. You're David. I'm very sorry about Eustace," I said, now feeling guilty about giving the graphic details earlier of what Eustace looked like when I had found him murdered in his own home.

"Not your fault, man," he said quietly with his deep voice. "You did good by him. You found his stuff and returned it. You're honest, man."

"Thanks," was all I could think of to say.

Pink Shirt joined the conversation. "David received Eustace's possessions after he died. This included his business papers, although that's perhaps a bit too grand a description for them. As you know, he did a number of under-the-counter type jobs and he was creative in the way he recorded it, to say the least.

"Seeing Clinkie's men take the Audi and workshop apart and the beating they gave Piotr, which would have ended up with him dead if we hadn't intervened, I am convinced that the polonium never made it into that car. Like you, I believe that Eustace hid it somewhere close to home and died before he could stash it in the Audi. I think he must have left

clues and I think you are the man to find and interpret them, which will

lead us to the polonium. That's what my boss thinks as well, which is lucky

for you because we are taking you back to Blighty, meaning that you will

stay alive for the time being."

Chapter Thirty-Five

"Let's go," Pink Shirt said, and with that, David got out from the back and went into the driver's seat.

"Have you got your passport?" Pink Shirt asked me. I felt in the side pocket of my shorts and was relieved that it was still there. It was one of my few remaining possessions, along with my wallet and phone. The cash in my backpack left in the Audi and the rest of my gear was just a distant memory.

"Yes," I answered tensely.

"Good, one less thing to bother about." He then took out his phone and rang someone called Sandra and asked her to make the arrangements. David started the SUV and drove towards the main road. A few minutes later, Pink Shirt, who was still sitting next to me in the back seat, read a text on his phone and told David that everything was in place. David nodded without turning round and concentrated on the road. Something inside me told me that we were on our way to the airport, and a few minutes later that feeling was confirmed as I saw the first of many signs pointing the way. It didn't take long before we were on a slip road approaching the airport and we pulled up in the drop-off point outside the terminal building. Pink Shirt got out and held the door open for me.

"You are in David's capable hands now," he said as he held out his hand and I shook it. I'm not sure why, perhaps because I wasn't yet dead. David took a small black leather shoulder bag out of the boot and he and Pink Shirt exchanged nods. Pink Shirt got in and drove off as we entered the airport building.

"First stop, some shopping," David said, and we went to a gift shop. He selected a backpack, newspaper, crime novel and T-shirt and paid for them. "Go to the toilets, give yourself a wash and put the new shirt on. You're stinking, man. We'll get you some deodorant when we get to duty-free."

I'd only had my Tenerife T-shirt on for a few hours, but I suppose the stress of it all had caused me to sweat more than usual. I had a quick wash in the sink in the gents, changed shirts and felt a little better. It crossed my mind to do a runner, but the relaxed way in which I had been transported to the airport suggested that they knew how to keep me in their sights if needed. David had told me to put everything in my new bag as I needed to look like a traveller and at least have hand luggage.

I came out of the gents and actually had to look for David, who was speaking on the phone with his back to me. He finished his conversation and we walked towards check-in. There was a small queue which quickly went down and we checked in on a machine. David had to show me what to do with my passport and what buttons to press. We then went through security and headed straight to duty-free. We had three hours until our flight.

"Buy the best one," David said with a slight smile as we approached the after-shave area. I could tell that he was being professional and trying to keep his distance but got the feeling that he was a good guy and might actually like me. I selected a bottle of Calvin Klein and David took it, had his boarding pass scanned and paid.

"Hungry?" he asked.

"A little," I answered. To be honest I wanted a beer first. We went to a bar and took a seat in the corner. I didn't get the feeling that David was trying to hide. After we sat down I asked him if he wasn't worried about Clinkie's guys following us.

"No, all the ones here are dead," he said with an enigmatic smile. Well that's that then, I thought. A waiter appeared, and I ordered a club sandwich and pint of lager. David went with a baked potato and fizzy water. We got talking and David was responsive to my gentle probing. He told me that they had several people staking out Piotr's workshop. They had been watching Piotr and me since my arrival so knew what was going on. They saw what happened when Piotr was snatched and acted quickly. They already had people in place around the workshop who remained there while others followed the Audi. It was taken to a place near to the disused factory where we had just been with Pink Shirt and the car was taken apart. Piotr never gave them anything. The guy in the Liverpool top was the chief henchman and laid into Piotr, who took it and didn't respond. After an hour of threats, violence and frantic searching of the car and several phone calls, they left for the workshop. Liverpool top and his wife left in one car and Piotr was taken by another three people in a second car.

David's gang acted fast. Pink Shirt was out at shore waiting for a signal. When he received it, his boat was on its way to the harbour. As soon as he got off and made his way to the café, the gang swooped and killed Liverpool top and his wife, then did an assault on the building coming in from the back. They killed another three of Clinkie's men inside, which explained Jonjo and his two friends' hurried departure. Pink Shirt had left an explosive device on their boat which could be set off from a phone signal. I then realised that I actually saw Pink Shirt set the bomb off as he spoke and laughed on the phone while sitting at the table in the café. It struck me that the crewman and the pilot must have been killed along with Jonjo and his fellow gang members.

"Did Clinkie have his own boat?" I asked.

"No, they chartered it."

"Was everyone on the boat killed?" I asked rather unnecessarily.

"Yes, of course, man," David replied as he tucked into his food.

He obviously regarded the crew of the charter boat as the collateral of war. I wanted to ask more, particularly about what would happen to Piotr and Cassie, but David's mood darkened. He seemed slightly agitated and I guessed he was a bit annoyed with himself for letting his guard slip and telling me so much. I didn't want to get anyone from this gang annoyed because I'm sure he wouldn't bat an eyelid if I were to become the next bit of collateral damage.

Chapter Thirty-Six

We finished our meal in silence. There were still two and a half hours to go. David received a text and then said, "What am I thinking about? Let's go." He got up and I dutifully followed as we made our way to a VIP area. "I forgot that I'm working for a big man now. Let's take advantage," he said as we approached the Executive Lounge.

He searched amongst a large collection of cards in his wallet before finding the one that he wanted. He gave it to the receptionist, who scanned it and said, "Thank you, Mr Brown."

He wasn't using his own name, not a surprise I suppose. "Please give a day pass for my colleague," David asked. She asked to see my boarding pass then scanned my permission onto the same card and that was it, we were in. The tastefully decorated lounge was spacious and around half-full. We took our seats at a table and I noticed the buffet-style serving area for food and drink. "Want a drink?" I asked David.

As I was looking at one of the many flight information screens, it suddenly dawned on me that Brygida and Ania would be arriving here soon. I desperately wanted to know what had happened to Piotr and Cassie and what would happen to Brygida when she got to Tenerife. I decided to take the bull by the horns and asked as I handed David his orange juice, "David, you know my full story and the role I played in Clinkie finding out about Piotr and where he was based. He also knows about Brygida, who is Piotr's wife. They're arriving here in a few days. Will they be safe?"

"I already told you that all of Clinkie's men on the island are dead, and Clinkie will know that as well. He won't have any men tailing her."

I let out a sigh. "Thanks, David. That's great, thanks a lot. Will Piotr and Cassie be OK?"

"Well that depends on you." My heart sank.

"What does that mean?"

"You better be useful when we get back to the UK, and they'll be fine."

"But I don't know anything about where Eustace would have hidden the polonium."

"Well let's get you started," David said, and with that he took out his phone and made a call to Sandra, telling her to send over the *stuff*, and then read out a number from his lounge card and hung up. He then got up, walked over to the fax machine and waited for a couple of minutes before it whirred into life. He came back to the table with six sheets of paper and handed them to me. He looked at the flight screens info and said, "You've got two hours before the flight, so use the time well."

I looked at the fax copies of handwritten notes and continued looking at them with a growing sense of unease as I was expected to uncover something that no one else had been able to, and this was to guarantee the safety of others. I didn't know what to say or how to start, and perhaps because of this I blurted out, "What happened to the money? We found three hundred grand in the car."

"It's in the kitty," he said with a smile. "But Piotr and Cassie will get some of it to help them on their way if you play your part." That sort of helped my mindset.

"Did you have any idea what your brother was up to?" I asked.

"No, man. I knew he had a few shady deals, like we all do, but no, I never knew he was in so deep."

"How have you become involved with this?"

"That's a story for another day. Now you start using your smart mind, Professor."

Here we go I thought. When telling him and Pink Shirt everything, I mentioned that Kev Osborne called me *Professor* because I was a lecturer at a further education college.

The six fax sheets looked like they had been photocopied from an A4-sized diary. They showed a list of jobs that Eustace had got booked in:

listing the car make along with a date and notes indicating what work had been carried out, when the job was completed along with the price. In total there were sixteen jobs shown. None of them were for an Audi.

"What was your brother like?" I asked David.

"What do you mean?"

"Well, you're asking me to try and get into his head to work out where he may have hidden the polonium..."

"Keep your voice down," he said, staring at me, "walls have ears. It's hard to say, because I hardly knew him as an adult. As a boy he was impulsive, but he respected me, his older brother, and he was loyal."

"Was he logical? Did he like puzzles?"

David laughed almost mockingly. "Puzzles? No, man, growing up in Rema you had no time for puzzles. The main game was surviving."

"What is Rema?"

"It's where we were brought up in Jamaica. Part of Kingston. It's pretty wild."

"Ah. OK."

"There were no books in the house," David added. "We used our hands to survive. Eustace got good with engines just watching the guys keeping their cars on the road. When you were as poor as us, you couldn't do trade-ins. You kept your car running."

Up to now, my recurring image of Eustace any time I thought of him was how he looked when I turned up at his house and found him dead with a knife in his chest. Therefore, I found it slightly strange to get a feel for him as a person and not just a body. However, the fax notes and my brief chat with David were getting me nowhere.

Despite being under orders to crack the code and find the polonium, this all felt rather strange, and I certainly didn't feel like I was effectively a hostage. There was a smoking area in the terrace outside the lounge and I went outside with the fax sheets. It was a lovely afternoon and I tried to enjoy the warmth before I returned to an English autumn. I stood and leant against the barrier and looked out across the vast car park before finding a seat in the sun and started looking at the notes again.

The list of jobs covered the time that Eustace was working on the Audi, so the one thing the notes told me was that he was hiding this particular job and the taxman would know nothing of it. Looking at the first two pages of jobs, it was clear they had been done relatively quickly whilst similar-looking ones after them were taking much longer, no doubt because he was spending time on the Audi as well. A thought struck me;

as well as working on the Audi he was screwing Cassie! That's how so much of this shit started. She was part of Kev Osborne's gang and got set up as an instructor at the Nelson Leisure Centre in Ealing. This was the facility that I used, as did Eustace, and where Piotr was employed as a part-time cleaner. Kev found out that Eustace was working on behalf of a Russian gangster to hide the polonium and Kev tracked him down using Cassie as bait.

As I thought this, I said, "I bet she knows."

"Sorry?" a man at the next table said.

I looked across at the middle-aged man and his wife who had their newspaper open at the crossword page. I think it was the *Daily Mail*. "Nothing, Tourette's," I said, and hastily returned inside. They looked at me blankly and returned to their puzzle.

"Get Cassie on the phone," I said to David breathlessly.

"What?"

"I need to speak to Cassie, she might be the key."

"What do you mean, man?"

"Did you know that Eustace was screwing her?"

"Yes," he said quietly. I suddenly realised that David had genuine reasons to despise Cassie as she had been part of the set-up that killed his younger brother. She didn't plunge the knife into him, but she set the scene. I then wondered that if I solved the riddle set for me whether David would then exact his retribution.

I gave him some background. "She told me about trying to get info on the polonium from Eustace for Kev, but she never had enough time to look. The additional polonium wasn't in the Audi and it won't be in any of these cars," I said, waving the fax sheets. "Over the time those jobs were done, Eustace was at the garage, the leisure centre or his house. There is no way that he would have hidden it in the garage, which wasn't his property and had lots of people coming and going, and while some of the leisure centre staff were lazy, I think he wouldn't have risked hiding it there. The most obvious place there would be a locker, but they will all get opened and cleaned once a in a while, so no not there. I think Eustace will have made a hiding place in or next to his house. It wouldn't have to be big and it could be made or set up quickly.

"We need to speak to Cassie to get a feel for the house and any ideas on hiding places. Does she know that you're Eustace's' brother?" I asked.

"Not yet," he replied. It sounded ominous.

"Can you do it?" I asked.

"Do what?"

"Call her?"

He got up and headed towards the terrace. "Let's do it out here," he said.

I followed him out and we passed the couple from earlier who were looking at me even more suspiciously now that I was accompanied by David. We made our way to the far side of the terrace and leant against the barrier with our backs to the tables. David took out his phone and called one of his contacts, who answered immediately. From the way he was talking I guessed it must be Pink Shirt. The phone at the other end must have been passed to Cassie, as David said, "Just answer the questions that you are going to be asked and no small talk. You got it?"

He then said to me, "You heard what I just told her, well the same goes for you. Just ask the questions you need and don't try anything you might regret."

"OK," I said. "Hi, Cassie."

"Hi."

"You OK?"

"Been better."

"They looking after you...?"

Before I could hear her reply, David snatched the phone from me. "I told you no small talk. Now ask the lady the questions you need and no small talk."

"Sorry, sorry, I'm just nervous, you know." I got the feeling that the middle-aged *Daily Mail* couple were watching us intently.

"Hi, Cassie, it's me again." I think I was now on loudspeaker at her end. No doubt Pink Shirt was listening carefully. "Now, I have some questions. We need to find something that Eustace has hidden. Everyone thought it was in the Audi, but it wasn't, so we need to find it. If we do, then that would help me, you and Piotr." David was looking at me intently. "I know you tried to find things for Kev when you were there." I saw David flinch in my peripheral vision. "Where do you think he would hide something valuable?"

"Is this the polonium?" she asked. I wanted to show David and Pink Shirt that I was playing ball and so simply said, "It doesn't matter to you what we are looking for, I just need some ideas of his hiding places."

"I looked in all the usual places, but he didn't have anything in drawers or under the carpet as far as I can remember."

"Did he have a shed outside?" I interjected.

"Yeah, but it was just an old wooden one, and I doubt he would have hidden anything there."

"What about the utility room?" I asked forlornly. I was desperately racking my brain trying to remember the layout of Eustace's house. I had only been in it once and that was under extreme stress.

"No, it was tiny and didn't even have any shelves, just the washing machine and his toolbox that sat on top of it."

"OK."

"Sorry I can't be of any more help," she said, somewhat playing to the gallery.

"No, you have been very helpful, Cassie. Keep in touch."

"Yeah," she replied.

I handed the phone back to David. "Well?" he said, as he put it in his pocket.

"Very handy," I said.

"Yes?" he asked with a raised eyebrow.

"Yes," I said. "I think I know where the hiding place is."

Chapter Thirty-Seven

It was the first time I had seen David excited. Most of the time his disposition varied in small degrees one way or the other, but now he was positively animated. The English couple were looking at us again.

"Let's get inside and I'll tell you," I suggested. We returned to our seats in the lounge.

"His toolbox," I said confidently.

"Toolbox?"

"Yes, if he was going to hide something, then that's where I think it would be.

"Why?"

"Because it's an everyday object, he would have had it with him a lot of the time and it would be easy for someone like Eustace to create a false bottom and put the polonium there. When you think about it, he was customising the car to carry the polonium, so at some point he had to take it to the car. What better way than in his toolbox?"

"Good thinking", David replied, then added, "you found three hundred grand in cash in the car – how would he have carried that?"

"I don't know and just now I don't care. You and your boss have asked me to try and find the polonium and Eustace's toolbox is my best guess. You took ownership of all his possessions – where is it?"

"Let me think."

"Well, he can't have had much."

"Yes, but remember I was in Jamaica."

"You came over for his funeral."

"Yes, I did. There were only six people at it including me."

I wish I had known Eustace, he seemed like a lovable rogue, but when he died, all his so-called friends and acquaintances were nowhere to be seen.

"I took some family photographs and arranged for a house clearance. I stayed there a few months and then sold it and went back home. One of the people at the funeral was the garage owner. He told me a few stories about Eustace, and I told him he could have Eustace's tools because they were of no use to me," David explained.

My heart sank. Although it was good to know where the toolbox was, I had history with Doug, the owner of Zach's Garage. I had broken into his garage to get to the Audi, and he knew this, as did the police.

Subsequently, they had used him as a source of information in the locality.

"Shit," I said.

"Why are you saying that?" David asked.

"Because Doug the garage owner is in the pocket of the police – DI Stevenson to be precise. There is no way I can go near the garage without him giving the police the nod. Let's put that to one side for a moment. When you gave Doug the toolbox, did you physically hand it over, and what did he say he would do with it?"

"Yes, I took it to the garage. I got a taxi there because the box was heavy."

"Did Doug say he would use the tools? I'm worried that he may have taken the tools he wanted and then chucked everything else out."

"He said that some of the tools were specialist and he was going to use them. He also said that Eustace had looked after all of them so well and that they would be good for his apprentice."

"So, it looks like the toolbox is still around, and in the garage," I said hopefully. "We need to work out a plan of how we get it from the garage. It won't be easy. I bet you Doug has ramped up his security." Just as I said this, I noticed on the departure board that our flight was being called.

"Well, we can think about what we do on the plane," David said.

Despite us being in the business lounge, I hadn't realised that we were flying business class until we arrived at the gate, and I followed David as we walked around the snaking line and went to a much smaller queue and were boarded in minutes. We were in the third row and had wide seats with a table between. This was certainly a step up from the budget flight cattle truck I had experienced on my way out. I definitely seemed to be under the wing of a different class of criminal.

David and I settled in as the flight continued to board. I noticed the English couple from the lounge as they went past and was pleased to see that they weren't in business class; they must have just bought a lounge pass. The man stared accusingly at me, as if to say *how are you in here?* If only he knew.

Finally, boarding was complete and we were ready to go. As soon as the seat belt signs went off, I was up to the toilet to relieve my extremely full bladder. By the time I got back to my seat the crew were serving drinks and snacks. David had got me a beer and some peanuts.

"Thanks," I said as I sat down. It was now time to start thinking. I knew the layout of Zach's Garage very well. At least I did from two years ago; it may well have changed because I hadn't been back since. It was a single-storey block in a small industrial estate and had two large rollover doors for where the vehicles went in and a small domestic-sized door to allow access into the reception area. Given the involvement with the polonium work carried out in the premises, which Doug had been unaware of at the time, I expected he would have installed CCTV cameras, both to prevent break-ins but also perhaps to monitor what was going on in his garage.

"First things first," I said to David. "What colour, style and size is the toolbox? You said it was heavy to carry."

"It was an off-red colour and bashed, so there were bits of metal showing through and some rust at the edges."

"Size?"

"About this long," he said, as he held his arms apart about a metre wide. And this deep..." He indicated about a third of a metre. "It had a big handle the length of the box, and when you opened it, it..." He struggled for the word.

"Concertinaed?" I suggested.

"That's it – it opened, and the shelves spread out," he said, widening his arms. I knew what he meant.

"OK. I can picture what it looks like. I think it's called a cantilever toolbox. The problem now is to find it," I said with a weary smile, which David returned.

I ordered a red wine. "Hey, you better watch your drinking, man," he said softly.

"Don't worry, this will help me think," I replied. "I'll pace myself. This is too important for me to screw up."

"OK, I trust you," he replied.

I took out the fax sheets and stared at them intently for want of anything else to do. I hoped somehow that they would magically generate a flash of inspiration. I glanced to my left and David was nodding off. I decided to try and get forty winks because no plan was formulating in my head, and I thought if I got some rest then I would be better prepared to start a plan. I closed my eyes and lay back in my seat. After a few minutes I felt myself drifting off. Suddenly I woke with a start. I had been dreaming, and in my dream I was in the Bridge Café, which was situated across the road from the industrial estate that housed Zach's Garage. In my dream, Gladys, the genial elderly waitress, was bringing me a bacon roll and coffee. There was someone with me, a female who kept changing. It might have been my sister, or it might have been Vicky – it seemed to be an amalgam of both of them. However, that got me thinking and I began to formulate a plan.

The dream reminded me of when I had drawn Doug away from the garage previously. I knew him from the leisure centre, and he was a middle-aged *lad* with a far higher view of his attractiveness to woman than they had. I think he would have called himself a lady's man. He was the type who would boast of his pulling power in the changing rooms to his mates and make leery remarks to female staff, all the while thinking they enjoyed such banter.

Over two years ago, when Vicky had phoned the garage with a sexy voice and a fictitious sob story regarding her car breaking down, Doug was out the garage in minutes to rescue the damsel in distress, freeing the way for me to do my stuff. I felt that a similar approach would work again, but he needed to be away for a good while to allow us to search the premises. We also needed to search the most likely places first and work systematically. About thirty minutes later, David woke up and I gave him the outline of my plan, which he nodded along with.

"We need you to get someone to play the Vicky role and make the call," I told him.

"No problem," he said. "We'll arrange that when we land."

"I think it's best if one of us goes into the garage and the other acts as lookout."

"Agreed," he said. "You go in." I knew he would say that, but I couldn't really argue as I knew the layout of the garage better than him.

"OK," I said. Strangely, I didn't feel at all nervous at what faced us the next day. Perhaps I was getting used to this life. Suddenly thoughts of Maggie flashed into my mind.

"David, you know I told you that my boss had been kidnapped and that was how Vicky forced me to steal her papers from Clinkie, which really put me in this shit?"

"Yeah. What of it?"

"Well, as soon as I knew Clinkie was on my tail, I ran. I have no idea if Maggie is safe. Could you or your guys help free her if she's still being held? She was being held by Vicky, who has probably fled."

"One thing at a time," he replied. "Let's concentrate on our job tomorrow."

There was nothing more to be said, so I sat back and tried to relax and enjoy the rest of the flight. Being business class, and with only hand baggage, we were in the Gatwick South Terminal building in minutes after landing.

"I'll get us transport. You wait there," he said, pointing at a bookshop which was one of many retail outlets in the terminal. I had become quite the traveller over the past few days but still found it strange to find such an array of high street shops at an airport, thinking on the basis that airports are for people travelling and not shopping. I browsed in the window and switched on my phone, which had been off since Piotr and I had headed off in the Audi that morning. It was strange to think that it was the same day as so much had happened since then.

There were three missed calls from an unknown number, and I noticed a voicemail message had been left. I pressed play and it was from DI Stevenson. He told me he needed to speak to me urgently and gave a number to call. Suddenly my anxiety levels reached previous levels. I had used up the last of my magic pills in the café when we toasted Piotr and had gone over five hours without resorting to them, which was probably a record for me in times of stress, but I was now suddenly desperately craving them. I saw a chemist on the other side of the concourse and hurried over to it.

I couldn't get my prescription drugs there so had to settle for the most effective-looking anxiety suppressors on the shelf. I bought a bottle of water, and as soon as I was out of the shop I washed four tablets down with a large glug of water and made my way back to the bookshop. David was standing angrily glaring at me. "Where were you, man?"

"I didn't feel well. I needed something from the chemist," I said, pointing at the water and tablets.

He inhaled deeply but didn't ask anything about what was wrong with me. Instead, he told me he had hired a car as we walked to the pickup point. David went over the formalities with the assistant and we got in the car; he keyed a postcode into the sat nav and we set off. It was now approaching eight o'clock. "Where are we heading to?" I asked.

"We have a hotel booked," he replied dryly.

"OK," I replied. He obviously wasn't in a talking mood, so I looked out of the window as we left the airport and joined the M23.

The traffic was relatively light, and we were soon on the outskirts of London. David had the radio on very quietly and we hadn't exchanged a word since we left the airport. I began to get my bearings and recognise where we were. I looked at the map on the sat nav and could see that we were heading for Hounslow. In another fifteen minutes we reached our destination, which was a budget hotel. He parked and we went to reception and picked up our room keys, which were booked under Mr Brown and Mr Steel. We were in adjoining rooms on the third floor. When we got out of the lift he said, "Dump your bag, freshen up and I'll see you in the bar in thirty minutes."

"OK," I acknowledged.

I could have kicked myself for not buying any toiletries when I was in the chemist at the airport. I had a quick shower and used the stuff stuck to the wall, which was actually all right. I then put on the same clothes I had just taken off and made my way downstairs to the bar. Surprisingly, David was already there. He got up from his seat, gestured for me to sit down and went to the bar and returned with a pint of lager for me.

"You know how to get me going!" I said with a half-smile.

"Enjoy," he said. "You hungry?"

"Not yet," I replied.

"Me neither."

And then we got talking. It was strange that for the whole time in the car from leaving the airport he didn't say a word, but now he started and couldn't stop. "Sorry for earlier," he said.

"What do you mean?" I asked.

"It wasn't you, but coming back into London got me thinking of Eustace and then of my life here when I was young. I was thinking of my father and my mother. She died when we were young and still living in

Jamaica – that's why we came here. My father tried his best. He was told that it was the land of milk and honey, but it wasn't like that. When we arrived, we didn't get the friendly welcome we thought we would. No man, instead we experienced racism and discrimination – we didn't know what that was until we got here. And as for the weather...

"My father managed to get us a flat in Lambeth, but I didn't think of it as a proper home because it was hard to make friends with British people. My father went four months before he got a job, yet when he was in Jamaica he was told that he was needed and would get employment straight away. When he arrived, lots of companies said they didn't want black people to work for them. He went to the employment exchange every day and lots of the jobs had 'NCP' on them. Do you know what that means?" he asked me. I shook my head. "No coloured person." I shook my head again, this time sadly.

"Me and Eustace were bullied at school because of the colour of our skins. That didn't last long though because I fought back; no one was going to treat me and mine like that, but it got me in trouble, I was always in trouble. Eventually I had to leave when I was only twenty. I never came back, man, I never came back. Not, not..." he paused, sighed and blurted out, "until my brother's funeral..." and then tailed off. "Sorry man," he said as he dabbed at his eyes then continued, "The thing is, I settled back into life over there, but my brother and father were over here. I got married and we had two kids and she didn't want me to have anything to do with Britain, even though my family were there. She was born higher up than me. Her father was a head teacher and she made me aware of that. I was always trying to keep up with her and she often put me down. I don't know what she saw in me. We got married because she was pregnant, and she didn't want to shame her family, who didn't like me. It was all about them. She was into the Church and I couldn't get into that, man. We always fell out about it. She would dress them up in little suits and make a big performance every Sunday and I stayed in the house.

"We got divorced nearly ten years ago and I haven't seen my sons since. What kind of a father am I? Now I'm here, I don't know what to do, man. I don't feel at home or wanted here or in Jamaica. I don't know what to do."

"Is that how you have got involved with Pink Shirt and his gang?" I asked quietly.

"Yeah. I'm sorry, I've said too much," he said sadly. We sat in silence and finished our drinks. I tried to imagine how it felt for David and Eustace as two young boys without their mother arriving in this cold, unwelcoming country. Also, their poor father struggling to look after them having travelled in expectation of a better life, only to be met with prejudice and hostility.

After a while David asked softly, "Do you want to eat?"

"No thanks," I said.

"Me neither. Let's go up," he said. "We have a big day tomorrow."

I nodded and we made our way silently to the lift. We said nothing in the lift. However, as we went up, I had an image of two small confused, cold and lonely boys in Lambeth. I had the urge to give David a hug, and when we got out, I did. We then went to our rooms.

Chapter Thirty-Eight

The next day we met in the restaurant. I was starving, not having had any tea the previous night and also being a bit hungover, and so went for the large fry-up option. We said nothing about our conversation from the night before or our hug, but I didn't feel embarrassed and I don't think David did either. I felt that we both had a better understanding and relationship, which would hopefully help us in finding and getting the polonium back and bringing our personal nightmares to some form of resolution. I felt this may be as good a time as ever to mention the missed calls and message from DI Stevenson, so I went for it, "There's a message from the cops on my phone."

"When was it left?" he asked without looking up.

"Yesterday."

"What was it about?"

"It was Stevenson, the cop who handled Vicky and Eustace's case. He didn't say, just that I had to call him as soon as I got the message."

"When was the last time you spoke to him?"

"Probably about nine months ago. You might have seen me leaving the court with him two years ago, after the verdict."

He nodded and asked, "What do you think it will be about?"

"It must be Vicky."

"You'll have to call him back some time, because if he really wants to speak, he can track you down if you have your phone on, but let's wait until we've got what we want today."

"OK," I said as I switched my phone off.

"What are our plans for today?" I asked.

"We'll check out of here in around thirty minutes and then pick up Sonia, who will make the call. I hear that she's good."

"Why does she have to come with us, could you not just get her to phone Doug?"

"No, we need her with us just in case we need to react and pass messages to her."

"OK, no worries."

"We'll go the café..."

"The Bridge Café?" I interjected.

"Yes, we'll have a coffee, watch the industrial estate and take it from there."

"David, one obvious flaw in the plan that has just dawned on me is that even if Doug falls for the phone call and heads off, there will probably be an apprentice still in the building and possibly customers as well."

"Well, that's why we stake it out first. Sonia doesn't phone him until we know the coast is clear. If there is an apprentice then use your good brain, Professor, to work out a way to get his toolbox."

We went back to our rooms, and as I gathered my stuff, I realised that David was involved in this because of his brother. He was no doubt involved in criminal activities, but at a comparatively lowly level, and his experience of planning something like this was probably less than mine. That realisation had occurred too late to affect our current plan, apart from making me think on how best to nab the toolbox should I manage to get into the garage while Doug was out.

I met David back in the foyer. He went to reception to check out and we then walked the short distance to the car park. Neither of us said anything. David started up the car and we were on our way. "Where are we heading?" I asked.

"Not far."

We drove on in silence and then the text alert went on David's phone. He briefly looked at it and said, "She's ready."

We drove for another five minutes and then pulled into the car park of a supermarket. A middle-aged woman with sharp features and dyed blonde hair walked over to the car and got in the back seat. She would have looked at home in *EastEnders*.

"Hi," she said flatly.

I turned round, smiled and replied, "Hi." She looked blankly at me with her hard eyes. I felt uncomfortable as I turned to face the front, and David didn't help as he said nothing. I didn't like her perfume, which I knew would give me a sore head. We continued on our way and were soon in familiar territory. My heart rate increased, and the butterflies started swirling about in my stomach as we passed the Nelson Leisure Centre and headed towards the industrial estate and the café opposite. "There is some waste ground up ahead that you can park in," I told David. We approached the café and saw that it was boarded up and looked like it had been that way for a while.

"There goes my coffee," David said dryly.

"If you take a right here as if you are going into the industrial estate, there's a lane immediately to the right where we can park and watch the garage," I told him. He followed my instructions and we stopped before a row of wooden lock-ups from where we could see the garage through a metal fence.

"OK, this will have to do. Let's see what's happening," David said. We watched the garage for fifteen minutes and didn't see any activity. It was open, the two roller shutter doors were up, but we couldn't make out anyone either in the office or the workshop. I put the window down and thought I could hear radio music being played. Just then I heard a ringing sound. It was the garage phone being amplified by a large bell on the wall of the workshop. A figure made its way into the office and picked up the phone. It had been a while since I had seen him, but I was sure the figure was Doug. He spoke for around a minute and then made his way back to the workshop.

"OK, Sonia, go for it," David instructed.

She keyed in the number, and as she did so David told her to remember and hide the call. "Don't teach your granny to suck eggs," was her response. She put the phone to her ear. Seconds later I could hear the workshop bell ring again and Doug make his way back to the office with his body language suggesting that he was getting pissed off at the interruptions. I could just hear Doug say *Zach's Garage* on Sonia's phone when he answered.

"Hi, I wonder if you can help me?" Sonia simpered. She certainly sounded better than she looked. "I'm in a bit of bother. I have had a breakdown not far from you and wonder if you could come out and have a look. My husband is away on business and I've taken his Jag. He's not going to be happy about that as it's his pride and joy. I just wondered if you could come and have a look. I would make it worth your while."

She was good. I could only make out Doug's head so I couldn't read his body language. Hopefully there would be a stirring in his loins any second now. I couldn't hear any response from Doug because Sonia held the phone tight to her ear. Suddenly she said, "Shit. He said he doesn't do pickups and hung up on me."

I could see Doug still holding the phone. The call had lasted for about a minute and now he made his way back to the workshop.

"Well, that's that then. What the fuck do we do now?" I said with a resigned sigh.

"Mind your language, there's a lady present," David replied. His expression told me he was serious.

"OK, sorry, but what do we do now?"

"Christ, you two ain't exactly the Krays, are you?" Sonia said dismissively. "Up till now you haven't told me what you want from the garage, just that you want this Doug character out of the way. Why don't you tell me what it is and maybe I can come up with an idea? I've been round the block you know."

I didn't doubt it. She had probably been round it several times.

"It's a toolbox," I said. "A red toolbox, a bit bashed and about this length," I held out my hands, "and this depth. It will be quite heavy. There's something in the box that we need. It will be well hidden, so we need the full toolbox."

"OK," she said, "and do you definitely know it's in there?"

"No," I said.

"Christ, we're doing well, ain't we," she said dryly. "So, the first thing we need to do is find out if the toolbox is there. Correct?"

"Yeah," I replied.

"Right, you two get out of the car and make yourself scarce. I'm heading over there to have a look."

Finally, David spoke. "Slow down, lady, what do you propose?"

"What I propose is that I drive over there in this car, flutter my eyelashes, act helpless and ask if I can book an appointment. Once that's done, I will act all coy like and ask to use the ladies. On my way there and back I'll have a look for your toolbox."

It was probably the best we could do under the circumstances, but I couldn't help thinking that Sonia sounded better than she looked, and I couldn't see Doug acting all chivalrous towards her.

"Is there a ladies in there?" David asked me.

"There is definitely a customer toilet," I replied.

"Come on then, you two – out," Sonia instructed, and we dutifully complied.

"Don't overstay your welcome, and call or text if you need. We'll wait there," David said, pointing at a row of wooden garages. This brought back vivid memories from over two years ago when I was hiding from Doug after having broken into his garage. At that point I had been working with Vicky, who I thought was on my side. I banished this memory from my mind as we stood hidden behind the garages and watched Sonia drive towards Zach's Garage.

"We need to think what we do if she confirms the toolbox is there," I said somewhat unnecessarily.

"Also, what we do if it isn't," David replied. Good point, our Plan B was so thin that it made Plan A seem like *The Italian Job*.

Sonia had parked in front of the open shutter doors with the car facing out from the garage. I could see her in the office. It had taken Doug some time to make it there and I sensed the interruptions were frustrating him. This gave me a thought. "How can the garage function if the chief mechanic is always being called to answer the phone or deal with customers?" I asked.

"With difficulty," David replied.

"Exactly. I bet you the apprentice is off today, and Doug is covering everything himself. If the toolbox is in there, we'll just need to distract Doug and get it." As I was saying this, I could now only see Doug in the office so Sonia must have gone to the toilet. I kept checking my watch, and when it showed she had been over five minutes I started to get nervous.

"What do you think is happening in there?"

"Don't know," David replied. "We'll give it another couple of minutes before we do anything." Just as he said that, we saw Sonia getting in the car and slowly driving away. She gave a toot and a wave to the office as she left. She drove along the lane and stopped but kept the engine running. We got in quickly and she drew away.

"Well?" David asked. He was sitting in the front seat.

"Bingo!" she said as she manoeuvred the car into a parking position on the other side of the garages from where we couldn't be seen. She took out her phone, opened it up and showed us a photo of the toolbox. It was

sitting on a workbench and it looked exactly as David had described it.

Chapter Thirty-Nine

"Good," said David. "Is Doug the only one in the garage?"

"Yeah, he's the only one. When I came out of the toilet, which is disgusting by the way, and no way was I baring my arse to it," she was providing too much detail for me, "I went back into the reception area and there was no sign of Doug. That made it easy for me to have an excuse to wander into the workshop on the basis that I was looking for him to say thanks and bye. I saw the toolbox, but not him. I take it he must have been under a car. The downside is that the toolbox is at the far side of the workshop, so it won't be easy to do a snatch and beat a hasty retreat."

"I seem to remember a fire exit on the back wall — is that right?" I asked.

"Yeah, it is," she replied. "It would be a good getaway option, but you would need to cross the workshop to get the toolbox first."

"Do you think Doug would recognise you?" I asked David.

"Of course, I'm Eustace's brother, I gave him the toolbox. He's not going to forget me that quickly."

I felt a bit stupid with my last question, so I tried to redeem myself with my next contribution.

"There's a pile of pallets in the yard next door. Let's set them alight to act as a distraction. Sonia, you drive back to the garage and tell Doug you have lost something... your purse or phone or whatever, and ask if you can have a look in the toilets. Under the cover from the smoke from the pallets, we," I said, pointing at David, "kick in the fire exit, grab the toolbox and escape under the mesh fence. Hopefully the fire brigade will arrive as we are leaving, which will further distract Doug."

"Full of bright ideas ain't we?" was Sonia's sarcastic response.

Her attitude was bugging me. "Can you come up with anything better then?" I asked accusingly.

"How do you and him break down the door and get under the fence?" she asked.

"We go to a merchant and buy a set of wire cutters and a crowbar," I responded forcibly.

"You're overthinking it," she replied.

"What do you mean?"

"Setting a fire is too unpredictable, and will the smoke distract anyone? More chance it will attract people either to gawp or for do-gooders to help. Breaking in through the fire exit door makes sense as you can quickly and easily get the toolbox. Getting in and out of the yard under the fence and back to the car in the lane should be the plan."

"So what do we do instead of a fire then?" I asked sarcastically.

She ignored my tone and added, "Like I said, when I came out of the toilet Doug was already back in the workshop. That gave me time to have a brief look round the office. I found his bookings diary and took a few pictures." She took out her phone and scrolled through a few, which were pictures of the jobs lined up for Doug over the next few days.

"So, what do we do with them?" I asked.

Before she could reply, David said, "Pretend to be one of these customers and get into a discussion and keep Doug on the phone."

"You've got it in one, Einstein," she said. "We will take the car to the lane at the back of the workshop. You cut the fence, I'll phone, when he answers I'll signal and keep him in discussion while you two break the door down and get the toolbox. You should be able to do that in two minutes. David, if you stay as lookout – you," she pointed to me, "get in and out pronto. I'll signal to David that the call is over, and he can let you know that he'll be on his way back.

"Right, let's get the tools," she said looking at me.

I nodded. I didn't like her attitude, but she knew what she was doing, and her plan was better. Just one thing though. "Have you decided who you are going to pretend to be from the list? Does it make a difference?" I asked.

"Yes. I'll choose what looks like a big job and big payer to get Doug very nervous about me pulling the plug and leaving a gap, so it makes sense to choose one from the next couple of days."

We approached and parked in the same supermarket car park as before. David handed me five twenty-pound notes and told me to get the gear.

"Are you not coming with me?" I asked in a slight panic.

"No need. One person is less noticeable then two."

"What am I asking for? I know nothing about tools."

David sighed and started playing about on his phone. "Have you got a pen?" he asked Sonia. She handed one over along with a small notepad. She was the only one of us with any sort of organisational skills. David wrote down four codes. The first two were circled. "Try these first," he told me.

"What do you mean, do I not just go in and look for the tools?"

"No, it's like Argos, you key in the codes and place your order then pick it up at the desk."

"OK – well which is which? Just in case I need to ask for help."

He wrote *cutters* against the first code and *crowbar* against the second. "Don't ask for help. If they don't have it, try the code below. Understood?"

"Yeah."

"OK. Get going."

I felt even carrying out such mundane tasks as buying tools was out of my depth. I had swallowed a few of my over-the-counter anxiety suppressors at breakfast and took in another two as I made my way into the shop. I tried to appear normal and went straight to a console, keyed in the codes and luckily both items were in stock. I confirmed my order, went up to the counter and paid. There was no banter from the guy serving me and within seconds I was walking back to the car with a set of wire cutters and a crowbar. I got in, and David turned round as Sonia started the car, and said, "Let's have a look."

I took the items out the bag, and he nodded at me. "Just the job. Have you decided who you're going to be?" David then asked Sonia.

"Yeah, there's a BMW 2011 1 Series 118d that's getting a new dual mass flywheel fitted tomorrow. Doug has pencilled in a price of thirteen hundred pounds. I'm going to ask why he isn't fitting a new clutch at the same time and how can he charge so much just for a DMF?" David nodded approvingly. I didn't know what she was talking about, she could have been speaking in Dutch.

"I don't want to be sexist," he said, "but how many women know about cars? Will he not be suspicious if you're asking anything technical?"

"You are being sexist," she said. "Leave it with me. I want that bastard on the end of a phone for over five minutes to give you a chance."

We were approaching the lane we had parked in earlier and slowly made our way to the area of fence nearest to the back of Zach's Garage. I recognised the unit next to the garage which had the pile of pallets I had been thinking of setting on fire. My nerves were racing and I felt like I was in a Guy Ritchie film just before the action kicked off.

"Right boys, go for it," Sonia instructed. I was warming to her because at least she knew what she was doing and had a confidence in her ability. We opened the car doors smoothly, got out and approached the fence. I was carrying the fence cutters and David had the crowbar. He had it up the sleeve of his jacket with the head resting in the palm of his hand. "I'll walk along to the end of the lane and back pretending to be on the phone to look normal. You start cutting and just do enough to let us get under," he told me.

"OK," I said as David walked away.

The wire cutters were surprisingly efficient, and I quickly made enough space for us to get through. My anxiety level was sky high and increased because I wanted David back straight away; he had obviously underestimated my fence cutting skills. He duly made his way back a minute later, signalled to Sonia and we were off.

I pulled the fence apart and scrambled through and he followed me. We stood up and walked as nonchalantly as we could towards the fire exit of the garage. When we were there, we looked over to Sonia. She picked up her phone and held it close to her face. I felt that I could hear my heartbeat. I could definitely hear the bell ring on the workshop wall. David looked cool, like he was ready. Christ knows what I looked like. The bell stopped and we looked over at Sonia; we could see her talking and she gave a thumbs up.

David used the handle end of the crowbar to use as a lever and got into the gap between the door and the frame on the hinged side. He might not have been great at planning, but his lifetime of petty crime showed as he made short work of getting the implement prised between the door and the frame. I was watching him and kept looking over to Sonia, who was doing lots of talking while giving me positive signs at the same time. With all his body weight, David used the crowbar as a lever and created enough space for me to get my arm through the gap and hit the push bar on the middle of the door and open it. Without a word, I opened the door out towards me and went into the workshop. There was no sight nor sound of Doug, and all that I could hear was a radio playing. I looked to my left along the back wall and could see the toolbox sitting on the shelf just as described by Sonia. I quickly went over, picked it up and carried it with both hands to the door. It was bulky and heavy, and in that short distance I banged my legs several times and nearly dropped it. My sweaty hands and rapidly increasing heartbeat didn't help matters. I went through the open door and kept going to the hole in the fence. To my relief Sonia was still speaking on the phone.

David was behind me. I think he was trying to close the door as best he could from outside to make it look normal at least from a distance, which might buy us a bit more time. Just as I was going through the fence, Sonia put her phone down and signalled for us to hurry up. I scrambled through, bent over and picked up the toolbox. David was right behind me and nearly knocked me over. We strode to the car and David ran round the front and got in beside Sonia. I pulled open the back door and heaved the toolbox onto the back seat, at which point somebody shouted, "Stop!"

I looked round and there was a male dog walker capturing me on his phone. I tried to cover my face as I got in the car, which took off before I could close the door. Sonia had us down the lane in seconds and then pulling into traffic on the main road. "What was that?" she said to me, looking in the rear-view mirror.

"Some bastard with his dog saw us and was filming me getting in the car," I said.

"Shit!" she said.

"Don't worry about that," David said, "let's keep moving." A few minutes later we were back again at the supermarket car park. Sonia parked and turned off the car.

"Thanks," I said as she got out. She winked and walked towards the shop. David hadn't said anything. He got out, climbed into the driver's seat and started the car. I was about to open the toolbox for an initial look while we were driving but he told me not to as we weren't going far and didn't need to draw attention to ourselves.

My heart rate was still going, but it was more now in anticipation than fear. In fact, I felt exhilarated. Our plan had come off and we might have the polonium. The only downside was the *might have* element. I couldn't wait to see if we did indeed have it. David drove in silence for a few minutes and then said, "Nearly there."

We skirted the park where I used to jog, in what felt like a previous life, and went in an entrance adjacent to it, which led to lots of allotments, and parked the car at the side of the road. "Let's go," he said quietly, and we got out with me humping the toolbox as we walked towards the row of allotments. We got to the third one and hadn't passed anyone; there was someone further up who hadn't appeared to see us. We approached a small hut in allotment three and David took a key out and opened it. "This was Eustace's," he said.

Well, that was a surprise. "I never knew he had an allotment. He could have used this as a hiding place," I said.

"Not secure enough, "David replied, "and I searched it before I came to you for answers."

"OK," I acknowledged.

He closed the door and signalled for me to open the toolbox. I set it on the floor and opened it up. A couple of the tools from the top shelves fell out as I opened them up. I hurriedly got all of them out then picked the metal box up and held it upside down to ensure there was nothing else in it. A couple of screws and a small role of grubby tape fell to the floor and that was it. I felt for any fastening locking or unlocking devices inside and outside, concentrating on the base, but couldn't find anything. I handed it to David. He couldn't find anything either.

"The last box was soldered. He might have done the same here," I said.

"You might be right," he answered. "Give me a hammer and a chisel."

David then got me to hold the toolbox hard against the floor as he kneeled and hammered the chisel along the junction of the side and base of it. Eventually the side started to come away and soon it was a case of pulling it away to leave the base. When we had separated the base, it was clear that we had found a hiding place as it was around two inches thick and obviously a false bottom.

David stopped to mop his brow and catch his breath. "Give them here," I said, and took my turn with the tools to try and break the seal.

"Wait a minute," David said, "how may toolboxes have a cover on their base? As he said this, he took it off me and dragged a chisel across the vinyl cover. It created a line which allowed him to tear across it, and after a few attempts all the vinyl was off and there it was: a small slide mechanism.

"He always was a devious little shit!" David said with a wistful smile.

He slid the mechanism then opened the hidden compartment, and sitting inside the base was a small box. I had seen one of these boxes before and knew what it would contain. Four small metallic-looking bottles sitting in a hard foam base. We looked at each other and both gave small smiles of relief.

"OK, let's leave the toolbox here. We need to get away," David said quietly.

We locked the hut and went back to the car.

"What about the guy that filmed us?" I asked.

"Don't worry, he's small fry. This is a hired car in a false name, and we're leaving it soon. A theft of a toolbox from a garage won't make it into the local paper."

"I suppose," I said, feeling slightly relieved. "Where to now?"

"Kings Cross. We're off to meet the boss."

"OK," I said. I was perhaps beginning to get used to this criminal life, I thought. The reason for this was that I didn't need my anxiety tablets and had sprouted an erection that could support a wet duffle coat. I wonder

what Sonia would have said to that.

Chapter Forty

David calmly drove through the lunchtime congestion to the drop-off point at Kings Cross and we dumped the hire car, went through the formalities and then walked the five minutes or so to the station.

"Where are we going?" I asked.

"Northallerton."

"Where's that?"

"North," he answered unhelpfully.

We walked up to a ticket machine, where he put his card in and collected our tickets.

"Well done, lady," he said, looking at the tickets.

"What do you mean?"

"Sandra, the boss's secretary. She's put us in first class. We're on the three thirty."

I looked at my watch. It was just after one thirty, but it felt so much later.

"I know what you are going to say," he said. "Let's go for a beer!" he added with a grin.

We went out of the station to a large ornate bar between Kings Cross and St Pancras. It was mainly frequented by office workers with very few obvious travellers present. I was gasping for a pint and went looking for a table while David went to the bar. I managed to get a corner table in an alcove, which was perfect. David arrived with the beers as well as crisps and peanuts.

"Just as well the boss is paying me well," he said, "because this cost a fortune."

"Am I meeting the boss?" I asked.

"You sure are, we're going to his house."

"In Northampton?"

"No, Northallerton."

"Yeah, got it."

I lowered my voice. "David, I travelled on the Tube with polonium the last time, and afterwards I read up about it and just about shat myself. Are you aware of how dangerous this stuff is and the risks we are taking?"

"Look, man, we have no choice. We'll have a seat and table in first class. I'll keep the box on me at all times and we'll try and avoid others."

"But we're going into first class and we'll be stinking. We haven't changed for a couple of days."

"Sandra will sort us out when we get there. In the meantime, I'll get us some deodorant and aftershave from the chemist in the station."

"OK, sounds like a plan. Do you want another?" He looked at my empty glass and his drink, which was barely touched.

"You must be thirsty, man."

I returned with another beer and a large brandy for him. "I didn't ask for that," he said.

"Executive decision," I replied.

"The boss won't be happy with me drinking on the job, especially with our dangerous cargo."

"When do we get there?"

"Just after six."

"That's ages."

"Well, no more for both of us after these."

"OK," I agreed reluctantly. "I'd better phone DI Stevenson," I said. "Are you OK with that?"

"Yes, but then switch the phone off. Keep the call short."

I took out my phone, switched it on and noticed another missed call from a withheld number. I played back Stevenson's message, noted the number he had given in his message and then called it. It was answered on the second ring.

"Greg – where have you been?" Stevenson asked.

"Trying to lie low," I said.

"It's about Vicky," he said.

"I thought it would be," I replied with a sigh.

"She's dead."

"What?" I exclaimed.

"Vicky. She's dead."

"For fuck sake," I said a bit too loudly, which caused a couple at the next table to turn and look at me. David signalled for me to quieten down.

"How?" I added.

"It was suicide, Greg. She knocked back a bottle of scotch and dozens of pills."

"Whereabouts? Where did you find her?"

"In a hostel in Ealing Broadway."

"Who found her?"

"The cleaner."

I found it hard to believe that she had killed herself. I remember at uni Vicky hated whisky, and once, when we had a trip to Edinburgh at New Year, she drank a lot but never touched any whisky. However, she had changed so much over the years, maybe this was another change caused by her mind flipping. I realised I hadn't read the email she sent when I arrived in Tenerife. It was still in my deleted folder.

"I was going to call you," I lied to him. "She turned up on my doorstep a few days ago and blackmailed me. She had kidnapped my boss and was going to have her killed unless I did stuff for her."

"What stuff?"

Time to get creative. "She wanted me to find Piotr. She knew about Brygida and how I was friendly with her."

"So, what did you do?" he asked.

"I tried but couldn't find anything, so I warned Brygida then went into hiding," I said convincingly.

"Where have you been?"

"It doesn't matter right now where I've been, but I think my boss may still be held, because Vicky had at least one accomplice. I think she may be in the West London Action Group warehouse at the back of the office in Uxbridge Road. Her name is Maggie Gray. Can you help?"

"You should have told me earlier."

"How could I? I didn't know Vicky was dead. I was running away from her."

"Right, we'll check this out. Where are you?"

"I'm in town. I'm heading back to my flat soon."

"Keep your phone switched on and I'll call later."

"OK," I said, and hung up.

"Vicky's dead," I said to David flatly.

"Good, the bitch that killed my brother has got what she deserved," he said quietly and evenly.

It wasn't actually Vicky that killed Eustace, but I wasn't going to say that just now. With finding the polonium and Vicky being dead, the chances of returning to some form of normality seemed to be improving. Hopefully Stevenson would find Maggie, I thought, as I tried to work out how long she had been held for and realised that it was almost a week.

I hated so much about what Vicky had done to me. Things that had seriously screwed me up and would affect me for the rest of my days. I still couldn't comprehend how she set me up for Clinkie's boys, but did I want her dead? No, I don't think I did. I went into my deleted items, found her email and read it. I then read it again more slowly. My eyes misted up, and by the time I had read it for a second time I was trembling.

"Read this, read this," I blurted as I handed the phone to David.

He read it and said, "Why should she tell you all this then top herself?"

"That's a good question. You should ask Clinkie Moore," I replied.

"You think they did it?"

"I'm sure they did," I said as I switched off my phone.

Chapter Forty-One

We got on the train fifteen minutes before departure smelling heavily of aftershave and deodorant, which we wore to mask our body odour. Our carriage was at the front of the train and we were the first people in it. By the time the train pulled out of the station there were only another three people in the carriage, so it remained nice and quiet. David said to me in a hushed tone, "Try not to attract attention. Let's stay in our seats as much as possible. It will take about two and a half hours, so try and relax. The boss will be pleased to see you."

I tried to follow David's advice, but I couldn't relax. The thought of Vicky dead was hard to take in. There was still a bit of me that felt sorry for her, and I read and re-read her message, which convinced me that she was not going to kill herself. It would be useful for Stevenson to see the message, but I wasn't going to do that until after my Northallerton visit and meeting with the boss. Despite Stevenson's request, I switched the phone off and stared forlornly out of the window. We were in the front seats on either side of a table with David looking down the carriage and me facing the direction of travel.

I decided that I must visit Vicky's family and tell them of the email she sent me. She may have contacted them before she died, but I doubted it.

It seemed like she was laying her cards on the table for me first. If I had answered her message when she sent it, I asked myself would she still be alive? I assured myself that my previous thoughts were correct, and she didn't kill herself; she was killed. David was clear on that as well. It was time to drop Clinkie in the shit. Not a thought that I would have considered twenty-four hours ago, but now if I was in the good books with the boss, not such a suicidal manoeuvre as it once would have been.

I looked across the table at David and he was busy on his phone. I switched my phone on to read Vicky's message again. There was a missed call and a voicemail. It was from Stevenson telling me to call him on the same number as before. I asked David if it was OK to call and he said it was if I kept my voice down and didn't get emotional. I had saved Stevenson's number and I felt my heart race as I searched for it and pressed dial. He answered straight away. "We've got Maggie. She's been taken to hospital for checking over. She seemed to be all right physically, very disturbed emotionally."

"Great, well not great about how she's feeling, but great that you got her. Where was she?" I replied clumsily.

"Where you said."

"Did you catch anyone?"

"No. It looked like she had been left on her own for a least a couple of days. You can imagine the state she was in."

"I can."

"Now we need to catch the bastards who did this and nail them."

"But I've already told you it was Vicky and an accomplice called Di. That's why she turned up at my door."

"We need to speak, Greg."

"Of course. Can I see Maggie?"

"Not yet."

"Maybe tomorrow?"

"We have to see how she is and what the doctors say and see if she wants any visitors. But I want to speak to you."

I guessed I would be staying the night in Northallerton, so I suggested that I met Stevenson the following afternoon. I suggested the pub I had met him in over two years previously when he told me of Kev Osborne's death. We arranged to meet at six o'clock the next day.

David had been listening in. "They found your boss then?" he asked.

"They have, thank God. As far as I can see, with Vicky gone and most of Clinkie's men, the only people that need to be dealt with now are Clinkie, his daughter and Di, who was Vicky's accomplice," I said quietly but excitedly.

"Don't try and overthink things just now," David said without looking up from his phone. I resumed staring out the window as I contemplated the good news about Maggie but worried about the impact this would have on such a nice, trusting, genuinely good person. The thought struck me that if it wasn't for me then this would never have happened. Just like if it wasn't for me Aunt Isa wouldn't have been kidnapped. It was nearly dark, and I could see my reflection in the window that there were tears in my eyes. David had told me not to get emotional, but I couldn't help it. I got up and made my way to the toilet, locked the door and burst into tears. I heaved several large sobs, which drained the strength from me as I sat on the toilet, head in hands. As they subsided and I started to regain my composure, I thought of my family, my life and the series of interconnected occurrences that had caused such a perfect storm.

I stood up, had a pee, washed my hands and face and went back to my seat with a resolution that meeting the boss was the first step in taking control of my life again. David looked up from his phone. He had been unusually busy on it and I wondered what he was up to.

An announcement informed us that the next stop was Northallerton. I didn't know what to expect when we got off the train but felt oddly relaxed. We had the polonium and Maggie was safe, although I suddenly thought of Brygida and Ania, who would be arriving in Tenerife in the next few days. I asked David about that and he told me to ask the boss. My sense of relaxation thus passed quickly because their fate, along with Cassie's, would probably be determined by the meeting I was soon to have.

I followed David out of the train. It was now dark and I hadn't got much of a view of Northallerton as we approached it, but it seemed like a pleasant enough market town. There were a surprising number of people getting off here and we followed the line off the platform through the station and to the car park outside.

David went straight to a dark blue Land Rover and we got in. He didn't exchange any words as he got into the front passenger seat. I sat in the back and the driver started the car. There was no music playing and I felt uncomfortable with the silence. David wasn't on his phone and looked straight ahead. Fortunately, the drive took only about fifteen minutes and we approached a place called East Cowton. We passed through it and then took a turning into a lane, drove for another few minutes and reached our destination. It was a steading-type development, not dissimilar to Clinkie's. The car stopped, the driver made no effort to offer any assistance, so we got out and walked towards the house. As we approached, the front door was opened, and a man indicated for us to follow him. We walked along the corridor of the tastefully decorated house. He knocked on a door and was told to come in. We followed him into a large lounge that was set up with the functionality of an office. This included a big desk that faced across the room towards bay windows with a panoramic view. The man sitting behind the desk got up and walked round it. I would guess that he was mid to late fifties with neatly trimmed thinning black hair which had a hint of grey at the edges.

"So, you must be Greg. I am so happy to see you," he said as he shook my hand and smiled. "And David, we have talked and sent messages, but it is good to finally see you in the flesh. Have a seat."

We both sat down, and the man who led us in stood at the doorway.

"Before we get down to business, would you like a drink?"

Music to my ears. "Can I have a beer please?" I asked.

"Of course, and you, David?"

"Just a water please, Sir Michael."

Sir Michael? What were we dealing with here? Sir Michael walked to his desk and pressed a button on his phone and said, "Sandra, please bring in a beer, a water and my usual snifter. Thanks." A minute later, an attractive elegant woman in a suit who appeared to be in her late thirties arrived and gave us our drinks. Sir Michael's snifter looked like whisky and ice.

"Thanks," he said as Sandra silently left. "So, David, show me what you have got," he asked benignly.

David took out the metal container from an inside pocket of his jacket, then laid it on a coffee table and opened the box. Sir Michael looked at the contents but didn't pick the box up. He signalled to the man at the door, who came over, took some pictures of it and then returned to his position.

Sir Michael then sat down in a comfortable-looking armchair and said to me as he contemplated his drink, "Now, Greg, I want you to tell me the whole story from when you found Eustace," he looked up at David as he said this, "until the minute you walked into this room. I have got all night, so you don't need to rush and don't miss anything out."

I started and recounted my story. The same one I had told to David and Pink Shirt yesterday, although I could now add that DI Stevenson had contacted me, told me that Vicky was dead, and I had told him about Maggie my boss and that she had been rescued. I told Sir Michael how bad I felt about Maggie and that I had asked Stevenson if I could visit her. It took me about forty-five minutes and Sir Michael didn't stop me once. When I had finished, he thanked me very much and said, "You have had a hell of a time." He had a soft steely voice and I tried to place his accent. There was a hint of Scottish, but worn away perhaps after living in England for a long time.

"What Vicky and her accomplices have done to you, and it looks like they have had their just deserts, has been unfortunate to say the least."

Well, that was one way of looking at it.

"I don't think for a second that she killed herself. She was killed on the orders of Clinkie Moore. I have been aware of you since you found the first lot of product over two years ago," he said as he pointed to the polonium. "Not just me, but several people in the same… ah *profession*…

"From the moment that Vicky Monteith was jailed, there have been moves afoot to track down the missing batch. You are absolutely correct that your boss being kidnapped is because of you." His eyes narrowed slightly. "Clinkie Moore had decided to join the big boys and kidnapping your boss was his message."

I looked blankly at him.

"My name is Sir Michael Gray and Maggie Gray is my daughter."

Chapter Forty-Two

Over the past couple of years, I have become used to surprises, but this was right up there at the top.

"Really?" was all that I could say.

"You have had a hectic few days," Sir Michael said. "Why don't you freshen up, and we can resume our conversation over dinner?"

He was so polite and apparently nice; it was hard to think of him as a crime lord, and he was also so different from Maggie. Sandra appeared and Sir Michael said, "Miss Courtney will show you to your room."

She gave a slight smile, which I returned and then followed her out of the lounge and along a corridor to an extension housing a couple of bedrooms that looked out onto a small patio. Sandra looked so efficient and well-presented that I felt like a tramp in comparison. I could detect a subtle perfume from her which made me feel self-conscious of how I must smell. "This one's yours," she said. "There's an en suite so you can freshen up." She pointed to a pile of leisure clothes on the bed. "Sorry, that's all we have just now. I will arrange some new clothes for tomorrow." She pointed to the phone beside the bed. "When you are ready for dinner, dial zero to let me know."

Before I could say anything, she turned and was gone. I tore off my clothes and went straight to the shower. There was an assortment of luxury body washes and shampoos that I used with casual abandonment. I checked myself in the mirror when I got out of the shower and was surprised that I didn't look too bad. I had caught some sun in Tenerife, which helped make me look a bit healthier than I probably was. I hadn't shaved for a few days now, but the stubble seemed to compliment my new tan.

The clothes that I had been left were boxers, cotton tracksuit trousers and an XL polo shirt. I put them on and was a bit swamped by the shirt, but everything else fitted reasonably well. It felt good to be wearing clean clothes. The trousers had pockets, but they weren't very deep, so I decided to leave my wallet, phone and passport in the room. There was a pair of open-backed slippers for me to wear on my feet. Sandra had said she would fix me up with clothes for the morning but hadn't asked my sizes. I guessed that as she was the go-to person in the organisation, whether it be for a flight booking, pair of shoes or anything in-between, she would just know what to order.

Although it felt good to be clean and in fresh clothes, I suddenly felt incredibly tired and was tempted to lie back on the bed. I resisted the temptation because I was also very hungry and keen to find out more about Maggie and where I fitted in the picture with Sir Michael. I picked up the phone and called. Within seconds Sandra appeared, and I followed her to the dining room. She was very attractive, which was masked somewhat by her business like appearance, and I was sure that when she kicked back she would be great company. A bit of me had hoped that she would at least have commented on me looking a bit better now or similar small talk, but she said nothing.

We went into the dining room, which was an open-plan configuration that led to a very large kitchen complete with matching Agas complimented by tasteful kitchen accessories.

"Ah! Greg, welcome," Sir Michael said in his soft voice. "Are you a wine drinker?"

"Yes," I replied.

"Good, Sandra, please get the Château Grand-Puy-Lacoste. Have a seat, Greg, we will eat in thirty minutes."

I could smell the aroma of meat and veg cooking, which got my juices flowing.

"You look a bit better," Sir Michael said with a smile.

"Thanks, I feel it. Is David joining us?"

"No, David has done a good job and you will see him in the morning," he said lightly.

Sandra arrived with two glasses of wine, which she handed to us and put the bottle on the small table near to Sir Michael. My glass was barely half-full, which was disappointing, but I suppose this was decorum. I was still finding it difficult to get my head round the fact that Sir Michael and Clinkie were basically in the same line of work. Sandra went to the kitchen and pulled a screen across which separated the rooms and then left from the dining room side.

"So, Greg, what are your thoughts?" Sir Michael started.

"Well, as I said before, Maggie is a great boss and a great person, and I am so pleased she is safe. I really want to see her as soon as possible because what she has been through will have been traumatic. She will need lots of help to recover." I could see a slight pulsing on Sir Michael's neck when I said it. "Sorry if you think I'm being rude, but I find it hard to believe that she is your daughter, as you appear so different."

He gave a slight smile and said with a sigh, "Yes, you're right. She has always had a rebellious streak. As a teenager it was ban the bomb, Anti-Nazi League and that sort of thing. All that increased when she went to university and became a tree-hugging *Guardian* women's page devotee.

She never liked my line of work." I looked at him quizzically. "Greg, I am a reputable businessman. I started off in scrap metal in Lanarkshire then branched out into garages before moving down here and securing a large share of the car insurance market. You have to keep moving and adapting as competitors come along and new ways of working evolve. I branched out to home insurance and travel cover, then when it got too congested, I moved into debt recovery." I could see why Maggie didn't want to follow her father into the family business. I was thinking of saying that when Sir Michael added, "Of course, coming from my background and working in the areas that I have done, you build up rivals and enemies. You need allies and you need to know your enemies. That's how I have got to this position and how I intend to stay here. It sometimes means working on the fringes when required and calling in favours. That's why we needed the product."

I nodded. "What is your actual business now? What is debt recovery?"

"You know when someone parks in a supermarket and stays too long, well they are issued with a fine. The process is contracted out to companies to identify the car and owner and then pursue them for payment of the fine. It will start off at say thirty pounds but double after twenty-eight days and so on, so it is in their interest to pay it quickly. My company, Lukrace Assets, is one of the largest in the UK. It is recognised as a standard bearer in the industry and the reason for my knighthood last year."

I found it all very depressing that a business built on harassment and misery, staffed mainly, I guessed, by minimum wage call handlers, had a guy at the top who trousered millions and got a knighthood to boot.

"There have been ups and downs, but on the whole my business life has been a success. Where I have regrets is my family life, and yes, of course, it has been impacted by my work. I have loved and always will love Maggie. We don't see eye to eye, and in fact we haven't spoken since I was informed of my knighthood. I expected that she would have been pleased for me, even if she doesn't agree with the honours system, but oh no, she gave me a tirade and said that she would have no more to do with me if I accepted it. It was always Maggie and me arguing and her mother acting as peacemaker, but Lillian died of breast cancer three years ago, so she wasn't around to see me knighted or keep our family together."

I couldn't think of anything meaningful to say and so asked, "Do you have any other children?"

"No, Maggie is an only child," he said as he refilled our glasses. Thankfully he didn't stick to protocol and filled my glass to the brim.

I took a large swallow and savoured the drink. I was feeling a bit lightheaded, caused no doubt by lack of food, stress, tiredness and now this lovely wine. Perhaps it was this that caused me to say, "I have a feeling that you and Clinkie have history. You mentioned Lanarkshire earlier."

"You've got it in one," he said. "He's a mean, vicious, jealous bastard. We're both from Carluke and we've known each other most of our lives. He's a bit younger than me and as I was getting things going, he was starting out. To be honest I made it difficult for him as I didn't want the competition, so I used my influence with local councillors and friends in the police to take an interest in his affairs. We had a major falling out many years ago, and even with me moving south he has never let it slip. His problem is that he may be ambitious, but he likes publicity, is one dimensional and easy to read."

I waited for him to tell me more, but he moved at a tangent. "This, this," he looked for the right word, "this situation has been of Clinkie's doing and is ultimately what will finish him."

I waited for him to say more but he didn't. "I am meeting the police tomorrow," I said. "DI Stevenson."

"I know, and that isn't a problem. In fact, it is part of the solution," he replied. That made me feel better.

"I want you to tell him about Vicky and her relationship with Clinkie. Tell him about Clinkie Moore's daughter in prison, tell him about Di, tell him about Piotr and Brygida and Cassie. Don't mention Tenerife and don't mention the product, of course."

It was strange, as it was almost like an actor not mentioning *Macbeth* and calling it the *Scottish Play*. Sir Michael had not once called it polonium; it was always *the product*. Perhaps he thought that if he mentioned it, it would bring him bad luck and his house of cards would come tumbling down.

"Stevenson said to me it was suicide," I said.

"Typical plod," he replied. "Show him your email from Vicky and drop the seed that it was Clinkie who did it. Also, I want you to get access to Maggie and pass a message from me to her.

"What will happen to Brygida, Piotr, Ania and Cassie?"

"Don't worry. We have kept Piotr and Cassie apart. Cassie is resourceful and so we have given her some of the cash from the car and she is off. We'll keep half an eye on her, but she isn't really on anyone's radar."

"Is that David's job?" I asked. He didn't answer, but added,

"Piotr and his family will take a bit more work, but we'll see them all right."

"Will they stay over there?" I asked.

"The less you know the better," he replied.

"But what about if Clinkie comes for them, or me again?"

"Clinkie won't be a problem. His team is severely depleted after Tenerife. I have had eyes in his camp for a number of years and am clear on the position. When the product is handed over, Clinkie and his gang are no longer an issue. Time to eat?"

I wasn't sure if it was a suggestion or an order. As we got up, Sandra appeared in the dining room and opened the sliding screen.

"Roast beef and Yorkshire pudding," Sir Michael said. "I thought it would be appropriate given that we are in Yorkshire. Sandra and a guest will be joining us for dinner. Sandra, please ask our guest to come through."

She left and returned a minute later with our guest. I had met him once before. He didn't seem surprised, but I was. It was Norrie.

Chapter Forty-Three

"You two have met before of course," Sir Michael said rather mischievously.

"Aye," replied Norrie, avoiding eye contact with me. I didn't say anything. Sandra brought over a large platter with a side of roast beef and various bowls of vegetables to the table. I couldn't see if there was a chef in the kitchen or if she had cooked it.

"Shall I be dad?" Sir Michael asked. He appeared to be in a playful mood. I couldn't imagine sitting like this with Clinkie. He carved and served our slices of meat and we helped ourselves to the veg. Sandra had opened another bottle of wine; we filled our glasses and Sir Michael said, "Time for a toast to Greg, for all that he has done."

We touched glasses and I felt slightly giddy. The food was delicious. As I was in the good books, I felt it acceptable to compliment the cuisine. "This is lovely – who cooked it?"

Sandra looked bashful. "Sandra here. She is our go-to girl," Sir Michael said with a smile.

"Well, Greg, you're probably wondering what this particular gathering is all about. So, I suppose it is time to start talking about Clinkie and what will happen tomorrow. As I have told you already, Clinkie and I have had a long-running dispute caused by Clinkie's petty jealousy and stubbornness. That allied to Clinkie's overinflated self-worth regarding where he is in the pecking order has caused complications. It is what has prevented me from stepping away completely from some dubious business practices." I guessed that trading polonium fitted in under this heading. "Things have been getting worse these past few years and so I needed some eyes in the camp. We looked around and found Norrie. He has fed us snippets as and when required. However, his worth to us rocketed as soon as Vicky was banged up and got in tow with Suzi Moore. That put the ball in our court and meant that we were playing with a stacked hand."

I was getting a bit confused by the mixed metaphors. "Have you been on Vicky's tail from when she broke out of prison?"

"Yes, and yours as well from the moment you commenced employment with Catering Solutions."

"Did you follow me from Clinkie's?"

"To an extent."

"What does that mean?"

"Did you not question how you an amateur, if you pardon the expression, managed to get into the office of one of Scotland's crime barons, as the red tops would call him, steal valuable papers and then escape?"

"I had actually. I thought I was good," I half joked.

"The place was covered in CCTV and there was security all over the place. The head of security laid it on a plate."

I now thought of Norrie in a different light, considering what balls it must have taken to do that. I looked at him and he was definitely less furtive than when we last met. "How long before Clinkie found out?" I asked him.

"It wasn't until late afternoon the next day. Jonjo found out almost straight away but he didn't want to ruin the wedding. He put the word out to get you and, because the Ka had a tracking device fitted, they thought that would be easy."

"Why did Jonjo leave a message and tell me to get back up the road?" I asked.

"It wasn't Jonjo, it was me."

"How did you get my number?"

"From Di," he replied. "Jonjo didn't take her call in the lead up to the wedding, so she left a message for me to pass on. She told me that Vicky had got someone a role with Catering Solutions and gave me his name, address and phone number."

I suddenly realised how lucky I had been. If Jonjo had spoken to Di, then I would be dead. As I tried to push that thought out of my head, the penny dropped. "You wanted me to run so you could follow me and be taken to Piotr and hopefully the Audi and the polonium?"

"Bingo, you got it in one," Sir Michael said.

"It sounds stupid I know because I'm not used to all of this, but what if you had lost me?"

"There was never a chance of that," Norrie said.

"How come?"

"I put a tracking device on you in Clinkie's. We didn't want you staying at your flat, because they would definitely have gone looking for you there."

I had thought I was so smart, but of course, and as ever, I had been played all along.

Sir Michael jumped in. "Suffice to say, Norrie made a sharp exit from Clinkie's employ on Saturday morning and will not be returning."

"What will be happening?" I asked.

"That's not your concern."

"I mean tomorrow."

"Call DI Stevenson when you are on the train about an hour from London to confirm your meeting and tell him again that you want to see Maggie. It should go without saying that you make no mention of me. I will give you an envelope tomorrow that contains a message for Maggie that I want you to give her."

"OK," I said. "I would like to visit Vicky's parents. Do you have any objection to that or me telling the police?"

"That's not a problem. In fact, it will be helpful," he said.

I didn't know what he meant but was glad of his agreement. It struck me that I would need to know when Vicky's funeral was because I wouldn't want to turn up on the day or find out that I had missed it. Also, I realised that I should try and contact her parents to let them know that I wished to attend. I mentioned this to Sir Michael, and he said to leave it with Sandra, who would do the necessary.

"Now, does anyone want dessert?" he asked.

"No thanks," I said, "I'm full."

Sandra and Norrie declined as well.

I had lost track of time but was aware of how tired I was. We indulged in some small talk before I said, "I don't want to be rude, but it's been a long day. I think it's time for bed."

"By all means. Sandra, please escort Greg," Sir Michael said.

I hoped that Sandra would drop her work façade, but no chance, and as soon as we got to my bedroom door she said goodnight, turned and was off. No night-time peck on the cheek then.

I slept like a baby and woke to the sounds of the countryside outside. I switched my phone on to check the time and saw that it was 8.45. I switched the phone off again, got up, showered and dialled zero on the landline. Sandra was along straight away and took me back to the dining room. David was there, but there was no sign of Sir Michael or Norrie.

Sandra handed me an orange juice, indicated where I should sit and asked if I would like the full English. I did of course. It duly arrived and I scoffed it down. She cleared all the breakfast dishes away. I asked where Sir Michael was, and she told me he had left on business. She then said, "He has asked me to check that you are clear on what to do today when speaking to the police."

"I am," I said.

She left the dining room and returned a few minutes later with an envelope and handed it to me. "This is for Maggie and no one else. Don't let the police know it has come from Sir Michael." She didn't say how I would achieve this, as I guessed there would be someone on guard at the hospital ward.

"There are new clothes for you in your room. I took the liberty of disposing of the old ones." This took me aback slightly. Firstly, deciding to get rid of my stuff without asking; then the thought of her seeing the state of my pants. It would be hard to look her in the eye again.

When David and I returned from our bedrooms with our stuff, we said goodbye to Sandra in the hall and were driven to the station by the same silent man who had picked us up the night before. I didn't see Norrie before we left. It was a bright autumnal early afternoon and I looked out of the window taking in the pleasant rural scenery. We soon arrived at the station, and my sense of calm disappeared as we waited on the platform after I switched on my phone and noticed a missed call from home. My parents had never called me on my mobile, so I felt this must be some form of bad news. I checked to see if a voicemail, text or email had been sent but there was nothing. It had been a while since we had spoken, and I decided I would call them after I had met Stevenson and hopefully seen

Maggie. Calling them now would be too much of a distraction. I switched off my phone and waited for the train, which surprisingly arrived bang on time.

Sandra had booked us in first class again and I settled into my seat with David this time facing the direction of travel and me looking the other way. We were on the 14.00 and would arrive in London just before five. I unfolded the paper Sandra had printed off that gave details of Vicky's parents' address, and details of her funeral, which was set for eleven o'clock on Friday morning at Liberton Cemetery in Edinburgh.

I was going to ask David lots of questions but couldn't be bothered. I decided that after I had met Stevenson and hopefully Maggie, I would raise the question with him regarding Piotr and Cassie to hopefully be convinced they would be safe. After that I would visit Vicky's parents, not fearing that Clinkie would be on my tail. I looked out of the window for most of the trip, feeling more relaxed than of late. David was either on his phone or sleeping and the train journey passed quickly.

When we arrived at King's Cross, David told me to phone him when I had finished my meeting with Stevenson and go to the pub where we had been the day before. I agreed and asked for some money. He took out a roll of notes from his trouser pocket without protest and handed them to me. I made my way to the taxi rank, got a cab and was soon at the Victorian pub which was in a lane off Regent Street. I hadn't set foot in it for over two years and it looked just the same. The circumstances that I was meeting Stevenson under were similar to the last time as well, in that we were hopefully at the end of a very bad chapter and looking to move on. The pub was busy with office workers who had finished for the day and I had a slight wait at the bar before ordering my drink. I managed to find a free table. I was early but that gave me time to go over my story in my head and get it straight, finish my beer and get another before Stevenson arrived. I also had a little look at the roll of notes David had given me and was pleased to see that it totalled one hundred pounds. I checked my phone, which showed that it was ten past six. I had never known Stevenson to be late. However, before I could start panicking, he arrived. He looked round and I stood up and waved. He smiled and gestured to ask if I wanted a drink. I gave the thumbs up and pointed at my lager. He came over with the drinks, put them down and shook my hand before taking a seat.

"Well Greg, when we had that drink near the Old Bailey, I can't say I expected this."

"Me neither," was all I could say.

"So, tell me all about it," he said.

I gave my story for the third time in two days, but this time it was much shorter as I didn't have to recount the events from two years ago, which he obviously knew. I started from Vicky turning up at my door and took it from there. I made no mention of finding where Piotr had gone and then visiting him and Cassie. Instead, I kept elements of truth such as having to go to Clinkie's to steal documents for Vicky but made out that this was because she believed that Clinkie knew where the polonium may be and that the details were in the safe.

"What documents did you steal?" he asked.

"There was a fake passport and a driving licence, but I didn't look too closely as I had his men on my tail."

"How did you escape?"

I told him about the darts match, my lucky find of cash in the jacket and subsequent flight to London.

"Very resourceful. I'll choose to ignore the bit about the cash in the stolen jacket."

I gave a weak smile and said, "Yes, but by the time I got home there was a message from Clinkie telling me to get my arse up the road. And that's why I headed off pronto."

"Where did you go when you thought that Clinkie was after you?"

"My parent's house," I lied, as I avoided eye contact and looked at my pint before drinking it. He could tell I was lying but didn't pursue it. Stevenson seemed quite relaxed despite me showing him Vicky's email and my talk of Clinkie. I told him that I believed her email and that I thought it was certain she was murdered, probably on Clinkie's orders. I told him of my plans to visit Vicky's parents in Edinburgh, as despite everything, I felt the need.

"Why didn't you do anything about it then," he asked?

"The email? Because at the time I thought that Clinkie was on my tail. After all I had done and the risks that I took at Clinkie's, I was livid with her, so when the message came through, I read the first couple of lines and felt it was self-pitying crap, so I deleted it. It was only when you told me about her being dead that I retrieved the message and read it in full. I think it explains a lot."

"Or it could be self-pitying crap as you first thought. Her prints were on the glass and whisky decanter," he replied. "When are you planning on going to Edinburgh? Do you know when the funeral is?"

"Yes, it's on Friday. I want to see Maggie first and then head up there."

"Well, you can't see her tonight, but the good news is that you can see Maggie tomorrow. She told me that her parents are dead and that you are one of her closest friends. She is a bit fragile, so be warned."

That was good news, but I found her description of me surprising. We were close colleagues, but she was my boss and I had never socialised with her on her own, just occasionally as part of the team. I barely knew about her personal life, and all she knew about mine were the basics that I was obliged to disclose.

"Can I see her first thing in the morning?" I asked. "That will give me time to get up to Edinburgh afterwards."

"That should be fine. I'll check and let you know. She is in Charing Cross Hospital. Let's provisionally set a time of 10am tomorrow. I'll be there to take you to her ward. Have you contacted Vicky's parents?"

"No. I have their address. I know it isn't ideal, but I was going to go to their house tomorrow as soon as I get off the train to offer my condolences." It sounded so lame when I said it. I had made the decision when my stress levels were fluctuating wildly, and in the cold light of day it didn't seem like such a great idea.

"Greg, for someone who can crack codes, you haven't really given this a great deal of thought, have you? They may not even want to see you.

After all, like it or not, you are associated with her crime and punishment, so to speak."

He was right, and all I could do was shrug.

"Luckily for you I still have some contacts up there, although they tell me that Police Scotland is a shambles since they amalgamated."

"What do you mean?" I asked blankly.

"Well, there used to be regional forces such as Lothian and Borders and Strathclyde. A few years ago, they were amalgamated into one force for the whole of the country called Police Scotland. There were lots of redundancies and golden handshakes resulting in a force with no cohesion and lots of things slipping through the gaps. If it was Clinkie, as you say, then he will get away. There aren't the same links between coppers like we used to have. It's all politically driven. They go for the easy targets so some poor sod who tells his ex to fuck off in a text gets arrested and stands trial for domestic abuse whilst the council estates are like the wild west and drug deaths escalate. Everything is fine for the pen-pushers because the arrest rate tables meet requirements.

"As I say, I don't have many close contacts now, but there is a guy I have liaised with on other matters over the years. I'll give him a phone and see if he can give us a contact."

Stevenson took out his phone, asked me to get him a pint and dialled. By the time I returned with our drinks he had finished his call. "That was quick," I said.

"There's a guy called Murdo McNeill who is a retired assistant chief constable. He's a friend of the family and acting as a kind of unofficial liaison officer to keep the parents shielded from the press and rubberneckers. I'll send him an email giving the background and let's take it from there."

As I watched Stevenson very slowly typing his message to McNeill, I couldn't help feeling that he was being almost too helpful. I sensed that he wanted the Clinkie murder theory kicked into the long grass and me seeing Vicky's parents may get me to drop that accusation in respect of their feelings. Finally, he sent the message.

"I have given him the background on this and told him you are going. I haven't mentioned Clinkie yet but have told him of your previous involvement with Vicky and how she set you up and was involved in your aunt's kidnapping." He picked up his glass and had a drink. I nursed my drink because the glass was almost empty. "One for the road?" he asked as he got up. I nodded.

We spent another twenty minutes or so chatting, with Stevenson doing some gentle probing over Vicky and Maggie, but not with any degree of intensity. "OK, time to go, see you tomorrow," he said.

"Yeah, thanks for your help," I replied.

I returned to King's Cross and met David for a pint as arranged. He was already there and was sitting at a table with a suitcase.

"Where you off to?" I asked looking at the case.

"This is for you," he replied. "Get yourself a drink and the usual for me."

I returned with the drinks and sat down. "So, what's this for then?" I asked.

David replied, "Sandra has bought you some more clothes and something to carry them in. You're going to a funeral, so you've got to show respect."

"Is Sandra here?" I asked hopefully.

"No, man," he said, smiling. "Click and collect. She clicked and I collected."

I looked in the case and it held a white shirt, black tie, trousers, socks and underwear, as well as a pair of dark brown hush puppies. "Wow, she thinks of everything," I said.

"She sure does," he replied. "How did your meeting go?" I told him and also that I was meeting Maggie the next day at Charing Cross Hospital. "Good, let me call Sandra. Get us another drink."

By the time I had returned, he confirmed that she had booked return train tickets to Edinburgh leaving on the 13.00 tomorrow. She had also booked a local Travelodge for David and I to stay in overnight.

"Why can't I just go home?" I asked.

"It might be being watched by cops or what's left of Clinkie's men, so best stay away for now. The good news is that there's a decent Indian nearby, so let's finish our drinks, get something to eat and have an early night."

"Sounds like a plan. We're not sharing a room I hope."

We went to the hotel and checked in. Once again, we were in adjoining rooms, which were on the first floor. David followed me into my room and said, "We're nearing the end of the road. Tomorrow, you go to Scotland, meet the family, then come home and get on with your life." With that, he handed me an envelope. "Open it," he instructed. I did and there was a bundle of cash in £50 notes.

"That's ten grand," David informed me. It wasn't as good as the 100k that slipped through my fingers in Tenerife, but it would do I supposed. "It's from Sir Michael and he sees it as closure."

"Tell him thanks," I said.

"Right, dump your bag and let's eat."

Despite the line of work he had ended up in, I couldn't help but warm to David. We had only been together for a few days, but I liked his company. I felt sorry for him as well and would have liked to have known Eustace. I planned on trying to get to know David better over the meal. I had managed to tease out of him that he would be staying in the UK and doing odd jobs for Sir Michael if required, but as he had sold Eustace's house, he would have a reasonable amount of capital to play with. I asked about the *product*, as Sir Michael would refer to it. "Why would he want that?"

"He doesn't want it for himself," he explained. "He's too clean. To him it's a product for trading. And what will he trade it for? A favour of course."

"A favour, what kind of a favour?" I asked.

"No need to know, man."

I knew I would get no further with that line of enquiring and so asked how he had got in tow with Sir Michael, and he explained that it was because he wanted to avenge the death of his brother. Sir Michael's guys had tracked him down after Vicky's trial at the Old Bailey. I asked if he understood my reasons for visiting Vicky's parents and if seeing the email she sent me helped explain her actions in later life, and he told me that he forgave Cassie because she was swept along with things, but Vicky chose her life and made her own decisions. When I raised her childhood, he replied, "Eustace and I had a shit childhood, but we didn't kill anyone."

I left it at that and then asked him about Pink Shirt, but he gave no details there. We made small talk for the rest of the meal. The service had been very prompt, the food delicious and before I knew it we were done. We got back to the hotel by nine thirty and I went straight to bed and slept surprisingly well.

The next day I met David for breakfast as arranged, after which we headed back to our rooms. He held out his hand and we shook. "You are a good man, Greg, and you did right by my brother. Best wishes, man."

I gave him a hug and said, "Thanks for everything, David. I really hope things work out for you."

We looked at each other for a few seconds then went to our rooms. I was glad to get in because I could feel my eyes misting up and didn't want David to see me crying.

Chapter Forty-Four

I packed, putting my small bag where I had stashed most of the cash that David had given me inside the new suitcase, careful to avoid creasing my new clothes. I put my trainers in the suitcase and put on my new shoes. I made sure I had the envelope that Sandra had given me to give to Maggie and put that in one of the pockets of my cargo jeans and zipped it closed.

I then checked out and headed for the Tube. As I made the walk from Barons Court station to the hospital, I tried to think of what I would say to Maggie. I was so glad that she was safe and was looking forward to seeing her, but I was now extremely nervous. After a few minutes I arrived at Charing Cross Hospital and Stevenson was waiting outside the A&E entrance.

"Morning, Greg."

"Morning," I replied.

"Before we go in, what time is your train?" he asked.

"One o'clock," I replied.

"Right, save these," he said, and read out a phone number and email address for Murdo McNeill. "Give him a phone from the train to let him know you're on time. He has suggested that you see the parents as soon as you arrive. He says they won't want any extra burden the next day. He feels that you appearing to forgive Vicky may be of comfort to them. Get a taxi from the station, which will take around twenty minutes. Got that?"

"Yes."

Stevenson radioed someone then said, "Let's go," to me. As we went into the hospital, I remembered that I should get something for Maggie and bought a box of chocolates from the gift shop. Stevenson knew his way about, and after a long walk along a corridor on the ground floor we took a lift to the third floor, had another long walk to a reception area, where he was obviously expected as the receptionist barely looked up as he flashed his credentials and she let us in. The ward had individual rooms and we went to the first of them, which had a uniformed officer sitting outside who immediately got to his feet. Stevenson nodded to him and asked me, "Are you ready?"

"Yes," I said croakily. I had a small cough to try and clear my throat. Stevenson tapped on the door and opened it slowly. A nurse turned, smiled and beckoned us in. Stevenson stood to the side and I entered the room. "Hi, I'm Greg," I said to the nurse.

"Hi Greg, I'm Jenny. Maggie's been looking forward to seeing you."

I smiled again and walked over to Maggie's bed. She had a radio on the cabinet at the side of the bed, which I think was tuned to Classic FM, but it was so quiet it was hardly worth being on. I was surprised that she looked more or less the same, remembering that when I had visited Isa after her ordeal I hadn't recognised her. I went towards the bed with the chocolates in my hand and the nurse intercepted, taking them from me.

"Greg, oh Greg, how are you?" Maggie asked. She raised her arms and we did a sort of awkward hug.

"I'm fine. Maggie. More importantly, how are you? God, I'm so glad you're safe. It must have been terrible."

"Yes – you know where I was kept? The WLAG warehouse. I really can't understand it."

I thought she was going to say more but she didn't. Her mind seemed to drift, so I said, "I'm sure the police will get to the bottom of it, but it wasn't a random act. I would like more time with you and hopefully we can get that over the weeks ahead." She nodded. "But there have been all sorts of things happened that I either don't understand or have time just now to explain, but I have this for you." I took the envelope from my trouser pocket and handed it to her and then sat down in the chair next to her bed.

"Thanks," she said, as she took it from me with a quizzical look on her face. She opened the envelope, looked at the card and rested it gently on the cabinet. I noticed that it was her first card and immediately felt guilty at not getting her one. There was a handwritten letter in the envelope as well and Maggie read it, folded it and put it beside the card.

"So, you know who my father is," she said wistfully.

"Yes," I said. My dry throat had returned.

"I don't know what more to say," she said.

"I met him for the first time two days ago," I said. "Obviously I don't know him, but I'm sure he loves you and that he misses you and your mother every day." As I said this my eyes misted over and so did hers.

"Oh Greg," she said. "I don't know what to say."

"Maggie, you need to recover first and then I can tell you more. If I can be of any help with your father then please let me know. But you need to get well. God knows, you know my back story and you have been so supportive of me and now I want to do the same for you."

"What about WLAG?"

"It will survive, but let's worry about you first, OK?"

"OK," she said. The main difference was her voice, which was so much quieter and less enthusiastic than before. We tried to make small talk, but it was difficult. I hoped she wouldn't ask what my plans were for the next few days as I would find it difficult to lie and not tell her about Vicky's funeral. Luckily she didn't ask. She was obviously fragile anyway, but whatever was written in the note had affected her.

"Maggie, I'm going to go now. But I'll keep in touch with the police and see you again soon."

She nodded and we hugged again. I left the room slowly and gave a small wave to Maggie, which she returned. Stevenson was still outside. "How did that go?" he asked.

"Much as expected I suppose." We didn't speak any more as we made our way downstairs and out of the hospital.

"Right, Greg, we'll go our separate ways. Keep in touch." As he said this, he held out his hand and I shook it.

"Sure," I replied.

"Give my best to Sir Michael," he said with a wink.

I was about to reply and then thought better of it and just said *bye* and turned to make my way back to the station. When I got to King's Cross, I visited the same pub that David and I had gone to for the last two days. The barman recognised me as I bought my pint. I drank it quickly and got a second, which I drank with a bit more respect while I sent a text to David telling him I had given Sir Michael's envelope to Maggie. Then I went to the station to get the train to Edinburgh. As ever, Sandra had got me first class and I settled into my surroundings. The carriage was just about full, which was disappointing.

I settled into my usual travelling mode of staring out of the window and stayed like that until we were well out of London. There was someone sitting across from me, which was inhibiting because I wanted to phone home. However, I didn't want him to hear, so I went to the toilet, locked the door and called from there. The phone was answered by my mum.

"Hi, Mum," I said.

"Dad has had a stroke."

"What?"

"He's very poorly. He's in hospital. He's asking for you."

"Oh my God."

"Where are you?" She was being so cool towards me.

"I'm on a train, Mum."

"Where are you going?"

"To Edinburgh."

"Why are you going there?"

"It's a long story," I said and then made the mistake of telling her that I was going to Vicky's funeral.

"How could you?" she screamed.

"She's dead. A lot of things happened to her when she was young that caused her to be the way she was, and I suppose this is some form of closure."

"Closure? Closure? Don't give me that wishy-washy crap." I was shocked at her language. "She was the bitch that killed his sister. Your dad is fighting for his life in hospital and you are going to her funeral?"

"Mum, Mum, please let me explain, please. There are reasons, Mum — I'll explain. I'll be with you tomorrow by teatime. I'll be home tomorrow night. I love you." I think she had hung up before I had finished though.

I phoned David and asked him to get Sandra to book me a Birmingham train ticket. "Hey, you can't leave me alone?" he said with a laugh. When I explained the reasons, his tone changed, and he expressed his sympathy. A few minutes later an email arrived with details of my train ticket for Birmingham, Sandra displaying her usual level of efficiency.

Ever since Isa's kidnapping, there had been something between me and my parents. My dad couldn't help but attach some blame to me, although as the months passed he had tried to hide it. My mother was generally more understanding but would always support him. I felt it was always me trying to make steps to reconcile relations with my family, but that these weren't reciprocated. Now I feared I had made a fatal flaw which would not be forgiven.

I stared out of the window and had a myriad of thoughts and memories such as Martina in Tenerife, the girls from the SECC who I met at Glasgow Airport on the way to London and of course Maggie. I wondered what the next few weeks would have in store for her and the charity and how much my colleagues were aware of the whole saga.

I thought of Vicky and read and re-read her email. The first time I had read it after Stevenson had told me she was dead; my initial instinct was to see her parents and tell them about her story. Now that I was on a train going to see them my resolve had slipped a bit. Yes, her story needed telling and the bastard who abused her strung up, but I was now doubtful that the day before her funeral was wise. I thought that instead I would tell Murdo McNeill because he would know the procedures for reporting this type of abuse case and may still have some connections in the force.

The details contained in her email were shocking and must of course have affected her for the rest of her short life. When I cast my mind back to when we met at uni, she never appeared vulnerable, quite the opposite; now I saw this was a front. In my unscientific mind I saw it as her putting her demons in a box and then trying desperately to keep the box shut forever.

Thinking of Vicky made me wonder if I would ever have normal relationships at all. I thought of the money David had given me on behalf of Sir Michael and considered going back to Tenerife to see Martina.

Norrie crossed my mind as well and I speculated what he'd be up to. It must have taken serious guts to double cross Clinkie. Was he suitably comfortable that Clinkie would soon not be a problem due to Sir Michael's influence being greater than Clinkie's?

I even thought of Martin Stafford and wondered if he had insurance for the Audi and also if he would just be Elvis for a while until he replaced his Tom Jones and Roy Orbison outfits.

Before I knew it, the train left Newcastle and I sent a text to McNeill, got a coffee from trolley service and sat back and stared out of the window. A while later my text was acknowledged.

I felt rough and wanted to freshen up before I met Vicky's parents, so when I arrived at Edinburgh Waverley station, I looked for a chemist to buy wipes and breath freshener. On my way, I noticed a headline in the *Daily Record* as I passed a newsagent.

Crime Boss Killed.

I bought a paper, went to the chemist and got my stuff, after which I went to the taxi rank and hailed a cab. I read out the address to the driver, who was very chatty, but I only half-heartedly responded to him as I quickly read the front-page article, which stated that Clinkie had been killed in a car crash the previous day when the Mercedes sports car that he was travelling in and being driven by Derry Byrne was in collision with a truck. Both occupants of the car were killed instantly, the driver of the truck was unscathed. There was also a two-page colour spread in the centre of the paper which was standard tabloid fare: summarising and eulogising Clinkie's life, accompanied by pictures of him alongside various Scottish footballers, boxers and TV stars.

It dawned on me that this was no accident and that I had been put up in the Travelodge the previous night so that I would be nowhere near my flat when this was carried out in case any of Clinkie's remaining gang blamed me and looked for retribution. David's mention of *a trade* resonated, and the penny dropped. Sir Michael had used his connection with me to get the polonium, aware that Vicky could be used as bait and killed by Clinkie, then the polonium would be handed over and in return Clinkie gets dealt with. The result being no connection between Sir Michael, Maggie and Clinkie. How neat.

As I was thinking this, the taxi drew up in front of a large Victorian villa on a wide leafy avenue. "That's us here, pal," the driver said.

"Thanks," I said absently, and handed over one of the £50 notes from David and got out.

"Not want your change?" the driver asked. I shook my head and the taxi sped off. I messaged to say I had arrived and stood awkwardly outside the house. After about five minutes the front door opened and a grey-haired man in his sixties came out and said, "Greg?"

"Yes," I replied.

He gave me a firm and unusually long handshake. He looked me squarely in the eye and said, "Mr and Mrs Monteith understand why you would like to see them, but they are naturally very upset. You were a friend of Vicky's and appear to forgive her and they appreciate that, but they may not show it when you meet them." Typical cop speak I thought.

"OK," I said.

"Let's go in," he said. We walked slowly into the house, which had a large ornately tiled vestibule where he told me to wait. He went to a door, tapped lightly on it, went in then returned a few seconds later and beckoned me to follow him in.

Mr and Mrs Monteith were sitting in the room, which smelled nicely of freshly brewed coffee. Neither of them got up as we entered. "This is Greg Stewart," McNeill said.

Mr Monteith gave a small nod, pointed towards a small couch and replied, "Have a seat." We both dutifully sat down. The atmosphere in the room made me feel nervous.

"Coffee?" he asked.

"No thanks," I replied. I actually wanted one but couldn't bear the thought of holding their twee china cup in my shaking hands.

"I'm fine thanks, Ian," McNeill said.

They were the archetypal upper-middle-class couple. Him well-groomed, thick greying hair, with the look of a Rotarian and golfer; she the blue-rinse wife who supported his career and brought up the kids. I had expected a cool reception, but the atmosphere in the room was worse than expected.

I was introduced by McNeill who explained that I had known Vicky for nearly twenty years and despite what had happened she had always been important to me. He made it clear that I was grateful to be allowed to meet them, which made me bristle, and I wondered what they would have said if they knew what she had been up to before she died.

Mrs Monteith finally spoke. "Thank you, Murdo. Yes, Murdo is right. We are very tired and terribly upset. Plus, the press keep hounding us and Murdo has been very good at keeping them at bay.

"You are of course welcome to come to the funeral if you wish."

Their middle-class resoluteness was staggering, I thought. She referred to it as the *funeral* not *her funeral* or better still *Vicky's funeral.*

"We will never know what caused all this over the past few years. It has put a terrible strain on us all. She always wanted her own way from a very young age. Remember dear that we told her she could get a puppy when she was ten, but we gave in and she had it at six." Mr Monteith nodded sympathetically. I noted that they were sitting some way apart.

I got thirty minutes of this, which was enough. I managed to drop in some positive anecdotes, which seemed to be well received, but my overwhelming feeling was that they were going through the motions and wanted this over. I was sure they grieved for their daughter but felt they wanted this chapter over along with the shame it brought. I had hoped Vicky's sister might have been around because I may have got some empathy, and if I had got a chance, I might have mentioned to her the email that Vicky had sent to me. I shook hands with both of them and left. McNeill offered to give me a lift to my hotel.

On our way to his car, McNeill suggested we could go for a pint after I checked in. However, I just wanted to get to my hotel, which was a Travelodge in the Old Town, and go for a few pints myself. I had found the visit difficult and stressful, which was compounded by the news about my father. I wanted to call home again and then wallow and I didn't want any company. I thanked him for the offer, explained about my father and we made small talk on the way to my destination. I warmed to him a bit and decided that once I had seen my dad and tried to repair relationships with my family I would give him a call and tell him about Vicky's email and ask if he could take steps to report her claims.

I checked in, dumped my case in my room and immediately left in search of a pub. The receptionist had given me directions to the Grassmarket, which was less than ten minutes' walk away. I vaguely remembered this area from when I had visited as a student with my gang, which of course included Vicky. Despite it being autumn there were lots of tourists around in the picture postcard surroundings, quite a few of whom were sitting at tables outside the many bars and restaurants. I found a small bar that looked dark inside, which fitted the bill, and went in and got my first pint. I sat down and immediately phoned my mother but there was no reply and I left a message. I then tried Fran, my sister, and left messages on both her mobile and landline. Despite everything that had happened over the past few days, I had managed to cope without my prescription drugs for over a day. However, as I now contemplated my family I was gripped by a crushing anxiety. I got another pint and phoned Stevenson, not that I had anything to tell him, but I wanted to speak to someone who knew me. I told him about the meeting with Vicky's parents and that I hadn't mentioned my theory about Clinkie to them, asked him if he knew of Clinkie's demise, which he did, and told him about my dad. He told me to forget Vicky's funeral and get back down the road to my family.

After that call I was in two minds about what to do. I sent a text to my sister asking how things were and asking her to call me. I did a small pub crawl visiting a few hostelries in the area and then slowly made my way back to the hotel. My sister hadn't replied, and my evening of drink and reflection had not solved any problems for me, so I went to bed as confused as I had been when I woke up that morning.

Chapter Forty-Five

The alarm on my phone woke me at nine thirty. I showered and was disappointed with myself that I had forgotten to buy anything for shaving despite having been in a chemist the day before. I put on the clothes that Sandra had bought me, which all fitted perfectly.

I went for breakfast, and despite not having had a proper meal the night before was not particularly hungry. There was a fry-up option available, but I chose some cornflakes and a coffee. I felt nervous and uncomfortable in the restaurant and quickly finished my breakfast and returned to my room. I went to the bathroom and gagged up a mixture of coffee and cornflakes into the sink.

I tried phoning my mother and sister again, but still got no reply. I racked my brain to think of a neighbour of my parents or other relative that I could contact but couldn't think of anyone that I knew whose number I would have. With a sigh, I got up, tied the black tie that Sandra had got me then packed my case and checked out. I asked the receptionist to book me a taxi, but she told me it was easier to go outside and hail one. She was right, and within a couple of minutes I was in a cab heading for Liberton Cemetery.

The taxi driver, noting my destination and attire, was respectfully quiet. It was a bright morning and I took in the sights as we made our way through Edinburgh's Southside. My phone pinged. I grabbed it out of my pocket and saw I had a text from my sister.

It simply said, *Dad has passed.*

I gasped and gripped the phone. I couldn't believe it. Instinctively, I called my sister, but there was no reply. I gave out a loud sigh that sounded like a wail. The driver eyed me warily in his mirror as a jumble of thoughts swirled about in my head: *My dad is dead. I will never see him again. He is dead. He is in Birmingham and I am in Edinburgh.*

I felt like jumping out of the car. Just then we stopped, and the driver told me we had arrived. I handed over another fifty-pound note without a word and got out. I had a primal urge to see my mum. I phoned her, but still got no answer and left a garbled message. I wanted to go home, to the house that I grew up in, but instead I was here. My instinct was to go straight to the station and get home, but as I was thinking this, the funeral cortege arrived. I tried to be rational and accept that I couldn't bring Dad back and I would be home soon.

It was a large gathering, and with shaking legs I fell in step and followed the other mourners to the family plot. Most people tried their best to get a spot with a view. I didn't care and stood right at the back, but I actually had a decent view because I was on the brow of a large slope. The undertakers respectfully took Vicky's coffin from the hearse, and I struggled to comprehend that she was in there. I thought back to only a few days ago when she was flesh and blood. I thought back to her message which I had initially deleted. I then thought of my dad and that he was dead as well. I started crying and a few people nearby looked at me sympathetically. I then thought what had caused my dad's death – was it the stress, was it his sister's death? And who caused that? *It was you, Vicky. It was you...* I screamed in my head.

The coffin was put in place and the minister made a brief speech which I couldn't hear clearly. I watched whilst the chosen family and friends took their place beside the grave and each took a cord to hold and symbolically help lower Vicky's coffin into the ground. I was momentarily blinded by a flash of sunlight reflecting off a large ring that Murdo McNeill was wearing on his right hand.

Along with the others, he gave a small bow as the coffin settled in the ground and the cords were drawn away and lifted up. McNeill then gave what appeared to be an involuntary shudder, before straightening himself and walking towards Vicky's parents, where he hugged and comforted them both.

I turned round, hurried out of the cemetery, flagged down a taxi and headed for the station. Fifty minutes later I was on a train to Birmingham and sat idly playing with my phone as I mulled over the impending meeting with my family. However, I was getting increasingly distracted by the incessant chatter of two women who sat opposite me. They were probably a few years younger than me but behaved like excited teenagers as one in particular wouldn't shut up. She kept going on about her boyfriend proposing the night before and held up her hand to show off her engagement ring. This drew shrieks of delight from her friend, and as I watched, a shiver suddenly ran up my spine as seeing the woman's ring had made something click in my mind. I hurriedly scrolled and re-read Vicky's final email to me. Her mention of the ring had previously been of no significance, but now in a sickening flash I realised who Vicky's "uncle" was. I saw in my mind's eyes the flash of light reflecting off McNeill's ring and a welter of emotions ran through my head which I struggled to control. However, what, if anything, I was going to do would have to wait until after I had returned to the remains of my grieving family. I put my headphones on and gazed out of the window as the train continued

south.

Acknowledgements

Keeping with tradition - thanks to my wife Maggie and my sister Jenny; my ever reliable first and second proof readers. Also, to Allan Jardine for again coming up with the cover concept and design.

Richard Sheehan my Copy Editor has kept me on track and was always available to answer my many queries that usually arrived at short notice.

I am lucky to have had the counsel of an excellent writer, Mike Kernan and am so grateful for his knowledge, expertise and great ideas as well as him acting as a general sounding board. Mike has been a huge help in improving the narrative and driving me to the finish line.

Heather Suttie has been a massive support to me and many other writers through her Bookface book club and numerous other mediums and I feel privileged to know her and am extremely grateful for her tremendous support.

Similarly, John Ward and Kenny McCabe's knowledge, love of books and general enthusiasm is truly inspiring.

Thanks to Geoff Wightman for consistently believing in me over many years and to Nigel Rowe for his ongoing friendship and support which I value enormously.

Neil Kilgour has patiently dealt with my techy needs over the past twenty years and his support and friendship is much appreciated. His work on Consider It Done has been exceptional.

To Ron Anderson for spreading the word. Keep up the good work!

It has been great getting re-acquainted with the Largo boys and I promise to keep in touch!

To everyone who read Bobbing Heads, thanks for your time.

Printed in Great Britain
by Amazon

23953816R00245